KILT
DEAD

KILT DEAD

KAITLYN DUNNETT

KENSINGTON BOOKS
http://www.kensingtonbooks.com

Library of Congress Card Catalogue Number: 2007926730
ISBN-13: 978-0-7582-1639-7
ISBN-10: 0-7582-1639-4

First Printing: August 2007
10 9 8 7 6 5 4 3 2 1

Printed in the United States of America

KILT
DEAD

Chapter One

Liss MacCrimmon never felt more alive than when she was about to step onto a stage. As she waited in the wings, she drank in the essence of the theater hosting that night's performance, inhaling the mixed scents of freshly ironed costumes, stage makeup, and rosin. Even the slightly musty smell of the old velvet curtains delighted her senses.

Just behind her she could hear the soft creak of levers moving a bit stiffly on an old-fashioned light board as one of the crew tamed the antiquated system to his will. The members of *Strathspey* had presented their show on all sorts of stages. This venue, in a forty-year-old high school in a medium-sized town in New York State, was no worse than most and better than many.

The rest of the troupe—Americans, Canadians, and Scots bound together by their passion for Scottish dancing—wedged themselves into the cramped backstage area as their introductory music blared through the sound system, effectively drowning out audience chatter. Liss had peeked out earlier. They had a good crowd, considering it was mid-week and they were in an area without a large population of Scottish descent.

The company had launched its first tour eight years earlier on the premise that those who loved the romance of bagpipes, *Braveheart*, and kilts would take to the idea the way the Irish, and everyone else, had embraced *Riverdance*. *Strathspey*—named after one of the traditional Scottish dances—had fallen far short of the phenomenal success of that show, but the troupe still managed to get bookings in small venues fifty weeks out of every year.

To Liss it didn't matter where they performed, or for how many people. She got the same tingle in her toes, the same giddy rush of pleasure and excitement, whether they were in Boston, Boise, or Boca Raton. At the age of twenty-seven, she felt as much anticipation, as much enthusiasm for her career, as she had on the day she turned pro at nineteen.

Out front the recorded music came to an end. An expectant hush fell over the assembled spectators. Liss's pulse quickened and her heart beat just a little bit faster as she waited for the first stirring notes to be played on the Great Highland Bagpipe. She flexed one leg, then the other, rolled her shoulders, and took a deep breath.

The cue came right on schedule. This was it. They were on. A surge of adrenalin propelled her onto the stage.

Leading the others, Liss flowed with the music, her feet performing the intricate steps as they had thousands of times before. The rest of her body automatically assumed the familiar poses and her face wore a radiant smile. She whirled and leapt, reveling in the freedom and beauty of the dances. The company performed a variety of Scottish standards, from strathspeys and reels and jigs to sword dances and Highland flings, all woven together in a loose story of Scottish immigrants finding a new life in the New World.

When she danced, Liss was aware of nothing but the music, the other dancers, and her own joy. If she was short on sleep, or stiff from too much traveling, she could easily ignore those minor distractions. She was accustomed to performing in spite of aches and pains. Dancers lived with both day in and day out, taping up ankles and knees as necessary so the show could go on.

But this night, as Liss launched herself into the final round of step dancing, the "Broadway kick-line" the company counted on to bring the audience to its feet, something went terribly wrong. Her left foot came down awkwardly on the hard wooden stage. She heard a loud pop. Excruciating pain shot through her knee. If her arms hadn't been linked with those of dancers on either side, she would have collapsed.

Her smile frozen in place, Liss stumbled through the next moments of the dance, literally carried by the others until they could spirit her off stage. From the wings, while anxious members of the backstage crew got her to a chair, elevated her leg, and applied ice, Liss watched the company dance on without her. Although she knew they had no choice, she felt as if they'd abandoned her. When another wave of pain swept over her, it was deeper and more agonizing than mere physical torment. It was accompanied by the terrible fear that *this* injury was the one all dancers dreaded, the one that could end a career.

Impatience was Liss MacCrimmon's besetting sin. As a child, she'd opened her Christmas presents as soon as the brightly wrapped packages appeared beneath the tree. Even when what she was waiting for might be bad news, she always wanted to hear the worst quickly and be done with it.

She sat in Doctor Kessler's examining room, twisting a lock of dark brown, shoulder-length hair between her fingers, wishing she'd brought a book with her to pass the time. She suspected she'd be too fidgety to take in a single word she read, but anything was better than staring at bigger-than-life diagrams of the hand, the elbow, the knee, and the ankle.

The sound of the door opening brought her head up with a snap. Her heart sank as she read the expression on the orthopedist's jowly face. He hadn't been optimistic when he'd operated on her injured knee two months earlier, but she'd made such a rapid recovery after surgery that she'd convinced herself there was still a chance of resuming her career. Hadn't she just walked into the doctor's office under her own steam and with only the hint of a limp? She'd been hoping for a green light to go back on the road with *Strathspey* before the summer was over.

Her gaze dropped to the X-rays he carried under his arm.

Her X-rays. Her *life*.

"Give it to me straight," she said.

Dr. Kessler's expression turned even more grim and Liss felt the knot of tension in her chest pull tighter.

"For someone in almost any other profession, this would be good news," he told her. "You're healing well. Remarkably well. But you have plastic and metal in there now, Liss." He tapped the long, still-livid scar on her left knee. "A partial knee replacement is not designed to stand up to the high-impact step dancing you do for a living."

Liss held herself perfectly still. "If I continue with the physical therapy, surely I can—"

"If you keep up the strengthening exercises, in another month you'll be ninety-nine percent back to normal and flexible enough to do almost anything, but if you go back to dancing, that knee won't last. You'll end up needing more surgery. And every time you have work done on the same area, healing becomes more problematic. There are no two ways about it, Liss. You're going to have to find a new career."

Her hands tightened over the front edge of the chair as emotions flooded through her. She was on the verge of tears but she refused to let them fall. "No. Damn it, no! It can't end like this. I don't know how to do anything else. I don't know how to *be* anything else."

"Do you want to end up in a wheelchair?"

Liss's usual self-possession deserted her. She was adrift. Dr. Kessler's blunt assessment left her without an anchor.

For a moment, she couldn't breathe, couldn't speak. "Scottish dancing isn't just my career," she finally managed in a choked voice. "It's my life."

"I'm sorry, Liss, but you have to face facts. And you must have known all along that dancers don't keep working until they reach the normal retirement age."

"I know that. I do. But some of the others in the company are in their thirties. One is forty-one. I should have had *years* left."

"I realize this is hard," Dr. Kessler said, "but it isn't the end of the world. You could teach dancing." He registered her automatic moue of distaste and shrugged. "Manage a dance company, then. Anything but perform night after night." He leaned forward, his gaze intense. "With normal use, this new knee can last ten to twenty years without giving you much trouble. But if you abuse it, it *will* give out on you. Make no mistake, Liss, your days as a professional dancer are over."

For the next month, Liss continued to exercise religiously to strengthen her knee. She alternated between feeling sorry for herself and making plans. Most of them were impractical, but she told herself she might as well dream big. It wasn't impossible that she'd win at Megabucks. Then, founding an institute to promote folk dancing would make perfect sense.

She was almost through all the standard stages of grief before she realized she'd been in mourning. By then, she had acquired two things that promised to make her adjustment to life without performing a little easier. The first was a car, a quirky, three-year-old P.T. Cruiser. Liss had never owned a car before. She hadn't needed one. She'd lived in cities or been on tour since she was seventeen. The second was the offer of a job—temporary, it was true—but in a place Liss had once loved almost as much as she'd loved being part of *Strathspey*.

On a sunny Friday in July, Liss MacCrimmon returned to Moosetookalook, Maine.

Her first impression was that her old hometown looked smaller and more dismal than she remembered it. She supposed she shouldn't be surprised. It had been over ten years since she'd been back. She'd left shortly after high school graduation. A few months later, her parents had moved to Arizona. She'd had no reason to spend time in Moosetookalook after that . . . until now.

The low-fuel alarm dinged, startling her. Since she had just come abreast of Willett's Store, she turned in to gas up, noting as she did so that at least this one place seemed exactly the same. Two gas pumps stood in solitary splendor out front, both designated as "full service." Inside the small, square clapboard building—painted bright yellow—she had no doubt the Willetts still stocked everything from milk to mousetraps.

Ernie Willett shuffled out to fill the tank and wash her windows. He looked, as always, as if his teeth hurt.

"Know you, don't I, missy?" His dark, beady eyes narrowed as he inspected her.

Liss gave him a friendly smile and told him her name. Within the hour, she thought, the whole town would have heard she was back in Moosetookalook. If they didn't already know she was coming.

"You Donald and Vi's daughter?" he asked.

"Yes, that's right. I'm here to give my Aunt Margaret a hand in the shop."

Small towns in Maine being what they were, Liss was certain he already knew about her aunt's stroke of good fortune. Margaret MacCrimmon Boyd had been offered a free trip to Scotland if she'd fill in at the last moment for a tour guide who'd fallen ill. A frugal New Englander, Aunt Margaret had seized the chance. Then she'd payed her luck forward and asked Liss to manage her business for her while she was gone.

"Margaret Boyd." Willett's craggy, grizzled face hardened as he said her name.

The animosity Liss saw in his expression sent a chill along her spine. She didn't understand his reaction at all. Most people liked Aunt Margaret.

Willett leaned closer, his cold stare inspecting both Liss and the interior of her car. "Heard you had some la-de-dah job in the theater." His thin lips flattened with what Liss assumed was disapproval.

"I was with a dance company." The ache was still there. Every time she thought of all she'd lost, it hurt. "Could you fill it up for me, please, Mr. Willett?"

He slouched off to activate the gas pump, muttering under his breath. Liss caught the words "damn fool woman" and wondered if he was referring to her or to her aunt.

She dug her wallet out of her purse, then glanced into her side mirror. Willett was just dunking a squeegee into a bucket. He washed her back window, then rapped on the glass sunroof as he sidled past the passenger side on his way to the windshield. "Want me to do this peephole thing too?"

"No need." But his words made her look up. At one side of the opening she caught a glimpse of the highest rooftop of The Spruces.

Liss smiled as her memory filled in details. In her mind's eye she saw it as a postcard-perfect grand hotel. Against a darker backdrop of mountains and trees, white walls stood out in sharp relief. Four-story octagonal towers rose from each end of the building, flanking a central tower of five floors surmounted by a cupola. Built on the crest of a hill, The Spruces had dominated Moosetookalook from the moment it opened in 1910. It loomed over houses and stores, forcing its identity on the town below. Local folks called it "the castle."

In its heyday, the first half of the twentieth century, The Spruces had attracted the rich and famous, from divas to heads of state. The lure of fresh mountain air and pure spring water, combined with rail service, privacy, and luxurious accommodations, had once been enough to keep over two hundred rooms filled.

Sadly, The Spruces had been dying by the time Liss knew it. It had still hosted proms and weddings, and taken in long-term lodgers, but after years of barely making ends meet, the owners had finally shut its doors for good five years ago. The railroads had been long gone by then. Only one puny Amtrak line even reached Maine anymore. Air travel had made more luxurious vacation spots accessible, and at lower prices. Even the fresh mountain air had become suspect, thanks to acid rain from factories to the south and west.

Liss had paid scant attention to news of the hotel's closing at the time. She'd been busy with her career as a dancer. Her parents had already moved away. She'd honestly never expected to return to the small rural community where she was born. Then again, she'd never expected to blow out her knee and lose her livelihood, either.

Ernie Willett's quilted, blaze-orange vest hovered into view at the driver's-side window, jerking Liss out of her reverie. He wore that getup year round, she recalled, not just during hunting season.

The cost of the gas was even more startling. Owning her own car was proving much more expensive than she'd anticipated.

Liss handed over a sheaf of small bills.

Folding them with gnarled fingers, Willett gave her a positively malevolent look before he stalked back inside the store.

Liss stared after him for a moment, shaking her head. What an odd man. Obviously no one had ever told him that being courteous to customers was the best way to keep them coming back. Then again, if this was still the only gas station in Moosetookalook, he probably wasn't too worried about the locals going to the competition.

As Liss drove away, following the curve of the road toward the center of town, she shrugged off Ernie Willett's bad attitude. Now that she was really here, all the frustrations and disappointments of the last three months seemed a little less devastating. A sense of anticipation lightened her heart. She'd always been fond of Aunt Margaret. Although she hadn't visited her here, they had kept in touch by letter and email and seen each other at Liss's folks' house in Arizona. Liss looked forward to spending a little time with her aunt before Margaret left for Scotland.

And with more eagerness than she'd felt about anything in ages, she relished the prospect of immersing herself in the day-to-day operation of Moosetookalook Scottish Emporium.

*   *   *

The hum of a small engine from the quiet street below caught Dan Ruskin's attention. He'd been listening for it, he supposed, ever since Margaret Boyd told him Liss was coming home.

She drove a P.T. Cruiser. The choice surprised him. It was practical, but almost stodgy in appearance. He knew she wasn't a big-time movie actress or anything, but somehow he'd expected she'd pick a sportier ride. She'd had her own style, even as a kid, favoring colorful, flamboyant clothing and paying no attention at all to current fads and fashions.

"What do you suppose they call that color?" Dan's brother Sam asked, gesturing at Liss's car with the Ruskin Construction ball-cap he'd taken off to use as a fan. The roof of a three-story Victorian was a hot place to be on a steamy afternoon in late July.

"Tan?" Dan suggested.

"I was thinking . . . putty."

Dan chuckled. "Probably some fancy name for it. Champagne, maybe? I'll have to remember to ask."

"Yeah, right. Talk about cars. That'll go over big. Might as well discuss the weather."

"I could invite her up here to look at the scenery." Dan was only half joking.

From this vantage point, he had a spectacular view not only of the town square below, but also of the countryside around Moosetookalook. In the distance he could see a good chunk of the hilly terrain of western Maine. Every shade of green was represented in the abundant vegetation.

Some folks thought the fall was prettier, when sugar maples sported crimson cloaks and elms adorned in gold vied for attention with the variously hued mantles of birches, ashes, and alders, but Dan would take the vivid greens over reds and yellows and burnt-umbers any day. Every one was distinctive. Varieties of evergreen from balsam, to pine, to the spruces for which the hotel overlooking Moosetookalook had been named, contrasted prettily with deciduous trees in all their summer finery.

Of course the hardwoods were better for furniture-making.

"Does she know you bought her old house?" Sam asked.

"I've got no idea." Her parents had sold it to a college professor who'd taught at the Fallstown branch of the University of Maine. He'd since moved on. For the last year, Dan had owned the place. Eventually, he meant to turn the downstairs into a furniture showroom where he could sell the hand-crafted pieces he made in his spare time.

"You surprised she came back?" Sam snugged the ball-cap back into place.

Dan shrugged, still watching the car. "Ten years ago I'd have bet money she wouldn't. 'Never coming back,' she said when she left. Sure sounded like she meant it."

"Teenagers say a lot of things they later regret." Sam's eyes narrowed. "Do 'em, too. The way I remember it, you once had a wicked crush on Liss MacCrimmon."

"Yeah. In third grade. Showed my affection by putting a snake in her desk. She paid me back by stuffing it down the front of my shirt."

He'd still been attracted to her when they were fifteen or so, but Liss hadn't seemed to return his interest. He'd ended up going steady with Karen Cloutier instead. Karen had been cheerleader to his basketball player the last two years of high school. Perfect match, everyone had said. Too bad she turned so crazy jealous every time he even spoke to another girl. He wondered what had happened to Karen. They'd gone off to different colleges after graduation and lost touch. He hadn't thought about her in years.

He *had* thought about Liss MacCrimmon. Thanks to Margaret Boyd, he'd gotten periodic updates. The latest news was that Liss had taken a fall and banged up her knee pretty bad and that Margaret had invited her to Moosetookalook to finish recuperating.

"Why don't you go on down and join the welcoming committee?" Sam suggested with a knowing grin. "I can finish repointing the chimney."

Dan shook his head. "I don't like crowds."

As soon as Liss parked her car, her aunt came bustling out of Moosetookalook Scottish Emporium. A plump woman in her late fifties, she wore one of her trademark Scottish outfits, a white dress with a tartan sash. Her son Ned was right behind her. He was not one of Dan's favorite people. And Amanda Norris had popped out onto the porch of the house next door, one of the few in the area that did not have a retail business, or plans for one, on its ground floor.

Good old Mrs. Norris. She never missed a trick. And no one could miss her. Her pear-shaped body was encased in bright-pink sweat pants and an orange t-shirt decorated with a picture of a cartoon cat. Dan couldn't say for certain at this distance, but she was probably wearing her favorite blue and white jogging shoes, the ones with the fluorescent chartreuse shoelaces.

He wondered if she'd known in advance when Liss was due to arrive, or if she'd spotted the car from her watching post in the bay window. Perched on a strategically placed chair, Mrs. Norris kept an eye on the entire neighborhood. Dan knew that if he went down now, she'd be after him for news of his sister's pregnancy, his uncle's gallbladder operation, and the latest on the carpenter his father had fired for petty theft. Dan wasn't about to let himself be buttonholed by a nosy old lady.

He moved a little closer to the edge of the roof to watch Liss get out of her car. The last time he'd seen her had been high school graduation. He remembered her as a tall, slim seventeen-year-old with sparkling eyes that changed from blue to green, depending upon what she wore, and dark brown hair cut straight and shoulder-length. At first glance she didn't seem to have changed much. She was still willowy as ever. Dan had been one of the few boys in school who'd been taller than she was. Thinner, too, but he'd filled out since then.

Liss used one hand to brace herself against the roof of her car while she pointed her left toe and flexed that foot, apparently working the kinks out before she tried to walk. Dan was surprised to see that the few steps she took before she was enveloped in Margaret Boyd's welcoming hug were unsteady. Liss had always moved with remarkable grace. She'd never clumped when she walked, the way most people did. Just how bad, he wondered, had she been hurt?

Liss returned her aunt's embrace with equal enthusiasm. "You look great, Aunt Margaret. I like the new color." Her aunt's hair was an even more brilliant red than it had been when Liss had last seen her. "And Ned." She hugged him too.

Ned was only four years her senior, but that had been enough of a gap to create some distance between them. Her cousin had always regarded her as a pest, and he hadn't hesitated to tell her so.

"I can't stay," he said as soon as she released him. "I have plans. But Mother insisted you'd need help getting your things upstairs."

Liss couldn't miss the condescension in his tone or the slight sneer on his plain, square face, but she chose to ignore both. "My bags and laptop are in the trunk. The car's unlocked."

"Hope you didn't bring too much stuff. You're not staying all that long."

That was Ned—always the charmer. Liss's father claimed his sister over-indulged her only child and he was probably right. Ned thought the whole world revolved around him.

As Liss turned to watch her cousin saunter toward her car, she realized that a third person had come out to greet her. Aunt Margaret's next-door neighbor all but skipped down her front steps and across the tiny strip of lawn that separated the houses.

White-haired and bright-eyed, decked out in vivid colors, Amanda Norris beamed at Liss. "Well, dear, just look at you! I love the scarf. Is that chiffon?"

"Hello, Mrs. Norris. Yes it is." She'd found it in a vintage-clothing store during *Strathspey's* tour of the midwest.

"Snazzy. Just like you, my dear."

In addition to being a long-time neighbor, Mrs. Norris had been one of Liss's most memorable teachers. She'd taught third grade in Moosetookalook for more than forty years. Probably half the people in town had been her pupils, Liss realized. And after she'd retired, she'd continued to be involved with Moosetookalook's children. She'd been on the school board Liss's senior year and helped Liss get a scholarship to a two-year college that offered both a business degree and classes in the performing arts. When Liss had joined *Strathspey*, Mrs. Norris had sent her a congratulatory note, wishing her success in her new endeavor. She sent Christmas cards every year too, even when Liss did not.

"Now, I won't hold you up when you're getting settled," Mrs. Norris said, "but I want you to promise me you'll be over for a nice piece of apple pie just as soon as you have a free minute."

Liss didn't hesitate to give her word. Mrs. Norris made the best apple pie in the county.

"Amazing, isn't she?" Aunt Margaret asked as the sprightly little woman darted away again. "She was eighty-two her last birthday but she's still sharp as a tack. If you want to know anything about anybody in Moosetookalook, just ask Amanda Norris. She's better than a year's worth of back newspapers for catching up on what's been going on in this town."

"I'll remember that."

There *was* one thing she was curious about. At an angle, across the near corner of the town square, was the house her parents had once owned, the house Liss had lived in for seventeen years. It had been repainted but otherwise seemed unchanged.

She shaded her eyes against the sun to better see the two men working on the roof. When one of them waved, she automatically waved back.

"Any idea who that is?" she asked her aunt.

"Dan Ruskin is just turning away. His brother Sam is over by the chimney."

She remembered them both, especially Dan. His eyes were the color of molasses and even in high school he'd had the kind of smile that could send chills down a impressionable young girl's spine. "They do roofing repairs?"

"Didn't I tell you? Dan bought the place. He's fixing it up for himself." Aunt Margaret headed inside, leaving Liss to follow. Ned had already gone ahead with her luggage.

As she crossed her aunt's front porch, Liss wondered who Dan had married. Lucky woman, whoever she was. Dan was a nice guy. And that house was perfect for raising a family.

Then she opened the door to the shop and forgot all about Dan Ruskin as she stepped back into one of the best parts of her childhood. She'd loved spending time in Moosetookalook Scottish Emporium and it looked exactly as she remembered it. Aunt Margaret always had been a great believer in "a place for everything and everything in its place." The racks of kilts and tartan skirts still marched along one side of the big sales room. The opposite wall held its usual collection of bagpipes, practice chanters, pennywhistles, and drumsticks. Cabinets, shelves, and tables all displayed items with a Scottish theme. The place even smelled the same, redolent of lemon-scented furniture polish.

For the first time in three months, Liss felt alive again.

Chapter Two

"**B**efore Ned has to leave," Aunt Margaret said, reaching for a pad of lined yellow paper, "let me fill you both in on the plan."

They had gathered in the kitchen of the apartment above the shop, Liss and her aunt seated on stools at the center island and Ned leaning indolently against the counter. Liss's aunt was not as domestic as Mrs. Norris—the scent that usually lingered most pungently in the air was that of microwave popcorn—but the room still had a homey feel. Liss smelled something wonderful simmering in the crock-pot and she recognized basil growing in a container on the windowsill.

Aunt Margaret consulted the list on the top page of the tablet. "The boxes going to the games are ready to be loaded, so we don't have to get up until five."

Liss groaned inwardly at the idea of such an early start. She'd become accustomed to performing at night and sleeping late.

"I'm sorry about the timing. It would have been easier on you if you'd been able to work in the shop for a few days first."

"No problem," Liss assured her.

Instead of just going downstairs to open the shop on her first day, she'd be driving to the fairgrounds in Fallstown to manage the Moosetookalook Scottish Emporium booth at the Western Maine Highland Games. Five o'clock wake-up call aside, Liss looked forward to it. She'd always loved participating in their local Scottish festival.

"I'll have to leave for the airport by six. Ned will drive me, but by then Sherri should be here and between her truck and your car, you two should be able to get everything to the fairgrounds in one trip. You'll have until eight to set up the booth. I've already had the tables delivered."

Liss took a long pull on a glass of ice water. Aunt Margaret talked a mile a minute. Always had. But she was the queen of organization. Liss had no worries that everything to do with the business was under control.

"Any questions?"

"Who's Sherri?"

"Didn't I tell you? Sherri Willett works part-time for me. Has ever since she came home. Wasn't she in your class at school?"

Liss nodded. She and Sherri hadn't been close, but Moose-tookalook Elementary School was small. They'd all grown up together.

First Dan Ruskin. Now Sherri Willett. Liss wondered how many others were still around. Then she frowned, remembering that Ernie Willett's daughter had been even more eager than Liss to experience life beyond Moosetookalook, Maine. Sherri hadn't waited to graduate from high school. Just before Valentine's Day their senior year, after a quarrel with her father that had been audible to neighbors four houses away, she'd packed her belongings and taken off for parts unknown.

"How long has Sherri been back?"

"Let me see. Must be about three years now. Yes, that's right. It was just a month or so after that when Sherri's mother filed for divorce and moved in with her and little Adam."

"Back up. Sherri has a son?"

Margaret nodded. "Cute little guy. Must be four or five years old. And no, there's no husband in the picture. Not sure there ever was one. Hardly matters these days, does it? Except to Ernie, of course. He won't speak to her. Didn't want to acknowledge that his wife finally walked out on him either. And of course he blamed me."

"Because you gave Sherri a job?" She supposed that could explain Willett's hostile attitude.

"Go figure. Far as I can see, he drove both his wife and his daughter away with that temper of his. Do you know he had the nerve to come here and demand that I fire Sherri? I gave him a piece of my mind, let me tell you. It'd be a cold day in Hell before I'd let a nasty old goat like him bully me."

"I still say you should have had him arrested," Ned put in. "He threatened you and he broke stuff in the shop. At the least you should have sued him for everything he's got."

"What would I want with a gas station and convenience store?" Aunt Margaret scoffed.

"I don't know. But then I don't know what you want with a hotel, either."

"Hotel?" Momentarily distracted from the alarming picture of Ernie Willett resorting to violence in her aunt's shop, Liss looked from her cousin to her aunt. There was only one hotel in Moosetookalook. "The Spruces?"

"Joe Ruskin and his sons are taking most of the risks," Aunt Margaret explained. "I'm only a very small shareholder in the project. But when they finish fixing the place up and it re-opens, the tourists will come back. Moosetookalook's economy will revive. We'll all profit."

Ned snorted. "Or you'll go bankrupt."

"Have a little faith, Ned." Aunt Margaret kept her voice light as she chided him, but Liss saw the disappointment in her aunt's eyes. She wanted her son's support and approval and clearly he wasn't about to give her either.

Liss did not sleep well that night. In the hour before dawn, she dreamed she was dancing. She came awake with a small cry of distress as a restless movement sent pain shafting through her knee.

For just a moment, she couldn't remember where she was. She didn't recognize her surroundings. She thought she must be on the road somewhere, between one show and the next. Then her gaze fell on a framed photograph on the dresser—the MacCrimmons and the Boyds three years earlier at Christmas in Arizona. Awareness crashed in on her, bringing with it renewed grief for all she had lost.

A glance at the alarm clock told Liss it would sound in another ten minutes. She turned it off and rolled out of bed. After a quick trip to the bathroom, she consulted the to-do list she'd composed the previous night, then settled herself on the floor of Aunt Margaret's guest bedroom to limber up.

Liss had run through an abbreviated version of her physical therapy exercises the night before, but they had to be repeated daily. Warm-ups and workouts were nothing new. When she was on the road, she spent hours doing floor and bar exercises every day, not to mention running through actual dances. After her surgery, she'd designed a strengthening regimen for herself and now stuck to it religiously. Ignoring protests from her newly-healed knee, Liss forced her torso downward until her chest touched the tops of her legs, a position she'd once achieved with no effort at all. She was leaning forward to repeat the stretch when she heard a light rap on the door.

"Liss? Rise and shine!"

"Be right there, Aunt Margaret." Liss levered herself up off the floor and reached for jeans and a t-shirt. They'd do for loading boxes. After that was done, she'd take a quick shower and change into clothing more appropriate for selling Scottish souvenirs.

Coffee, cereal, and toast awaited Liss in the kitchen, but she barely had time to finish eating before Aunt Margaret, watching out the window, announced that Sherri had arrived and whisked Liss off to the stockroom. It had been the kitchen when the building was a single-family home. Now it was lined with floor-to-ceiling shelving and crowded with boxes and bins.

"Still making kilts?" Liss asked, nodding toward the bolts of fabric stacked on several shelves.

"Every once in a while. The profit margin is good." Years before, Margaret had tried to teach her niece the basics of kiltmaking, but Liss had lacked the patience to do complicated, exacting needlework.

"Hello, Liss." Sherri Willett, a petite blonde, had already begun carrying boxes out to the truck she'd backed up to the side entrance that led directly into the stockroom. The merchandise going to the fairgrounds was stacked beside that door, all neatly labeled.

Liss grabbed a carton and followed suit. She wasn't sure what to say to Sherri after the first greeting. Once she'd envied her, for her size if nothing else. Liss had spent her teenage years being the tallest girl in their high school. Not that she was a giant. But the other girls—and most of the boys, too—had been shorter than her five foot nine.

"Are you going to reunion?" Sherri asked.

Liss vaguely remembered sending a card back months ago to say she couldn't come. She'd expected to be on tour. With a sinking feeling, she asked when it was being held.

"Next weekend."

"I'm just not sure I want to . . . to—"

"Face the inquisition?" Sherri finished for her.

Liss winced. The truth was, if she could have attended her tenth high school reunion as a successful professional dancer, she'd have gone in a minute. Her present circumstances made her reluctant. What if her former classmates saw her return to Moosetookalook as slinking back home, tail between her legs—a failure, washed-up, a has-been?

"If you're worried about intrusive questions, don't be. Just tell them you're 'resting.' Isn't that what people in show business call it when they're between gigs?"

Liss couldn't help but laugh. "I don't know why I care what anyone thinks. I never used to."

From an early age, Liss had been totally involved in the peculiar hobbies her family encouraged. She'd taken lessons on the bagpipe instead of the piano. She'd learned the Highland Fling rather than ballet. And in lieu of participating in field hockey or basketball or softball or trying out for cheerleading, she'd entered Scottish dance competitions.

"Maybe I will go," she said. "It might be fun to find out what everyone is up to these days." With what she hoped seemed only casual interest, she asked. "So, who did Dan Ruskin marry?"

"Dan?" A note of astonishment came into Sherri's voice. "Unless he's eloped in the last twenty-four hours, he's still single."

"Really? What's he want with a house, then?"

"No idea. Maybe he's fixing it up to sell."

"Whatever happened to that girl he used to date?"

"Karen? Believe it or not she's an executive with a software company. She's also been married and divorced. Two kids."

Liss was still trying to imagine Dan as homeowner and Karen as a mother when Ned arrived, bleary-eyed and grumbling. He didn't offer to load boxes. When he'd gone upstairs after his mother's luggage, Liss and Sherri exchanged a look.

"Same old Ned," Liss said. "Such a sweetheart. Does he do anything to help out around here?"

"Oh, sure." Sherri's truck was full, so they began stacking merchandise in the back of Liss's car. "About six months ago, he made an all-out effort to convince your aunt to sell items with higher mark-ups so she'd make bigger profits. He ordered these. Suggested retail price is twelve dollars plus tax."

She opened one of the boxes they'd just carried out. Inside were refrigerator magnets with a bagpipe and thistle design. When Liss pushed on the spot marked "press to play," the first few bars of "Scotland the Brave" sounded in a tinny imitation of a bagpipe.

"This is just . . . tacky."

Sherri shrugged. "Your aunt is betting that a good many of the folks at the games will think it's a perfect memento of the day. She's knocked the price down to five bucks apiece in the hope we can get rid of them."

"Sounds like a plan to me."

They'd just loaded the last of the stock earmarked for the Highland Games when Aunt Margaret emerged, purse and passport in one hand and cash box in the other. "Here you go, Liss. Keys to the house are inside, along with plenty of change. Sherri's name is on the bank accounts so she can pay any bills that come in."

"I hate to see you leave so soon," Liss whispered as they

embraced. "We've barely had time to catch up." Dozens of unanswered questions remained, not the least of them concerning her aunt's surprising involvement in the renovation of "the castle."

"You take Amanda Norris up on that offer of a piece of apple pie and gossip," Aunt Margaret urged, nodding toward the house next door. A flutter of movement at the bay window indicated the retired teacher was awake and keeping an eye on them.

Aunt Margaret was on her way moments later. Liss watched Ned's car until it turned the corner, then took a moment before going inside to shower to appreciate the beauty of the day.

She hadn't really had the chance to study her surroundings the previous afternoon. Early morning light gave all the old houses around the square a mellow look. Directly across from her aunt's store, one large brick edifice stood out in a sea of white clapboard: the municipal building. It housed the town office, the police station, the firehouse, and the public library. As for the town square itself, picturesque didn't begin to describe it. It contained everything people expected of a rural New England town—gazebo-style bandstand, monument to the Civil War dead, flagpole, even a playground with a jungle gym, a slide, a small merry-go-round, and swings big enough for adults.

When she had time, Liss promised herself, she'd take a stroll through the old neighborhood, but right now she had to get a move on. The Highland Games were scheduled to open in less than two hours.

"Look quick!" Sherri shoved a pair of binoculars into Liss's hands and pointed toward the athletic field.

Liss managed to adjust the focus in time to see Pete

Campbell throw the *clachneart*—the Scottish version of the Olympic shot put.

Most people would have kept their eyes on the twenty-eight pound granite stone Pete held at shoulder height, wondering if it would break the local record of thirty-five feet. Forewarned by the laughter in Sherri's voice, Liss watched Pete's kilt. He spun three times in a circle. Each rotation sent the fabric billowing higher. The final revolution, just before he let go of the stone, lifted the hem above his thighs.

A traditional Scot wasn't supposed to wear anything at all beneath the kilt, but this was an American version of the Highland Games and Pete Campbell, though he'd passed on the more usual cut-offs and bicycle shorts, wasn't about to risk arrest for indecent exposure. Swim trunks patterned in fluorescent purple and chartreuse flowers winked at spectators for a split second before the concealing folds of the Campbell tartan settled back to knee level.

"Oh, God!" Sherri had watched through a second pair of binoculars. "Did you see that?" Her cheeks were bright pink. "He said he'd wear them but I didn't think he would."

Grinning as much over Sherri's delight as at Pete's unconventional choice of attire for the Stone of Strength competition, Liss waited on the next customer. "That will be ten dollars and sixty cents," she told a middle-aged brunette wearing a MacDougall tartan sash over jeans and a camp shirt.

While the woman searched her pockets for exact change, Liss shoved a damp lock of hair out of her face, tucking it behind her ear. For the most part she'd been able to ignore the heat and humidity. The hot, sticky weather wasn't exactly a surprise, not in late July, but Liss did wish she wasn't dressed in an ankle-length wool skirt and a long-sleeved blouse.

Suck it up and keep smiling, she told herself. It was part of the job to be a walking advertisement for the store's line of Scottish women's wear. At least the smiles came easily. They'd had a steady stream of paying customers ever since the gates opened.

Liss wrapped her customer's purchase, a ceramic mug decorated with a thistle, the symbol of Scotland, in tissue paper, sliding both it and the receipt into one of the small red bags Aunt Margaret special-ordered with "Moosetookalook Scottish Emporium" emblazoned on both sides. She watched the woman trot off, package in hand, toward the clan tents, and felt a sense of satisfaction. Business was brisk. Aunt Margaret would be pleased.

Both Liss and Sherri were busy for the next half hour. Sherri was still ringing up sales when Liss finally managed a short break. She used it to take in the sounds and smells and sights peculiar to Scottish festivals.

A very welcome breeze carried a snatch of song in a clear soprano voice above the general hubbub of the crowd. According to the program, a series of performers were scheduled throughout the day.

The same stirring of fresh air also brought a variety of smells wafting Liss's way, including one that made her stomach growl. Nothing in the world smelled better than freshly baked scones. They'd always been a weakness of hers.

The area around the Moosetookalook Scottish Emporium booth was a virtual forest of tents and awnings. Along one side were vendors of goods and food. Clans and societies, together with registration centers for various events, dominated the other. Liss had a good, if distant, view of the athletic field used for sports competitions and the parade field where everything from the performance by the massed bands to the sheepdog trials took place.

Along with the chatter, laughter, and occasional cheers

of the crowds, bagpipes skirled. Now and again Liss picked out a few stray notes of a reel or strathspey being played by the lone piper assigned to accompany the dancers. She was too far away to see the stage set up for that competition and thought that was probably just as well. Watching young girls do what she no longer could would be difficult.

Distance didn't help, however, when she recognized the current tune as "The Battle of the Somme." She'd danced to it on dozens of stages just like the one at the other end of the fairgrounds. A flash of memory assaulted her with painful clarity. She was nine years old and wearing *Arisaidh* dress, an outfit that had evolved as a sort of national costume for female dancers after the organizers of the Aboyne Highland Games in Scotland refused to allow women to wear the kilt. Liss's version of *Arisaidh* dress consisted of a gathered skirt and a green velvet jacket that laced up the front. A plaid in MacCrimmon colors was attached to the waistband at the back and came up and over her right shoulder to fasten to the jacket with a brooch that displayed her clan crest. She moved gracefully and energetically with the music, feeling no pain, easily beating out the competition in the Scottish lilt.

"Liss?"

Sherri's voice brought Liss back to the present with a jolt. Feeling as if someone had just doused her with cold water, she shivered and had to take a moment to reorient herself.

"Do you need to sit?" Sherri's worried gaze fixed on Liss's hip-shot stance.

Liss straightened abruptly. She was not supposed to favor her left leg. Shifting position and gears, she forced a smile. "I'm fine."

She was, too. Keeping busy was the best cure for any

ailment and the morning's flood of customers had resumed. Liss sold a cashmere scarf while Sherri rang up a
pewter figurine of a bagpiper and two kilt pins.

"I want that," said a young man in shorts and a t-shirt
decorated with a Scottish lion. He pointed to a small dagger, silver mounted and hand carved, in its own leather
sheath.

"Do you know the traditions associated with the *sgian
dubh*?" Liss asked as she wrapped the knife. "*Sgian dubh*
translates as 'black dagger' and in the old days warriors
believed it should never be drawn and returned to its scab-
bard without spilling blood. Later, when the English passed
laws prohibiting Scots from carrying weapons, they ex-
empted the *sgian dubh* from the ban. Their reasoning was
that one of these little knives was only big enough for a Scot
to slit his own throat with, and that was a *good* thing."

"TMI, lady," the young man said. "I'm buying it to use
as a letter opener."

"Too much information," Liss murmured when he was
gone. Granted, not everyone found Scots trivia as fascinat-
ing as she did, but why would someone attend a Scottish
festival if he didn't have any interest in Scotland's history
and traditions?

"Only his opinion," Sherri said. "Don't let him get you
down."

"No, he's probably right. I do go on. Do me a favor? If
I start to babble again, smack me."

"I think you should babble all you like. You really
know this stuff cold."

"That doesn't mean other people want to hear it."

"Hey, when you're passionate about something, you
have to share, right?"

A new customer arrived and began flipping through a
box of Scottish-themed bumper stickers. "You got any

more of these?" he asked Sherri, holding up one that read "Old Pipers Never Die. Their Bags Just Dry Up."

"Another of Ned's selections," Sherri whispered before she dutifully trotted over to help out.

Liss turned her attention to a woman examining a row of figurines—piper, drummer, soldier—each six-and-a-half inches tall and all in Highland dress. She blinked in surprise when she recognized Mrs. Norris. "Well, hello again. I didn't expect to see you here."

"Oh, I can never resist coming to take a look around. I won't stay long. Too much going on. But I did want to see how you were doing." For her jaunt to the fairgrounds, the retired teacher wore stretch denim and a loose, sleeveless top. The jogging shoes were the same ones she'd had on the previous day.

"Things are going just fine, Mrs. Norris."

"Had a scone yet?"

Liss laughed. "Imagine you remembering that!"

"Oh, I never forget a thing, dear. In fact, I seem to recall something a little naughty about you."

"I can't imagine what."

"Can't you?"

Liss shook her head, truly baffled. "I wasn't exactly a wild child."

"Well, we all have our little secrets. And I know most of them."

"Now *that* sounds ominous," Liss teased her. "Should I be worried about blackmail?"

"Too risky. That would make you a threat to me, if you were murderously inclined, that is." Mrs. Norris lowered her voice. "I was reading a mystery novel the other day in which a character is stabbed to death with a little dagger. I wonder if it could have been one of these?" She indicated another *sgian dubh*.

"Was the story set in Scotland?" Amanda Norris loved to read. Liss had seen her bookshelves. They were lined with mysteries, although romances ran a close second.

"Sixteenth-century England, but the victim was a Scot."

For once, Liss wasn't certain of her history. "I'm not sure they called it a *sgian dubh* that long ago, but I'd certainly think twice about crossing someone who carried a knife."

"This character should have thought twice about carrying one himself, since it was his own weapon that was used against him. Still, he got what he deserved. That's as it should be." She nodded sagely. "You'll get your just desserts, too, Liss MacCrimmon."

At Liss's blank look, Mrs. Norris leaned in, again lowering her voice to a whisper. "That piece of apple pie, dear. It's still got your name on it."

Chapter Three

For the first time all day, there were no potential customers in sight. Liss sank gratefully down onto a stool and fished under the counter for the cooler she'd packed with lunch. It was just after one in the afternoon.

Her knee ached a bit, but as a dancer she was accustomed to ignoring pain. Just now she was more concerned about easing the hollow feeling in her stomach. She hadn't eaten a bite since that quick breakfast at sunrise.

With a sigh, she pulled a container of strawberry yogurt out of the cooler. "Want one?" she asked Sherri.

"Yuck."

Silently agreeing with that assessment, Liss peeled back the top and dug in. She tried to imagine she was eating a warm scone dripping with butter. It didn't work. She couldn't even pretend the yogurt was one of the flavored scones, best eaten plain. "I have a feeling I'll be giving in to temptation before the day is out," she muttered under her breath.

Sherri popped the top on a can of soda and squinted toward the athletic field. The Stone of Strength competition was long over but two other events were in progress at opposite ends of the field, the caber toss and the sheaf throw.

Even without the binoculars, Liss could see the action

well enough. Each caber was nineteen feet long and weighed a hundred and twenty pounds—most people compared them to telephone poles. The object of the competition wasn't distance, but to toss the caber end-over-end so that the small end fell directly away from the competitor. The sheaf toss was an event that involved tossing a sixteen-pound sheaf of hay, encased in a burlap bag, over a bar . . . using a three-tined pitchfork.

"Hammer throw is next," Sherri said, consulting a program. "Pete's entered in that one, too."

"Not my favorite sport," Liss said. The hammer, a metal ball attached to a wooden handle, weighed a little over twenty pounds and had been known to fly more than a hundred yards when well thrown. "One year I stood too close to the field. A contestant lost his grip on the hammer and I swear it was coming straight at me. I let out a shriek and threw myself flat on the ground."

"Were you hit?"

Liss shook her head, a rueful expression on her face. "The only thing damaged was my dignity. The hammer didn't land anywhere near me."

She could smile about it now. At the time she'd been mortified.

"So," she said, scooping out the last of the yogurt, "do you have a special interest in Pete Campbell?" Liss remembered him slightly. He'd been a couple of years ahead of them in school.

A haunted expression came over Sherri's face. "What would be the point? I come with too much baggage."

Frowning thoughtfully, Liss tossed the now empty container toward the trash can. "Because you have a child?"

"That's part of it. The other's my job. And his. It's complicated."

"I'm a good listener," Liss offered. "What does working

in a shop that sells Scottish imports have to do with any-thing?"

"Oh, not that job. I only work part time for your aunt. My full-time job is as a corrections officer for the sheriff's department." Before Liss could ask for further explana-tion, Sherri's gaze shifted, moving to a spot over Liss's shoulder. Her eyes widened. "Oh-oh."

"What?" Liss turned her head to look but saw nothing that alarmed her.

"Jason Graye is coming this way. He's got to be the most obnoxious man in Moosetookalook."

"Never heard of him."

"He only turned up in this area a couple of years ago. One of those move-in-and-take-over types. Lives in Moose-tookalook but owns a real estate company here in Fallstown. Got himself elected president of the Rotary Club and a selectman."

"Ah, an entrepreneur!"

Sherri grinned. "Yup."

Liss fixed her salesperson smile in place and reached her side of the counter just as a man and woman came abreast of the booth. Graye looked to be forty at most, with a hawk nose and strong jaw. His companion was younger, but not by much. Of medium height and slender, she'd styled her strawberry blonde hair into an elaborate twist that kept it away from an oval face dominated by pouty lips and rather pretty hazel eyes. Liss glanced at her hand, looking for a wedding ring, but didn't see one.

"The lady wants a kilt," Jason Graye said. He had a brusque manner and although he wasn't quite tall enough to loom over Liss, he thrust himself into her space in a way that made her hackles rise. She wondered if he tried to in-timidate everyone, or only those he considered his inferi-ors.

Hiding her irritation behind the facade of a helpful salesclerk, she invited him to come around the counter and take a look. A narrow aisle allowed access to several racks of clothing, including ready-made kilts. The rest of the sales space consisted of a series of display tables arranged in a square under an awning.

From the rack holding an even dozen, Liss selected a kilt in the red, green, yellow, blue, and white Royal Stewart tartan and held it up for their inspection. "This one is beautifully made."

Graye reached in front of his companion and flipped the price tag over. His eyes widened. "Three hundred dollars! For a skirt?"

"For a *kilt*," Liss corrected him. "Kilts are tightly pleated at the back and take eight yards of material to make. The apron front has to hang just right. Length is important, too. A properly-made kilt just clears the ground when the wearer kneels."

"That looks too big for me," the woman said, leaning in and nearly knocking Liss over with the strong perfume she wore. "What size is it?"

"They don't come sized the way women's clothes are. To be honest, the best way to make sure your kilt will look right is to have one custom made."

"And that costs more, right?" Graye made it sound as if he thought Liss was trying to bilk him.

"Yes, it does. And it can't be done overnight, but the results are well worth both the price and the wait. We have three sources for custom-made kilts. Kilts ordered from Canada arrive in ten to twelve weeks. Special orders to the kilt-maker we use in Glasgow take longer."

"And the third choice?" the woman asked.

"My aunt, the owner of Moosetookalook Scottish Emporium, makes kilts as a sideline. However, she is currently in Scotland. I'm afraid you'd have to wait three weeks just for an appointment to have measurements taken."

"Forget it. Come on, Barbara."

But Barbara was having none of it. Liss applauded her for refusing to let Jason Graye boss her around even as she winced at the whine in the other woman's voice. "You promised, Jase. You promised me a kilt."

"That was when I thought we could get one off the rack." Unspoken was the qualifier "cheap."

"You promised."

"All right. All right. Anything to shut you up. Order the damned kilt."

All smiles, Barbara turned back to Liss. "I don't like this plaid. It's too bright."

"In connection with kilts, the pattern is called a tartan, and these days each clan has one or more of its own. Do you have any Scottish ancestors?"

"I don't think so." Her face fell, momentarily giving her the look of a small child denied a treat. "Does that mean I can't wear a kilt?"

"Not at all. The tartan I just showed you is called Royal Stewart and this—" she pulled out a kilt featuring darker hues"—is Black Watch. Anyone can wear either of these, which is why you often see them in the uniforms of bag-pipe bands."

Liss lovingly fingered the soft wool, debating whether or not she should elaborate on the terminology. What Barbara had called plaid—pronouncing it "pladd"—was rightly tartan and a plaid—pronounced "played"—was the rectangular woolen cape in a tartan pattern that was worn over one shoulder. TMI, she decided. By the same token, she didn't think she'd let Jason Graye in on the fact that some purists still insisted only men be allowed to wear kilts. That would cost Aunt Margaret a sale for sure.

"I don't like that pattern either," Barbara said. "Too dark."

Liss indicated the tartan in her own skirt, yet another available to anyone. "This is Hunting Stewart."

But Barbara's gaze had strayed to an assortment of tartan ties on a nearby rack. "What about that one?" The pattern she'd picked was dark green and blue with black and pink worked in.

"You're in luck." And so was Aunt Margaret. "This is called the Flower of Scotland and was specifically created for those who don't have Scots roots. I noticed just this morning that there is a bolt of this fabric in my aunt's stock room, so if you'd like to go ahead and place the order for your kilt, I can set up an appointment for three weeks from today. The deposit is a hundred dollars."

"What a racket," Graye complained.

"I want a kilt in this pattern." Arms crossed in front of her chest, Barbara gave him a look that said she wasn't budging until he agreed to Liss's terms.

"And I want to see this bolt of fabric first," Graye said, "to make sure it's quality stuff. And I want to see a sample of your aunt's work. Margaret Boyd, right? I know her."

Liss kept smiling, but it took an effort. "I'm not sure one of Aunt Margaret's creations is available. Every kilt she makes is pre-sold. They don't stay in the shop long once they're finished. As for the fabric, however, I'd be happy to bring the bolt of cloth here to the fairgrounds with me tomorrow, if that would suit."

"We won't be here tomorrow. Why not today? It's only sixteen miles to Moosetookalook. You could get there in twenty minutes."

"But to drive there, pick up the fabric, and come back would take closer to an hour," Liss pointed out. "I'm afraid neither Sherri nor I can spare that much time away from the booth."

Luckily, the number of customers browsing at the display tables supported her claim. Just now they could have used a third pair of hands.

"You could give me a key to the shop," Graye had the audacity to suggest. "Barbara and I can stop in on our way home."

"I'm sorry, Mr. Graye, but I can't do that. You'll have to wait until tomorrow."

Graye seemed prepared to argue further, but Barbara put a restraining hand on his arm. "We'll be back," she assured Liss.

Graye's expression was thunderous but he took his cue from Barbara and left. As they walked away, Liss could hear him muttering under his breath about the extra mileage he'd have to put on his car to make a second visit to the fairgrounds.

"But apparently it's okay for *me* to drive to Moosetookalook and back." Liss shook her head. There was just no accounting for some people's logic.

Sherri rang up a purchase for a falconer with a hooded hawk on his shoulder and then helped herself to another soda from the cooler. "I wonder why Graye's girlfriend wants a kilt in the first place. All those pleats just make women look fat. Now a man in a kilt, that's another matter. Men in kilts are to die for. Just look at Mel Gibson in *Braveheart*."

Liss opened her mouth to comment, then closed it again. If Sherri was like most people, she didn't care a bit that Mel's movie had taken appalling liberties with history.

* * *

Working with a steady rhythm, Dan Ruskin applied the final coat of varnish to an oak drawer. He knew Ned Boyd was standing in the open doorway of the carriage house he'd converted into a woodworking shop. He'd seen him cross the town square. Dan was ignoring him, hoping he'd get bored and go away.

"What *is* that?" Ned finally asked.

"Puzzle table."

"Could you be a little more specific?"

"It's a table purpose-built for putting together jigsaw puzzles. Folding legs for storage. Cover to keep cats, children, and other predators from knocking the pieces onto the floor. Drawers for sorting."

"Huh. You sell many of those?"

"A few." Two, so far. One to his brother.

Uninvited, Ned wandered around Dan's workspace, idly examining both the tools and the results of Dan's latest experiments in hand-crafted furniture. There were two decorative clocks with battery-operated works, one Shaker-style and the other Art Deco. Also a cradle, a rocking chair, a pair of high stools for use at a bar, and an earlier, less successful model of the puzzle table.

"Something you wanted, Ned?"

"Wondering about the hotel."

"What about it?"

"You really think you can make a go of it?"

"My dad does. So does your mother."

"A less charitable soul than I am might wonder if Joe Ruskin conned my mother out of her hard-earned life savings."

Dan stroked too hard with the brush, caught himself before he ruined the finish, and continued more slowly and with a gentler touch. "You want to be careful tossing accusations around."

"I'm just saying that a hotel and convention center in the middle of nowhere seems like a pretty shaky proposal. Might work in Portland or Bangor, where there's an airport nearby, but here?"

"Why not? Look at the Sinclair House over to Waycross Springs. That place is still going strong after more than a hundred years. So is the Mount Washington in New Hampshire and the Mohonk Mountain House in New York State."

"*Still* going. That's the difference, isn't it? That old wreck on the hill bled money for years before it finally went out of business."

Truth to tell, Dan had his own doubts about his father's pet project. The castle needed a lot of work and it would take more money than the investors now had to finance all the renovations. But just as Dan's dream was to one day leave the family business for full-time custom furniture-making, his father's was to retire from Ruskin Construction and run The Spruces. Forty years ago, as a young man, Joe Ruskin had worked at the hotel and fallen in love with the place.

Finished with one drawer, Dan put it aside to dry and reached for the second. He inhaled the familiar, calming smells of his workshop. Underlying the sawdust, the linseed oil, and the turpentine was the cedar with which he'd paneled the walls.

"I'm worried about my mother, Dan," Ned said. "What say you get your old man to let her out of the partnership?"

"That's between the two of them," Dan told him. "Last I heard, Margaret was enthusiastic about being part of the rebirth of Moosetookalook."

"She's getting on in years. She doesn't always know what's best for her."

Dan snorted. "Margaret hasn't even hit sixty yet. She's a

long way from being too senile to manage her own affairs."

"I'm not so sure about that. Why do you think she jumped at the chance to have all her expenses paid on a trip to Scotland? She couldn't afford the annual buying trip on her own this year. The hotel is a big draw on her cash reserves."

Leaving less for you to wheedle out of her, Dan thought in disgust. "Give it up, Ned. I'm not sticking my nose in."

This time he succeeded in ignoring his unwelcome visitor until the other man went away. Dan put Ned out of his mind, but he wasn't as successful at forgetting Ned's cousin. He'd been thinking about Liss MacCrimmon, on and off, ever since he'd seen her get out of her car the previous day.

She was putting in long hours at the fairgrounds. She'd be tired when she got home. A good neighbor would do something about that. Pizza, he decided. That was nice and casual and easy to come by. Louie Graziano's tiny restaurant was just a block away and he delivered.

That settled, Dan went back to work. From about six-thirty on, he'd keep an eye out for Liss's car. As soon as she returned, he'd go over and offer to treat her to take-out.

By the time Liss closed the booth at six, she was glad to see the day end. It had been exhilarating, but she was ready for a break.

With Sherri's help, she unrolled the sides of the awning to form a tent, tying them together and anchoring them to the ground. It was only after she'd sent Sherri home that she realized that wasn't enough protection. Although the canvas would keep rain out, it wouldn't be much of a deterrent to theft. Security guards patrolled the grounds at night, but they couldn't keep an eye on everything. Reluctant to take chances with Aunt Margaret's merchandise, Liss packed up the more valuable items and loaded them into her car to take back to Moosetookalook.

The thunderstorm that had been threatening all day hit when she was halfway home, forcing her to pull over to the side of the road and wait it out. With all the delays, it was nearly nightfall when she pulled up in front of the shop.

Liss slung the strap of her shoulder bag across her chest for ease of carrying, collected the cash box and the small cooler that had held her lunch, and got out of the car. She debated whether her aunt's stock would be safe locked in the trunk overnight and decided that thieves were unlikely to know it was there.

The streetlamps had come on, although it wasn't yet full dark. By their light, even before she made her way across the wide front porch to the store entrance, Liss could distinguish the huge, colorful sign directing customers to the Carrabassett County Fairgrounds for the Western Maine Highland Games. A smaller placard informed potential buyers that the store would be closed until Tuesday at ten. In this part of Maine, even in tourist season, most businesses that stayed open on Saturdays took Mondays off.

Liss's stomach growled as she let herself into the shop. She'd finally given in and bought herself a scone, but that had been hours ago. Her goals in life were simple just now—nuke a microwave dinner from the freezer and take a long, hot bubble bath.

Both, however, would have to wait just a little longer. Leaving the cash box and cooler on the counter, Liss threaded her way through the dimly lit shop to the stockroom. If she collected the bolt of tartan wool before she went upstairs, there'd be no chance she'd forget to take it with her in the morning. Jason Graye might be a royal pain, but his money was nothing to scoff at. His kilt order would yield a nice profit.

The sense of wrongness hit Liss the moment she opened the door.

Her fingers, already reaching for the switch, completed the movement, flooding the room with light. Harsh overhead fluorescent bulbs illuminated the scene with merciless clarity.

The Flower of Scotland fabric was no longer on the shelf.

It was on the floor, partially covering a very dead body.

Chapter Four

D an had just locked his workshop and started down the street toward Moosetookalook Scottish Emporium when he saw Liss stagger out onto the porch. Even in the uncertain illumination of the streetlight, he could tell that something was wrong. Shudders racked her slim frame as she braced one trembling hand against the nearest pillar.

Breaking into a run, he covered the distance in a matter of seconds. She gasped when he skidded to a halt at the foot of the porch steps, her eyes wide and frightened in a face devoid of color.

"Liss, what's wrong?"

With visible effort, she managed to whisper an answer. "She's dead. Dan, she's dead."

"Who's dead?"

Tears leaked out of the corners of her eyes. "Amanda Norris. She's in the stockroom. I just found her."

When Liss swayed, as if about to keel over, Dan grabbed her by the shoulders and gently shoved until she was sitting on the top step. "Stay right here," he told her, and went inside.

He knew where the stockroom was. He'd been in Margaret Boyd's store often enough to be familiar with the place. Besides, Liss had left the door open and the light on. He didn't have to venture past the doorsill to see that what she had told him was true. A bolt of fabric had tumbled from a shelf to land on the body, unrolling enough to cover part of it, but he recognized Mrs. Norris's fluffy white hair and her blue and white jogging shoes.

Dan swallowed hard. Blood stained the wood flooring beneath her head.

The sound of soft footfalls behind him had Dan whirling around, jumpy as a cat, but it was only Liss.

"Maybe I was wrong. Maybe she's not dead."

"You weren't wrong." Dan had no doubt on that score. The human body tended to void itself at the moment of death. He'd learned that when his grandfather passed away in the upstairs bedroom at his parents' house. He'd been seven years old when he'd walked into that room, sent by his mother to call her father down to breakfast. The smell had imprinted itself on his memory.

But he went to Mrs. Norris anyway, kneeling down so he could feel for a pulse. "Nothing. She's gone. Looks like she fell against the shelving." He glanced up, instantly spotting the blood staining one of the metal brackets that stuck out at the front edge of an upper shelf. "She must have hit the back of her head against the end of that at just the wrong point. A freak accident." He didn't really want to dwell on what might have happened. He had a strong stomach, but not for something like this. "Christ. I just talked to her this morning."

"Me, too," Liss whispered. She swiped at the tears staining her cheeks. "But what was she *doing* here?"

Good question, Dan thought. "You didn't let her in?"

"No. I just got home. I came back here for a bolt of cloth." A sob escaped her. "*That* cloth. I don't understand. How can she be dead?"

Her face was no longer ashen, but Dan suspected Liss

was still in shock. He wasn't feeling too steady himself. It was almost impossible to imagine Moosetookalook without Mrs. Norris. He went to Liss's side and gently steered her from the room, closing the door behind them.

Liss didn't seem to know what to do next. Dan wasn't sure either, but he knew who would. He reached for the phone on the sales counter. It took him two tries to manage 911. Liss wasn't the only one with the shakes.

A short conversation with a dispatcher yielded almost immediate results. After all, the police station was just across the town square. Jeff Thibodeau, a big, balding man who'd been on the Moosetookalook Police Force for as long as Dan could remember, came on foot. They could see him through the window as he loped toward them, ignoring the "keep off the grass" signs on the green.

"Stay put," he ordered, and went into the stockroom.

"She invited me over for apple pie," Liss whispered in a broken voice.

Dan reached over and squeezed her hand. "She made good pies."

"She made *great* pies."

Thibodeau returned, looking as shaken as Dan felt. "Do either of you know what happened in there?"

Liss shook her head. Dan hazarded a guess. "She tripped on something? Fell. Hit her head."

"I dunno, Dan. I can't see anything that would've caused her to do that."

Liss's eyes widened. "Surely you can't think . . . she wasn't—"

"Pushed?" Thibodeau didn't look happy about it, but he clearly had suspicions. "Seems like you'd have to hit your head awful hard to die from it."

"A freak accident—"

"Better let the experts decide. I'm damned if I know

what happened. But the back door's unlocked and she had no business being in there. Did she?"

"No," Liss whispered. "We were closed. The Games. I just got back."

In her agitation, she'd kept hold of Dan's hand. Now she tightened her grip. It was a measure of how upset she was, Dan thought. Liss MacCrimmon had never been the type to cling.

He was keenly aware of the irony. He'd wanted to get close to Liss for years, but this was a helluva way to do it. Murder? He couldn't seem to take in the possibility. Mrs. Norris was a pain sometimes, but she was harmless. What kind of monster would kill an old lady?

"Whatever happened here," Jeff said, "it's an unattended death. I've got to call in the M.E. and I think I'd better send for LaVerdiere, too." He reached for the portable radio attached to his belt.

"State cop?"

Jeff grimaced. "Yeah. Craig LaVerdiere. He's the one assigned to this area so this'll be his case. It shouldn't take him long to get here. He just lives over to Wade's Corners."

"Okay if I take Liss up to Margaret's apartment?" Dan asked.

"Yeah, sure. You need to stick around anyhow. LaVerdiere's going to want to talk to both of you."

Dan lost no time putting some distance between them and the body.

Once upstairs, Liss started to pull herself together. "I should make coffee."

"Probably a good idea. Looks like it's going to be a long night." Anything he drank right now would likely burn like acid, but Dan figured it would help Liss to be busy. He followed her into the kitchen and settled onto one of the high stools at the center island.

"Thanks for stepping in. I would have pulled myself together eventually. I had some idea of running across the square to the police station. But I'm glad you showed up. I just couldn't seem to wrap my mind around . . . I still can't."

"I was on my way here anyway," Dan said.

The hand measuring coffee into the pot stilled for a moment, then completed the task. She didn't turn around. "Why?"

"Figured you'd be beat after a day at the games. I was going to suggest sharing a pizza, so you wouldn't have to cook." He shrugged. "Seemed like a good idea at the time."

She started the coffee perking and rinsed her hands before joining him at the island. "That was a very nice thought."

"Hey, what are neighbors for?"

Her tentative smile vanished along with what little color she'd regained. Dan could have kicked himself. Confessing his plan to get reacquainted with Liss had been intended to take her mind *off* Mrs. Norris.

Liss studied her clasped hands for a moment, then abruptly excused herself. "I need . . . I'll be back . . . I just . . . make yourself at home."

She needed to be alone for a bit. Dan got that. And when, a few minutes later, he heard the shower running, he understood that, too.

The image wouldn't wash away no matter how hard Liss scrubbed.

The angle of the body. The wrongness of that cloth half covering it like some misaligned tartan sash. The blood. The smell. Bile rose in her throat. She had to brace one hand against the side of the shower stall until her insides settled again.

Even worse than stumbling upon a body was that the

dead woman was Mrs. Norris. She was a widow with no children, Liss remembered. In fact, she didn't have any living relatives. But she'd made all of Moosetookalook her family. Just because someone moved away didn't mean she forgot about them. Liss knew for a fact that Mrs. Norris still corresponded regularly with Liss's parents in Arizona. Amanda Norris might not have any descendants to mourn her, but there were hundreds of people whose lives she had touched. They'd be devastated by the news of her death.

She *had* to have fallen. A tragic accident. Anything else was unthinkable. No one would deliberately hurt Mrs. Norris. A small sound of distress escaped Liss at that horrible thought, barely drowned out by the cascade of water. She desperately wanted to believe Jeff Thibodeau was mistaken.

With hands that felt stiff and clumsy, Liss shut off the water, now gone tepid. She rested her forehead against the glass door of the shower. She didn't know how long she stood there, but she was chilled by the time a voice called her name.

"Liss? You okay?"

Dan. Dan Ruskin. She fumbled for a towel. Good grief. She'd been more addled by finding Mrs. Norris than she'd thought if she'd completely forgotten that she'd left him sitting in Aunt Margaret's kitchen. "I'm fine," she called. "Give me a minute."

Of all the ways she might have imagined getting reacquainted with Dan, this was *not* one of them.

"The state police detective's here." The note of warning in his voice made the hair on the back of her neck prickle.

"I'll be right out," she called.

She quickly finished toweling herself off, glad she'd remembered to grab clean clothes on her way to the bathroom. It did not take long to blow dry her hair and slip into a gauzy, ankle-length skirt and a soft, lacy camisole. She didn't bother with makeup. This was no time for primping.

Liss paused with her hand on the doorknob. Bracing herself for whatever new shocks waited beyond the relative security of the bathroom, praying no one would guess that her composure was all on the surface, she stepped into the hall.

A lanky blond stranger in gray slacks, white shirt, herringbone jacket, and conservative maroon tie was just coming out of her bedroom. He had a boyish face that made her think he must be younger than she was, but his attitude left no doubt as to which of them was in charge. "Where are the clothes you were wearing?" he demanded.

Taken aback, Liss just pointed. She'd hung her wool skirt on the back of the bathroom door and stuffed everything else into the hamper.

"Come into the living room," he ordered, leading the way. He gave the uniformed officer already there orders to bag up her discarded clothing.

Liss felt as if she'd been kicked in the stomach. He was acting as if he considered her a suspect. "What on earth—?"

"You found her, right?"

"Well, yes, but—"

"Why did you take a shower?"

Anxiety abruptly gave way to annoyance. "I'd just worked all day in the heat and humidity at the fairgrounds. Why do you *think* I took a shower?" She left the words *you moron* unspoken.

The sound of a throat clearing pulled her attention away from the detective. Dan sat on the sofa, a mug of coffee in one hand. His deadly serious expression sent a shiver down Liss's spine.

"This is Detective Craig LaVerdiere, Liss. He's in charge of the investigation."

Investigation—she didn't like the sound of that word. It seemed to confirm that Jeff had been right and Mrs. Norris's death wasn't an accident.

"Would you like some coffee?" Dan asked. He'd already poured a mug for her and set cream and sweetener out on the coffee table. He'd also unearthed Aunt Margaret's brandy, presumably to add a dollop of that to the brew.

"I'm through with you, Ruskin," the detective said when Liss sat down beside Dan on the sofa. "I'll have a statement typed up for you to sign tomrrow. For now, you can go home."

Liss wondered how much time she'd lost in the shower. Then again, she didn't suppose Dan had had much to say. As he'd already told her, he'd been at home until he'd seen her car and come over to suggest ordering pizza.

She frowned, suddenly acutely aware that Dan didn't know exactly when she'd arrived. If she needed an alibi, she was out of luck.

Don't think like that, she told herself. *This is all some horrible misunderstanding. Mrs. Norris fell!*

Dan made no move to leave. Instead he looked at Liss. "Would you like me to stay?"

"You've got no business—"

"Yes," Liss interrupted. She might be confused about some things, but she was certain she didn't want to be left alone with this aggressive detective.

As if to underscore the reason for her uneasiness, the uniformed trooper walked through the room carrying the bag that contained Liss's clothes. She assumed he was taking them away for some sort of testing.

"What's going on here, detective?" she asked. "I thought Mrs. Norris fell and struck her head."

"I ask the questions, Ms. MacCrimmon. You answer them."

"Very well. But Mr. Ruskin stays." She wasn't ashamed to admit that she felt less vulnerable with Dan beside her. Everyone needed a little support sometimes.

LaVerdiere gave her a fulminating glare but after a moment he settled into the chair opposite the sofa and retrieved a small, spiral-bound notebook from his breast pocket. When he'd turned on the small tape recorder sitting next to the brandy, he recited the day and time for the tape and identified himself. Then he asked Liss for her full name.

She gave it to him with a straight face. "Amaryllis Rosalie MacCrimmon."

He never looked up from his notebook, and she grudgingly gave him one point for sensitivity. The fanciful name her mother—Violet—had given her had always embarrassed Liss. As a child she couldn't even pronounce it.

"You say you were at the fairgrounds today?" LaVerdiere asked.

Liss doctored her coffee and took a tentative sip before she answered. "Yes. I was there all day. I left here around six-thirty this morning."

"The store was closed for the day?"

"That's right. It always is for the Highland Games. I set up and ran the Scottish Emporium booth."

"What time did the games end for the day?"

"Six."

His eyebrows lifted. "So you were home for some time before you discovered the body."

She shook her head. "I found her only minutes after arriving here. It took awhile to close up. Some of the stock had to be repacked and stored in my car. And the weather was bad driving back to Moosetookalook."

"What time was it when you entered the shop?"

"I don't know. I didn't look at a clock."

"Did you see anyone when you came in?"

"No."

"Do you know why the victim was in that storeroom?"

"No."

"Do you know how she got into the building?"

"No, although it would be easy enough to find Aunt Margaret's spare key. She always left it on the sill over the back door. Half the town probably knew that."

"I certainly did," Dan said.

LaVerdiere ignored him and asked Liss more questions she couldn't answer. The interrogation seemed endless and soon became annoyingly repetitive. LaVerdiere's tone, never exactly soothing, slowly turned downright hostile, as if he didn't believe a word she said.

"And no one can confirm precisely when you arrived back in Moosetookalook?" he asked for the third time.

Sick of his not-so-veiled hints that she'd been lying to him, Liss reached the limit of her patience. "Why don't you just say straight out what you *think* happened here?"

"Oh, we *know* what happened," LaVerdiere drawled. "The M.E. will confirm it with the autopsy but it's obvious from the angle of the body and the force of the blow that she didn't just stumble into those shelves by accident. She had help. Someone shoved her. Hard. Someone *killed* her, Ms. MacCrimmon."

"Well, it wasn't me!" Outraged by the ridiculous insinuation, she let her feelings show.

"You were here."

"I found the body."

"You'd be surprised how many times the person who reports a crime is the one who committed it."

"She was already dead when I got home! How many times do I have to tell you that?"

"Until you make me believe it."

"If she *was* murdered, I want her killer caught and punished even more than you do. I *knew* her. She was a part of my childhood, a good, kind, decent woman who didn't deserve to die that way!"

"So you say."

Left momentarily speechless by his gall, Liss just gaped at him.

Before LaVerdiere could make any further outlandish comments, a deputy sheriff stepped into the room. The state police detective clicked off his tape recorder and left his chair to confer with the other officer.

Liss scowled at the two of them, blindly at first. Then her gaze sharpened and she realized that she knew the man in the brown uniform. It was Pete Campbell, last seen hurling the stone and wearing a kilt over fluorescent swim trunks. The sense of unreality she'd had felt ever since she'd discovered Mrs. Norris in the stockroom ratcheted up another notch.

"Pete's a cop?"

"Yeah," Dan said. "Amazing, isn't it? Listen, Liss. You hang in there. You're right not to let LaVerdiere bully you. He's only picking on you because he's hoping for an easy solution."

"Somebody killed Mrs. Norris." Whispering the words aloud brought a painful tightness to her chest. "Somebody *murdered* her."

"LaVerdiere seems to think so."

"He seems to think it was *me*."

"He's barking up the wrong tree. Damn, I wish I'd seen you arrive home. I'd have been with you when you found her."

"Then that idiot would probably suspect both of us."

The "idiot" had finished his conversation. Pete, on his way out, stopped in the doorway to address Liss. "You want me to call Sherri for you?"

"I hate to bother her this late."

"She'll hear about it soon enough. She's on the eleven to seven shift at the jail."

LaVerdiere listened to their exchange with ill-concealed disapproval. "Is there a reason you're still here, Campbell? If not, I'm in the middle of an interview."

"No, you're at the end of one." Liss was fed up with LaVerdiere and his unwarranted suspicions. "I've told you all I know."

LaVerdiere gave her a hard stare. Liss glared back at him until he finally realized she meant what she said. Only then did he gather up the tape recorder and notebook. "We're not done. Don't leave town, either one of you."

Liss gave a short bark of laughter. "Literally? Because I need to be at the Highland Games again tomorrow and the fairgrounds are over in Fallstown."

"Don't leave the county," LaVerdiere amended, and stalked out of the apartment.

"What *is* his problem?" Liss asked Pete.

Pete checked to make sure the detective was really gone, then shrugged. "Sheriff says he's well trained. He just hasn't had much experience dealing with people."

"He has the sensitivity of an iguana. Is he always like that?"

"Abrupt?"

"Offensive."

"What can I say? He's an asshole, but we're stuck with him. You sure you don't want me to call Sherri?"

"Thanks, but no. I'll talk to her tomorrow."

He started to go but she called him back. "Was Mrs. Norris really murdered?" In spite of what Jeff had said, in spite of LaVerdiere's certainty, it just didn't seem possible.

"Looks that way. Someone from the A.G.'s office is here."

"And that means?"

"The district attorney's office handles most manslaughter cases. The attorney general is in charge of some manslaughters and all homicides. They must think murder's likely. Probably figure Mrs. Norris interrupted a robbery."

LaVerdiere *had* asked if anything was missing from the shop, but Liss hadn't been able to tell him for certain. She hadn't noticed anything. The cash register had already been empty because she'd had all the cash with her at the Highland Games. The cash box, she realized, was still downstairs on the counter.

"If he thinks a thief killed her, why is he picking on Liss?" Dan asked.

"She's handy." Pete grinned suddenly and seconded what Dan had already told her. "Good you stood up for yourself, Liss. Rule of thumb if you're being questioned—police can only talk to you as long as *you're* willing."

"Wish I'd known that an hour ago, but thanks."

"Try to get some rest," Pete advised, and let himself out.

"Do you want me to go, too?" Dan asked.

He was still settled in on the other end of the sofa, angled so that he was facing her. She mirrored his position and studied him. He wasn't remarkable looking—sandy brown hair in need of a trim, an ordinary nose and chin—but there was something solid about Dan Ruskin, something comforting. And it was oh-so-easy to get lost in those sympathetic molasses-brown eyes. She had to look away and clear her throat before she could answer him.

"I'd appreciate it if you'd stay a bit longer."

"No problem."

She felt herself relax against the sofa cushions in what seemed like the first tranquil moment she'd had all day.

The peace abruptly shattered when Detective LaVerdiere reentered the room. "One more thing, Ms. MacCrimmon. You'll have to be out of here within the next half hour. You need to vacate the premises for a couple of days."

Liss came to her feet in an indignant rush. "You can't kick me out. I live here."

"Not for the present you don't. Not until after we sweep the entire building for evidence. You can collect a few personal items to take with you, but leave everything else. What you do take will be inspected and inventoried before you go."

"And just where am I supposed to stay, detective? It's July during the Highland Games. There are no rooms available at any of the local hotels, motels, or bed and breakfasts."

"Not my problem." LaVerdiere said, and made another abrupt exit.

"Oh, well, thanks a lot. Maybe I'll just sleep in my car!"

"You could reconsider calling Sherri," Dan suggested.

"Sherri has enough on her plate without me adding to it." Not to mention a mother and a son already living with her. Liss wished Gina Snowe still lived in Moosetookalook. Gina had been her best friend, but she'd moved away years ago. "I guess I could bunk at Ned's."

"Liss, you—"

"No, probably not a good idea. If I stay with Ned we're likely to end up killing each other. We never did get along." She winced. "I don't believe I just said that. How can I talk so casually about killing? Joke about murder?"

"Cops do it all the time," Dan said. "It's a way of coping."

She shivered. "I'm not a cop. I'm a dancer. I'm in charge of Aunt Margaret's shop," she amended, and that triggered another concern. "They'd better not mess up her inventory."

"You can keep an eye on things if you stay with me," Dan said. "Nobody's using your old room."

The suggestion warmed her. She didn't want to think too deeply about why that should be so. Neither did she give herself time to come up with objections.

"I'd like that. Spending a few days in the house I grew up in sounds like heaven just now." Liss gave Dan the full benefit of her smile. "There's a lot to be said for the old and familiar."

Chapter Five

Old and familiar?

Dan reached into the refrigerator for a cold one. Not quite how he'd seen himself in relation to Liss MacCrimmon. He took a swallow of the beer and wandered back into his living room. It was pretty obvious Liss *still* didn't return his interest in her.

Bad timing anyway, he told himself, what with Mrs. Norris dead and—

"Damn! Lumpkin."

The thought of Mrs. Norris's bad-tempered cat took Dan straight to the picture window. Given the location of the streetlight, right in front of Moosetookalook Scottish Emporium, he had no trouble seeing that the number of police vehicles had multiplied and that there was crime-scene tape around both Margaret Boyd's place and the house next door.

Dan debated with himself, but not for long. He could almost hear Mrs. Norris's voice in his head, lecturing her third graders on their responsibility to the animals they claimed as pets.

He let himself quietly out of the house and wandered back across the square. So far, it looked as if everyone was in Margaret's building. Mrs. Norris's house was dark except for a light in her kitchen.

"Something I can do for you, Dan?" Pete Campbell loomed up out of the shadows, armed and dangerous.

Dan cleared his throat. "You the one assigned to keep gawkers away?"

"Pretty much. How's Liss?"

Just that quickly, the authority figure turned back into the old pal from high school. Dan let out a breath he hadn't realized he'd been holding. "Snoozing peacefully, I hope. I got her to eat something first, and she said she was going to take one of the pain pills left over from her knee surgery to help her get to sleep." It had been too late to order pizza, so they'd shared a can of Chunky soup and a bologna sandwich.

"You should get some shut-eye, too."

"Yeah. Right. When a neighbor gets murdered in my nice quiet village, I think a good night's rest is pretty much out of the question." When that neighbor was a woman everyone knew, everyone liked—well, tolerated, anyhow—he had to wonder whether anybody was safe from random violence. "What's going on in there?"

Pete shrugged. "They took still shots and videos. Medical Examiner did his thing. The body's gone to Augusta to be autopsied."

"But they haven't been into Mrs. Norris's house yet, right?"

"Right. Why?"

"Lumpkin's in there. I was thinking I could take him home with me."

Pete hesitated.

"Even LaVerdiere can't object to me giving an orphaned cat a home. Or does he intend to interrogate Lumpkin, too?"

"Now *that* I'd like to see. Come on." Pete held the yellow tape out of the way so Dan could duck beneath it and follow him toward the house. "Better you tackle that damned cat than me. Last time I stopped by to chat with Mrs. N., he bit me on the ankle."

Dan glanced at Margaret Boyd's place as they went in through Mrs. Norris's unlocked kitchen door. She'd had a good view of the entrance to the stockroom. If someone *had* been trying to rob the Emporium, knowing it was closed while the Highland Games were in session, Mrs. Norris could have seen the intruder find the key and enter the building. That much made sense. What didn't was her failure to call the police. Instead, she'd apparently gone right in after the thief. Why hadn't it occurred to her that she might be putting herself in danger?

"There he is," Pete said.

Lumpkin stood in the doorway that led to the hall: all twenty pounds of him. The big yellow tom blinked once at them, then plopped himself down and began to lick his tail.

"Yeah, I'm fond of you, too," Dan muttered. "Where's your carrier?"

They found it in the hall closet. A cage that looked much too small for a behemoth of Lumpkin's proportions sat on the overhead shelf along with a collection of ballcaps and other hats. Dan took it down, unlatched the front, and advanced on the cat, who was still engrossed in grooming, pointedly ignoring the upstart humans who'd invaded his house.

"Gotcha!" Dan came up with the cat under one arm.

Lumpkin took exception to being grabbed. Squirming, kicking, and hissing, he tried to break free. The carrier crashed to the floor when Dan had to use both hands to hold onto the cat.

"Good luck getting him inside that thing," Pete said. "Lumpkin doesn't like to be confined."

"He doesn't much like being held, either."

Flat-eared, teeth bared to the gums, the cat snarled. Dan took a good look at that feral expression, swallowed convulsively, and tightened his grip. Lumpkin kicked out with his back feet, hard, claws extended. Dan grunted and shifted position, holding both of Lumpkin's front legs in one hand and forcing the cat's back end tight against his chest.

He was reaching for the carrier when Lumpkin bit down hard on the soft, fleshy skin between Dan's forefinger and thumb. With a yelp, Dan dropped him.

"Now you've done it." Pete was trying not to laugh.

"You want to give me a hand here?"

"Sure. I'll hold the carrier."

Lumpkin led Dan and Pete on a merry chase through the house, but they finally cornered him in the small downstairs room Mrs. Norris had called her library. The walls were lined with tall bookcases. Seemingly without effort, Lumpkin went from the back of a recliner to the top of the nearest set of shelves. A looseleaf binder tumbled to the floor as he launched himself from there to Mrs. Norris's cluttered desk. A stack of computer printouts, a tissue box, and a remote control scattered as he landed.

"Close the door!" Dan yelled as the cat caromed off an end table and headed that way.

Pete slammed it shut, trapping Lumpkin in the room. He was climbing the drapes when Dan pounced, recapturing him. Pete had the carrier ready, but Lumpkin managed to brace all four paws against the opening.

Grimly determined, Dan pried them loose, claw by claw, and gave one final push. Lumpkin flew into the carrier. Dan closed and latched the grate on a yowl of protest.

"Well that was fun." Pete surveyed the chaos, shaking his head. "What a mess. If LaVerdiere sees the place like this, he's going to think somebody broke in and trashed it."

After first checking to make sure the catch on the cat carrier was secure, Dan set about putting the room back to rights. "The way I see it, there's no need for Craig LaVerdiere to know we've been here."

Pete thought about that for a moment, then said, "I need to get back outside. Can you finish cleaning up on your own?"

"No problem."

The fallen looseleaf binder had opened on impact, freeing the contents. Dan scooped everything up and took it over to the desk to line up the holes and put the pages back in order. He glanced idly at the printed words as the stack slid into place. He frowned as he recognized a name or two, but didn't take time to read more than a few sentences.

Ten minutes later, Dan was back home and Lumpkin had been freed from the much-hated cage.

"Here. Console yourself." Dan put a feeder full of kibble, also liberated from Mrs. Norris's house, in a corner of the kitchen. He filled a cereal bowl with water and set that down next to it. Lumpkin curled a lip at him but deigned to eat.

Dan went to the refrigerator for another beer.

What the hell, he wondered, had he gotten himself into? He didn't usually act on impulse, but somehow he'd ended up with two house guests. One of them was probably there for good.

Too bad it wasn't the one he'd *like* to keep.

Yawning, Liss wandered into the kitchen at ten minutes past six the next morning. She stopped short at the sight of a large yellow cat. "Well hello there, gorgeous. I didn't know Dan had a cat."

"Dan doesn't." Dan sounded disgruntled. "Or rather, Dan didn't. That's Lumpkin. He belonged to Mrs. Norris."

As unexpected tears welled up, Liss felt her composure slip. She'd given herself a stern lecture before coming downstairs. She'd intended to show a brave front, act as if she'd put finding Mrs. Norris's body behind her and could cope with whatever the new day might bring. *Fat chance!*

She bent down to scratch Lumpkin behind the ear. "She only had the one?"

Dan kindly ignored the hitch in her voice. "For the last couple of years, yeah. Remember when she had five felines in residence, along with a dog she named Not-a-cat?"

"She did enjoy her pets." Steadier now, Liss glanced at Dan over her shoulder. "Are you going to keep him?"

"Kind of depends on him. Right now he's not too happy to be here." Dan indicated a section of freshly shredded wallpaper.

"Poor baby. He's just upset. He'll settle down." She lifted the cat against her chest and gave him a cuddle. She smiled when he began to purr. That had to be the most comforting sound in the universe.

"He's smirking at me over your shoulder," Dan informed her. "I swear that cat hates me. He bit me on the ankle by way of greeting this morning."

"What did you do to him?"

"Me?"

"Yeah, you." It was a relief to find she could banter with Dan.

"I'll have you know I'm innocent of all but the noblest of intentions."

"You haven't been innocent since seventh grade."

Dan stared at her, bemused. "Okay. How did you come up with that?"

"You were thirteen when you cooked up that scheme to con the other kids out of their lunch money by claiming it would go to a charity to save abandoned puppies."

"It did go for dog food."

Liss turned to look at him and grinned. He was standing in front of an east-facing window. The early morning sun behind him had created a totally inappropriate halo around his head. "Yes, for your *own* dog."

"I found Freckles in a box by the side of the road. I rest my case." His gaze shifted to a spot behind her. "Damn!"

A small television on top of the refrigerator had been running on mute, tuned to a morning news program. Dan reached for the clicker and restored the volume.

"—and authorities here in Moosetookalook say the autopsy will be done in Augusta on Monday. Detective LaVerdiere, can you tell us anything else about the case?"

An attractive brunette ignored the state police public affairs officer to shove her microphone in Craig LaVerdiere's face. They were standing in front of Aunt Margaret's store. The sign reading "MOOSETOOKALOOK SCOTTISH EMPORIUM" was plainly visible in the background.

"We're investigating several leads," LaVerdiere assured her, giving the camera a phony smile. "We expect to have someone in custody shortly."

As one, Dan and Liss moved out onto the porch. From that vantage point they could plainly see that three news vans with satellite dishes were parked in front of the shop, along with several police vehicles. A crowd of townspeople had gathered and Liss recognized several of the neighbors . . . and Ernie Willett.

"I'm glad you suggested moving my car into your driveway last night," she murmured. "Unless Willett identifies it, no one will know where I am." No one would bother her. At least, not today.

"Come back inside," Dan urged. "Eat something. Get dressed. We'll get out of here as soon as you're ready."

"One thing's sure," Liss said with a sigh. "I'm not going to have time to worry about my little career crisis today. Murder is one hell of a distraction." Horrified by her own words, she clamped both hands over her mouth. "Oh, Lord! I didn't mean that the way it sounded!"

"Sit down, have another cup of coffee, and tell me about your career crisis. It will take your mind off Mrs. Norris."

As if he knew she needed reassurance, Lumpkin stropped Liss's ankles. She sipped the coffee Dan poured and scratched the cat under the chin. But when he went back to his food dish, she hesitated. Dan was watching her, a contemplative look on his face.

"What?"

"I've been wondering why you came back."

"To help Aunt Margaret. Good grief. How am I going to tell her what happened to Mrs. Norris?"

"You can't do anything on that score yet. She's barely had time to get to Scotland. So, you're here, helping out. You have that much vacation time?"

Very carefully, Liss placed the now empty coffee mug on the kitchen table. "Don't be coy, Dan. It doesn't suit you. I'm sure Aunt Margaret told you I had knee surgery."

"Yeah, she did. But she didn't say how serious it was."

Liss stared into the dregs of the coffee. "Serious enough to end my career."

She hated saying that out loud. There were days when she could almost convince herself there was still hope for her as a dancer. When she'd done her stretches that morning, she'd been nearly as limber as she was before the accident.

"I've devoted myself to dancing for so long," she confided, "that I'm having a hard time imagining I'll ever find another purpose, another passion to fill my life."

"Do you miss the touring, or just being on stage?" Dan asked.

The question made her think before she answered. "Both, but it's not being able to perform that really tears me up inside. I've considered going back in some other capacity, but I'm not sure I could bear watching everyone else on stage while I'm restricted to the wings. Even yesterday at the games, I stayed away from the stage where the dance competitions were being held. To watch others perform when I can't. . . ."

"Ever think about staying on here?" Dan asked.

"I'm not sure Aunt Margaret's shop can support another salesclerk."

Dan frowned. "Was Ned telling the truth? Did she overextend herself to buy into the hotel?"

Startled, Liss gave him a hard look. "What are you talking about?"

"Damn. I thought you knew."

"I know she invested in the castle, along with your father."

"Ned says she's going to bankrupt herself if she doesn't unload the hotel shares. Then again, it's *Ned* who told me that."

"Are you involved in that project too?" Liss asked.

"Only as free labor." He glanced at his watch. "I'm supposed to be out there this morning, but I'm going to give it a pass. Dad will understand, soon as he hears about Mrs. Norris."

Liss started to protest that he didn't need to stick around to babysit her, but Dan cut her off.

"I'm going to the fairgrounds with you this morning. Give you a hand packing up."

"Sherri can—"

"She's just coming off her shift at the jail. I don't think she's going to mind the help."

"I still have trouble taking *that* in. Sherri as a police dispatcher. Pete as a cop."

"Me as a good Samaritan?"

"Oh, no. I had you pegged. Man who rescues abandoned puppies and orphaned cats."

A loud pounding at the door prevented Dan from responding. Liss turned. Her first thought was that Craig LaVerdiere had come for her. *You're innocent*, she reminded herself. With the memory of LaVerdiere's interrogation still fresh, that thought wasn't much comfort.

"Sit tight," Dan said. "I'll get that."

Liss didn't know whether to feel relief or dismay when Ned followed Dan back into the kitchen.

"Why didn't you call me? I had to hear about it on the morning news." Ned seemed distraught and looked as if he'd thrown on the first clothing that came to hand after he'd heard the television report. The short-sleeved Oxford-cloth shirt looked odd matched with ratty old cut-offs.

"I'm sorry, Ned. It didn't occur to me." In all honesty, she hadn't given Ned a thought except to consider his apartment as a temporary refuge. She'd never seen the place, but she knew it was only a few blocks away above one of the old storefronts on High Street.

"It should have. After all, with Mother away, the business is my responsibility."

Very carefully, Liss put down the mug she'd just refilled

with coffee. "I rather think it's mine. Aunt Margaret left me in charge."

"Well what are you going to do about this, then? Are you still going to the fairgrounds today?"

"Yes. I'll pack up—"

"No. Keep the booth open. You'll do a land-office business when news of this gets out."

"Yes, with ghouls!" Liss couldn't believe what she was hearing. "Ned, that would be disrespectful to Mrs. Norris."

"You have an obligation to a live woman, not a dead one. Besides, it's not like we arranged her death for the publicity. Come on, Liss. The show must go on, right?"

"Wrong, Ned." Dan's voice was level but his eyes betrayed a temper rapidly coming to a boil. "Have a little concern for your cousin's feelings, why don't you? She's the one who found Mrs. Norris. Do you think she wants to spend the whole day fending off insensitive questions about the gory details?"

Not a picture she'd wanted to imagine, Liss thought, but Dan's blunt words had the desired effect on Ned. "Sorry, Liss," he mumbled, studying the floor.

"You didn't know."

Ned shifted his gaze to her face, trying his best to ignore Dan. "Thing is, we can't let Mother down. She's counting on us to keep the business solvent. There are going to be big profits today. Always are on the Sunday of the Highland Games. We can't afford to sacrifice those."

"Maybe I should call Aunt Margaret and find out what she wants me to do."

"No! Don't do that!" Ned's voice rose in alarm. "Why upset her? Just go to the games and open the damned booth."

"If you feel so strongly about it, why don't you do it?"

Dan's suggestion earned him glares from both Liss and Ned. Then Ned laughed. "Sorry, folks. It would go against my principles. I've said for years that the only Scottish import I want anything to do with comes in a bottle."

Liss rolled her eyes heavenward. What an asinine remark! Sometimes Ned sounded more like a spoiled frat boy than a grown man of thirty-one.

"I'll open the booth," she said, ending the discussion, "but I may not stay open all day. If things get to be too much, I'll close early."

Ned's relief was almost palpable. "Excellent! And don't you worry about breaking the news to Mother. I'll take responsibility for contacting her."

Liss told herself she should feel relieved. She had no idea what to say to her aunt. But she wasn't sure she trusted Ned to be accurate. As soon as she moved back into the apartment and reopened the shop, Liss decided, and had made certain nothing was missing from either, she'd call Aunt Margaret herself.

Chapter Six

Dan hadn't been to the Highland Games for years and wasn't all that excited about the prospect. The skirling of bagpipes didn't do a thing for him and he wasn't fond of crowds. But when he saw the light come back into Liss's eyes, watched her smile in spite of the ordeal ahead, he was glad he'd accompanied her from Moosetookalook.

They went in by way of the back gate, waved through by one of the security guards hired for the event. Liss drove straight to the booth Margaret Boyd had leased and parked behind it. Sherri's truck was already there.

Liss's joy faded. The two women got out and stared at each other. For a minute, Dan didn't know what to expect. Then they flew into each other's arms, hugged, cried a little, and engaged in a murmured exchange he didn't even try to interpret. He stayed by the car, well out of the way, until they broke apart.

While Liss dashed moisture from her face and blew her nose, Sherri gave the tent a hard look. "Well. So. Set up or tear down?"

Liss hesitated. "Ned thinks we should stay open. He reminded me that the rule of thumb in my world is 'the show must go on.' So we open. But it seems in bad taste to pretend nothing has happened."

"Most people won't have heard a thing about it." Sherri managed an encouraging smile. "They come from all over northern New England. They aren't interested in local news."

"It won't have made the Sunday papers, and this is the day most people sleep in. Chances are, they'll have missed the early broadcasts." Dan wasn't sure why he was backing Sherri up. Chances were also good that the news of Mrs. Norris's death had spread by other means.

"Besides, CNN rarely shows up this far north in Maine. They think the state stops a mile north of Kennebunkport."

It was an old chestnut, but Sherri's straight-faced delivery sparked a flicker of amusement in Liss's eyes and persuaded her to give the go-ahead to start unloading the stock she'd stored overnight in her car. When Dan's part in that was finished, Liss sent him off to buy scones.

"Terrible thing," said the scone-maker, who baked them fresh all day in a portable oven. Dan saw by the sign on her tent that she came from nearby Waycross Springs. As he'd expected, the Carrabassett County grapevine had been working overtime.

"Yes," he agreed, and placed his order.

"Heard Liss MacCrimmon was the one who found Mrs. Norris."

So much for the police keeping details quiet.

"She was here yesterday," the scone-maker continued. "Mrs. Norris. Saw her over there—" She nodded toward the Moosetookalook Scottish Emporium tent. "—talking to Liss."

Turning, Dan realized that the vendors could watch a good deal of what happened at the other booths, if they weren't too busy with their own customers to take notice. The scone-maker might not know just who he was, but she'd seen him arrive with Liss and help Liss and Sherri open the booth. That made him a prime target to pump for information.

"Had what looked to be a real intense conversation."

Dan ignored the blatant invitation to gossip. He had no idea what Liss and Mrs. Norris had talked about the previous day. Liss had mentioned seeing the older woman but not that it had been at the Highland Games. He paid for the scones, wished the baker a profitable day, and headed back across the midway.

Liss fell on the flaky pastries with murmurs of delight. "Comfort food!"

"Anything else I can do to help?"

"Ever work a cash register?" Two small ones had been set up and money transferred to them from the cash box Liss had insisted upon taking with her when she left the shop the previous night.

"Guess it couldn't hurt to learn."

"Good." The warmth in Liss's expression caught Dan by surprise.

"Brace yourself," Sherri warned as a distant fanfare sounded. "The gates just opened."

Customers descended in droves. For the next hour, Dan barely had time to draw breath. To his great relief, no one mentioned Mrs. Norris' death. He was just beginning to relax, in spite of the hectic pace and noisy crowd, when Sherri made a strangled sound. A familiar figure in blaze orange bore down on them—Ernie Willett, Sherri's father.

Willett shoved a woman customer out of his way without appearing to notice he'd done so. He glared at his daughter. "Are you crazy, working for these people?"

"Wh-what do you mean?"

"Lucky you're still alive!"

"Mr. Willett, please—"

Willett cut Liss off with an impatient gesture. "You stay out of this, missy. I'm talking to my girl here."

Bright red flags flew on Sherri's cheeks as she faced her father. "Why now, when you haven't spoken to me for almost three years? What do you really want?"

"Maybe I'm worried about you."

"Why?"

"Why? Why? I'll tell you why! A woman was killed in that shop. Could have been you."

Dan rounded the display table and caught Willett's arm, hoping to steer him away from the booth before his bellowing attracted any more unwelcome attention. "Settle down, Willett. There's no need to make a scene."

Willett jerked free, his gimlet-eyed gaze never leaving Sherri's face. "I hear it was Amanda Norris got herself killed. Nosy old busybody. Not surprised somebody bumped her off. But it could have been you, girl." He pointed one arthritis-riddled finger at her. "By rights, it *should* have been Margaret Boyd."

Liss gasped.

Dan stopped trying to use reason. He seized Willett by the shoulders and spun him around. "That's enough! You leave now or I call security to escort you off the fairgrounds." He'd have attempted it on his own except for the certainty that they'd end up in an undignified wrestling match. Dan wasn't even sure he could best the older man. Willett had a wiry strength and the stubbornness of a mule.

Liss had retrieved a cell phone from her purse. The woman at the scone booth was already talking into hers. No fool, even if he was hot tempered, Willett went still. Cautiously, Dan let go of him.

Willett straightened his vest, thrust out his chin, and stomped off. A smattering of customers watched him go, returning their attention to the wares offered by Moosetook-alook Scottish Emporium only after he'd disappeared into the crowd.

"So much for most people not knowing what happened," Liss murmured.

As the day wore on, Liss was too busy to worry about the chaos awaiting her when she returned to Moosetookalook. Only stray concerns crept in. She had to make sure Ned had called his mother. She had to find someplace to store anything they didn't sell today. She had to ask someone when she would be allowed back into the apartment and shop. But overall, the business of selling kept her mind off less pleasant topics.

During one lull it occurred to her to wonder why Detective LaVerdiere hadn't asked her for an inventory of merchandise. She'd told him that as far as she knew nothing was missing, but he hadn't followed up on that angle. She froze in the act of folding cashmere shawls a browser had left in disarray. Maybe he hadn't bothered because he really did believe she was the one who'd killed Aunt Margaret's long-time neighbor.

You had no motive, Liss reminded herself, falling back on her reading of detective stories for reassurance. *Opportunity, yes. Means, yes. But no* reason *to harm Mrs. Norris.*

She was surprised to find her hands clenching the soft fabric, twisting it out of shape. They were not quite steady as she smoothed the cashmere flat again and finished restoring the display to order.

She looked up to see Barbara, the woman who wanted Aunt Margaret to make a kilt for her, sidle up to the booth. There was an anxious expression on her face. Jason Graye didn't appear to be with her, but Liss had a feeling he wasn't far away.

"Did you bring the material?" Barbara asked.

Liss swallowed as her stomach knotted. She didn't want to remember the last time she'd seen that particular bolt of cloth. "I'm sorry. We had some trouble at the store yesterday while it was closed."

"That's too bad," Barbara said, "but what does it have to do with my kilt?"

"I'm not allowed to remove anything from the shop until the police have finished investigating." Liss wasn't certain what that involved, although she was pretty sure television's version of crime scene investigations was flawed. Screenwriters almost never got the details right.

Barbara's brow creased, and then alarm overspread her features. "Just what kind of trouble did you have?"

Graye came up behind his lady friend, a smirk on his face. "A murder, it seems. I've been hearing all about it. It's the talk of the fairgrounds, Barbara. I guess you won't be getting that kilt after all."

Liss cleared her throat. "There need be no more than a slight delay. After all, construction on the kilt couldn't have begun until my aunt's return from Scotland in any case."

She fought the urge to tell Jason Graye to take a hike. She was determined to complete this sale. If Aunt Margaret needed money as badly as Dan seemed to think, the least Liss could do for the cause was endure a few minutes with an obnoxious customer.

"How did she die?" Graye asked. "Shot? Strangled? Stabbed?"

Repulsed by the avid curiosity in his eyes, Liss took a step away from him. She realized she had no idea what to say. He already knew it was murder. LaVerdiere hadn't specifically ordered her not to discuss what had happened.

But Liss had no wish to dwell on the horrible discovery she'd made in the stockroom. She didn't even want to think about what she'd seen, let alone describe it.

"Talk to Detective LaVerdiere." Dan came up beside Liss, 6'2" of protective male. "He's the one in charge of the case."

Liss clenched her fists at her sides. She didn't need Dan rushing to the rescue. She was perfectly capable of handling a boor like Jason Graye.

Let it go, she warned herself. *Dan's one of the good guys.* He'd stepped in earlier, too, when Ernie Willett's diatribe had threatened to disrupt things.

Liss squared her shoulders and met Graye's sneer with a cold stare. "What you don't seem to realize is that the woman who died was someone I've known all my life. We are all deeply upset by her loss."

"Yeah. I can see that. So upset that you rushed right out here to open up for business."

Stricken, Liss had difficulty keeping her voice level. "We had a commitment to keep, Mr. Graye." And an obligation to the living, as Ned had said.

"Come on, Jase." Barbara tugged at his sleeve. "I want to go home."

"Yeah, yeah." As he had the previous day, he let her lead him away, but he was no happier about it than he had been the first time.

Liss breathed a sigh of relief when the two of them had gone, but the respite didn't last long. Another customer had overheard the entire exchange.

"Murder?" He gulped audibly, goggling at Liss with a look of alarm on his face.

Liss stared back, thinking he looked familiar. Then she remembered. He'd debated a long time over the purchase he'd made yesterday, using his indecision as an excuse to flirt with Sherri. She was probably the sole reason he'd come back today.

"Is there something I, or my assistant, can show you?" Liss asked.

"Naw. I just, uh—never mind." And he took off, almost running.

Dan watched him go, shaking his head. "Guess we've lost that sale."

She forced a smile. There were other customers waiting. "No big deal. I just remembered what he bought when he was here the last time. It was a bumper sticker, the least expensive item in the entire inventory."

By the time the Highland Games closed to the stirring sounds of the massed bands, there was only enough merchandise left to fill the back of Liss's car. She felt a pleasant glow of satisfaction at the success of the day.

"Happy with the receipts?" Dan asked as they headed for Moosetookalook.

"Astonished would be more like it. Except for the kilts, just about everything sold." Of all the shawls and skirts and ties, the pins and figurines, only a few of each item remained. They'd unloaded all the refrigerator magnets and most of the bumper stickers and even sold a couple of the "Learn to Play the Bagpipe" kits that included practice chanters and instruction books.

Liss drove in silence for a bit, through the familiar hilly landscape dotted with dairy farms, apple orchards, and the occasional disreputable-looking trailer. "I just wish I'd been able to talk to Aunt Margaret before we made the decision to open the booth."

"It wouldn't have done anyone any good to hang around the house all day."

"I could have gone with you to The Spruces."

"You got any construction experience?"

"I wield a pretty mean hammer backstage. We built our own sets, you know."

"I'll keep that in mind. And I'd like to show you the place."

As he talked about his father's plans for the old hotel, Liss let the words wash over her. She found his voice oddly soothing. In fact, having him around all day had been a pleasure. His presence steadied her.

Warning bells went off at the thought. It wouldn't do to become dependent on Dan Ruskin. And she sure wasn't looking for romance. Not now, when so much was undecided.

She stole a glance at him and felt an instant tug of attraction. Liss frowned. Where had that come from all of a sudden? And what was she going to do about it? She hadn't come to any conclusions by the time she pulled into Dan's driveway.

"LaVerdiere." Dan made the name sound like a curse.

Startled, Liss followed the direction of his glower. The detective was just getting out of an unmarked car parked in front of Dan's house. With a growing sense of dread, she watched him approach.

"Ms. MacCrimmon, we need to talk." LaVerdiere opened the car door for her and waited for her to get out.

"Let's take this inside." Dan didn't look as if he really wanted the state police detective in his home, but there was still one news van parked in front of Aunt Margaret's shop and who knew how many eyes were watching from windows around the town square.

Two officers followed them across the front porch and into the living room, LaVerdiere and a state trooper carrying what turned out to be a fingerprint kit. Liss submitted to the process without comment, as did Dan. It made sense the police would need to eliminate the prints of people who'd had a reason to be in the building.

The ink had a distinctive smell to it. So did the wipes she was offered to clean the black smudges off her fingers. Liss kept scrubbing long after every trace was gone.

"I'd like to hear your story again, Ms. MacCrimmon." LaVerdiere ordered his assistant to take notes.

"Do you badger everyone this way?" Dan asked him.

"As a matter of fact, yes. And you can both expect to be questioned at least once more by another officer."

There wasn't much they could say to that. Dan reminded Liss that she didn't have to talk to LaVerdiere, but she saw no point in putting it off. She just wanted to get this nightmare over with.

This time they sat on Dan's sofa instead of Aunt Margaret's, but the questions were the same. For almost an hour, LaVerdiere took Liss through the statement she'd made the previous evening. Sustained by the coffee and sandwiches Dan provided, she gritted her teeth and tried to remember everything she could, everything that might help them find out who had killed Mrs. Norris.

"You're sure that's the way it happened?"

"As sure as I was the last hundred times you asked that question."

He waited.

"Yes, Detective LaVerdiere, I am certain that's the way it happened. Is that all?"

"Not quite."

She repressed a groan when he produced several typed pages and skimmed through the contents. Inventory? That was Liss's guess.

"When was the last time you saw Mrs. Norris alive?" he asked.

She blinked in surprise, having expected a question about the contents of the stockroom or the value of items in the locked display cases. "I saw her the afternoon I arrived. Oh, and at the Highland Games, for just a few minutes."

"Yesterday?"

Liss nodded. It felt as if that encounter had taken place days ago. And it seemed like weeks since she'd been free of worry. Her thoughts drifted, longing for a relaxing soak in the claw-footed bathtub Dan had installed and about eight hours reclining on the excellent mattress on the antique bed that now furnished her old room.

". . . 'something a little naughty about you.' Do you want to tell me what she meant by that, Ms. MacCrimmon?"

"What?" Liss blinked at the detective, once again caught off guard. She played back his words, but they still didn't make sense. "I'm sorry, I don't understand what you're asking me."

He consulted the pages in his hands. "Mrs. Norris said 'Oh, I never forget a thing, dear,' and then made mention of 'something a little naughty about you,' and then said, 'we all have our little secrets. And I know most of them.' Do you remember those comments, Ms. MacCrimmon?"

"Yes, but—"

"And do you remember that you said something about blackmail?"

"We were talking about *books*," Liss protested. "Mystery novels."

"It didn't sound that way to the person who overheard your conversation."

"Well, obviously he or she only heard part of it." The pages the detective held were a deposition, she realized. Someone who'd been at the fairgrounds yesterday had come forward upon realizing that the woman Liss had been talking to had been killed in Aunt Margaret's shop a few hours afterward. The eavesdropper had added two and two and come up with five.

"He heard Mrs. Norris say you were 'murderously inclined.'" LaVerdiere added after consulting the typescript again. "Then she lowered her voice, and he missed most of the conversation, but he caught the end. Mrs. Norris said you'd get your just desserts, Ms. MacCrimmon. That sounded like a threat to the witness. Does to me, too."

"You're taking this completely out of context, detective."

"Explain it to me, then. What was the 'something naughty' she referred to?"

"I'm not sure. Besides, she was just kidding around."

"What do you think she meant?"

Liss stared out the window, trying to figure it out. Something she'd done during her high-school years, but what? As she'd reminded Mrs. Norris, she hadn't been the rebellious type. When had she had time? She'd been too busy to get into trouble back then, just as she'd been too busy with her career after high school to have much life outside the dance troupe.

Her view encompassed the town square. If she looked to the left, she could see Aunt Margaret's shop with Mrs. Norris's house beyond. Looking right, she had a clear view of more white clapboard houses and the impressive red-brick municipal building. Her gaze zeroed in on the second floor, above the town office. The library. Dolores Mayfield was Moosetookalook's town librarian. She was married to a no-account drunk who went by the nickname Moose.

"Oh," Liss murmured.

"Yes, Ms. MacCrimmon?"

"I did something stupid once, as a teenager."

She felt heat rush into her cheeks as she remembered.

Yes, that would fit Mrs. Norris's definition of "naughty." Unable to meet either the detective's eyes or Dan's, she blurted out her confession.

"I was scheduled to compete in a dance competition in Portland. A friend was supposed to drive me, but she had car trouble. My parents were away. I couldn't stand the thought of missing the competition, so I borrowed Moose Mayfield's old clunker of a truck and drove myself to Portland."

Liss thought she heard Dan stifle a laugh.

LaVerdiere gave her a hard look. "By borrowed you mean stole?"

"Yes, detective. I mean stole. And I am fully aware that I could have ended up in jail if I'd gotten caught. But I didn't. And I didn't think anyone knew about it. You see, Moose liked his beer. Since I refilled the gas tank before I brought the truck back, he never realized it had gone missing."

"Did you win the competition?" Dan asked.

"Yes." She dared a glance at LaVerdiere. No smile there.

"Good thing the statute of limitations has run out on that one," Dan said, *sotto voce*.

"Detective LaVerdiere, I can understand why what Mrs. Norris said, taken out of context, sounded suspicious." Liss felt a bit braver now that she'd straightened him out concerning the overheard conversation. "I can even comprehend why you were inclined to believe I might have some deep, dark secret. But why would you think that a nice old lady like Mrs. Norris was capable of blackmail?"

It was a particularly nasty accusation, one that outraged Liss on the other woman's behalf.

For a moment, she thought he wasn't going to answer. Then he leaned forward, holding her gaze. "We found evidence in Mrs. Norris's house that she'd been accumulating compromising information about a number of people. As to your conversation with her, Ms. MacCrimmon, I have only your word that car theft was the worst she threatened to reveal."

"She did not threaten—"

"It sounded that way to my witness. And if she did threaten you, then it follows that you had a reason to kill her. Perhaps you didn't mean to. A quarrel. A push. You were overcome by panic and ran. Is that how it happened, Ms. MacCrimmon?"

"You have *got* to be kidding."

"I never kid, Ms. MacCrimmon. She warned you you'd get your 'just desserts.' Isn't that right?"

"She wanted me to come over for a piece of her apple pie. 'Just desserts' was a play on words!" Liss balled her hands into fists to keep from acting on the impulse to grab him by the lapels and shake some sense into him.

"So you say, Ms. MacCrimmon."

She'd never heard a voice so cold. Just that quickly, an icy chill drove the heat of her anger away.

Oh my God, Liss thought. *He's serious. Detective LaVerdiere really believes I killed Mrs. Norris!*

Chapter Seven

When LaVerdiere finally left, Dan checked his watch, then reached for the phone. "What do you want on your pizza?"

"I'm not very hungry."

She looked like hell, but he didn't suppose she'd want to hear that. "You have to eat. Pick a topping or I'll go with anchovies."

That got a faint smile out of her. "Mushrooms and onions are my favorites, but order whatever you like. I'll only eat one slice anyway."

By the time he placed the order and disconnected, Liss had gone to stand by the window. He wondered what she was thinking about as she stared out at the gathering darkness. It had been just about twenty-four hours since her life had been turned upside down. Again.

"All set. Be here in half an hour. I figure you for at least two slices, so I made it a large. This is no time to count calories," he added, letting his admiring gaze skim over an enticing back view. She'd given traditional Scottish dress a pass for the second day of the Highland Games in favor of curve-hugging jeans and a camisole top. "You're not one of those women who's always on a diet are you? You look just fine to me."

"I'm not, no. But if I eat as much now as I did when I was dancing, I'll double in size within a year." She glanced at him over her shoulder and registered his doubtful look. "Think retired football player who doesn't continue to exercise at the same level."

"So take up a new sport. One that's easier on the knees. You can't just stop eating."

"I haven't stopped eating. I just watch what I eat. That's all."

He heard the thread of annoyance in her voice, grinned, and pushed harder. "So you say."

She turned to glare at him.

Better. Her lack of animation, the total apathy she'd displayed during the last part of LaVerdiere's interrogation, had worried him. She'd been holding her own. Then she'd suddenly gotten that deer-in-the-headlights look on her face and abruptly shut down.

It had been about the time LaVerdiere told her he wasn't kidding. Dan winced, realizing he'd just used the exact same words the detective had—"so you say."

"LaVerdiere is just blowing hot air. If he had a case against you, you'd already be in jail."

For a second he thought she was going to keel over on him. Her face lost every vestige of color. "They don't . . . he wouldn't . . ." Her voice trailed off, but for once Dan had no difficulty reading her thoughts. Anyone who watched television news shows knew there were people on death row who didn't belong there.

"Maine doesn't have the death penalty," he blurted.

She pressed her palms against her ears and closed her eyes. "This isn't happening. I'm going to wake up soon and find myself on the road somewhere. No bad knee. No murder." Bright spots of pink flared in her cheeks. "No you!"

"Damn it, Liss. I'm on your side. I'm trying to help." Crossing to her, he wrapped his arms around her and hugged, settling her head on his shoulder.

She went stiff as a board but he didn't let go. If anyone had ever needed cuddling, it was Liss MacCrimmon. After a moment, she gave a little sigh of resignation and relaxed against him. They stood that way, neither moving, neither speaking, until the doorbell buzzed to announce the arrival of the pizza delivery girl.

Liss ate three pieces of pizza, although she did refuse a soft drink in favor of plain water. Dan polished off the rest and waited until the box was in the trash and they were settled on the sofa again before he broached the subject neither one of them could afford to ignore.

"LaVerdiere's dead wrong, you know. About you and about Mrs. Norris. No way was she blackmailing her neighbors."

"Everybody has secrets, even if they're just silly little ones."

He chuckled. "Borrowed Moose Mayfield's truck, huh? Who'da thunk it?"

She punched him in the shoulder. "I'm not proud of it."

"But you wouldn't have paid a blackmailer to keep it quiet, either. Right?"

"Of course not." She almost smiled. "I can't imagine very many frugal Mainers would be willing to pay someone off just to keep them quiet about a youthful prank. Not in this day and age. Most folks around here would say 'go public and be damned' and that would be the end of it. Besides, you're right. I can't see Mrs. Norris eking out her retirement income with extortion."

"Still, if anyone knew where all the bodies are buried and who was carrying on with whom, it was Mrs. Norris."

"But what information she collected was hardly secret.

She didn't gossip, exactly, but if I'd asked her questions she'd have given me an earful over apple pie." Liss paused, looking thoughtful, then sent him a wicked smile. "I wonder what she'd have said about you?"

Dan, who'd gotten caught up in watching her eyes change from blue to green, didn't immediately react to what she'd said. Only when he realized she was waiting for an answer . . . or a confession . . . did he blink and pull back.

"No idea. I'm pretty sure I haven't murdered anyone lately and I haven't got a wife or girlfriend to cheat on."

"Ever fool around with married women?"

"No." And it bothered him that she could think he would.

She must have read his reaction in his face because she dropped her gaze, staring at her tightly clasped hands. "Sorry."

"Forget it. The foot-in-mouth thing must be contagious. Anyway, my point was that LaVerdiere is wrong about Mrs. Norris and he's wrong about you."

"I appreciate the vote of confidence, but as long as he's convinced I'm guilty, he's not going to look elsewhere for a suspect."

"He'll have to realize he's wrong eventually. Detectives report to the attorney general. Even if LaVerdiere doesn't, the A.G. will realize there's no case against you."

"Is that supposed to reassure me?" In her agitation, she couldn't seem to sit still. She jumped up and began to pace, her steps taking her the length of the living room and back again. "I can't just sit around and wait for LaVerdiere to see the light. I need to *prove* I'm not guilty."

"How?"

"Well, I can ask around. Find out if anyone saw anything."

"The cops will do that. Probably have already."

"What if they didn't ask the right questions? If they think I did it, they wouldn't have tried to find out who else was around yesterday."

He hated to douse the light of battle in her eyes, but if she interfered with LaVerdiere's investigation she'd only make things harder on herself. "Bad idea, Liss. It may even be illegal." He didn't know if that was true or not, since his only information on how the police solved crimes came from watching television, and he wasn't a fan of cop shows.

"It's the best one I have. And really, think about it. I know this town. Or at least I used to. And I know things Scottish. Whoever was in the shop, whoever killed Mrs. Norris, that person must have had some connection to Aunt Margaret or her business."

"How do you figure that?" His money had been on a stranger. He didn't want to think any of his neighbors might be a killer.

Liss came to a halt in front of the sofa, hands on her hips. "Because Mrs. Norris wouldn't have gone into the stockroom for no reason. She must have seen someone enter through the back door, someone who shouldn't have been there. There were no signs of robbery or vandalism. Maybe whoever was in there did plan to rob the place, but if Mrs. Norris had thought the intruder was there to commit a crime, she'd have called the cops instead of going over herself."

"I thought the same thing last night," Dan reluctantly admitted. "She could see the door to the stockroom from her back porch and it doesn't make sense that she'd take a foolish risk if she saw a stranger break in."

"So, it was someone she knew. Or at least someone she recognized and thought of as harmless. And I'm better equipped to figure out who that someone might be than

LaVerdiere is." Liss looked extraordinarily pleased with herself.

Dan caught her hand and tugged her back down onto the sofa beside him. Her determination to play detective alarmed him. He was glad she no longer seemed to be frightened or apathetic, but there was no sense going overboard.

"Think about this a minute, Liss." He angled himself so that he could look her straight in the eyes. He kept hold of her hand. "If Mrs. Norris thought this person was harmless, aren't you likely to make the same mistake?"

"I'm just going to check on one or two little things on my own. Come with me if you're worried I'll get into trouble."

"I'm not sure that would help much if a murderer takes exception to your snooping. I can't watch your back twenty-four/seven."

"I can take care of myself!" Blue fire in her eyes, Liss jerked her hand free in a sudden display of temper.

"Okay, Liss. If you say so." She'd been on a real roller-coaster ride since yesterday. Dan supposed he couldn't blame her for resenting his words of caution.

"Humoring the little lady, Dan?" She hopped up, dancing lightly on the balls of her feet. "Come on. Try to take me down."

Dan stood slowly, suddenly wary. "I'm not going to assault you."

"No, really. It's okay. Come at me like you want to grab me and strangle me." She bobbed and weaved like a prize-fighter, face alight with anticipation. Euphoria, he thought. A false sense of security in reaction to the emotions she'd been feeling earlier.

"This is—" He broke off when she jabbed him in the stomach.

"Chicken!"

"Fine," he wheezed, his breathing momentarily impaired. She packed quite a wallop. "Have it your way." Maybe she'd take the risk seriously if he resorted to brute force.

He moved fast, reaching for her. She moved faster. As soon as he made contact, she took a step back, disrupting his balance. Using his own size and weight against him, she flipped him neatly onto the sofa.

He landed on his back, hard enough to knock the wind out of him again. Her crow of triumph echoed in his ears. Closing his eyes, he stayed put. This was not the way he'd expected things to go. In fact, he'd probably made matters worse. Now she'd be convinced she could take care of herself.

Something touched his cheek, softly nuzzling. Dan smiled and opened his eyes, but Liss was right where she had been when she'd thrown him. Warily, he shifted his gaze to the left. Lumpkin gave him another wet-nosed nudge and followed up by licking him with a warm, rough tongue.

Dan sat up fast, swiping at the cat slobber on his face. "Sheesh! Talk about adding insult to injury." All in all, he'd rather the cat give him another bite on the ankle than turn affectionate.

Still smiling, Liss plunked herself down in the chair LaVerdiere had used earlier. "I feel much better now."

"I just bet you do."

"Mad at me?"

"No. But I'm still on record that this is a lousy idea. You aren't Nancy Drew. Or Veronica Mars."

"How about one of Charlie's Angels?"

He shook his head.

"Buffy the Vampire Slayer?"

He stood, as tense now as she'd been a short while ago. "Damn it, Liss. This isn't make-believe. There's a real killer out there, someone who's a lot more dangerous than I am. He—"

"Or she."

"—won't want to be found and won't be happy to hear you're asking questions."

"I'll be careful." As he watched, her expression turned deadly serious. "I have to do this, Dan. I can't just sit still and let myself be railroaded straight into jail."

Now it was Dan's turn to pace. If she *had* to do it, he'd have to help her, if only to keep her safe. She did need someone to watch her back. "If you're determined to ask questions of the neighbors, then we'll do it together."

"Five minutes ago you hated the idea."

"Still do, but I suppose there's no real reason we can't check out a few things on our own; make a list of everyone who was near the Emporium yesterday afternoon and evening. What would that hurt?" Nothing, he hoped.

"Thank you." She sprang out of the chair to give him an impulsive hug.

He didn't let go when she tried to step back. Instead his hands slid over the silky texture of her camisole and came to rest on soft, well-worn denim at hip level. Eyes locked on hers, he started to lower his head.

She jerked away, almost losing her balance as she broke free. "Now this, Dan, *this* is a bad idea."

"Sorry."

"No, you're not."

"I'm sorry you're not interested."

"I didn't say that. I—" She stopped speaking and shook her head. "Bad timing, okay? It's been a long day and I just hit the wall." She headed for the stairs, talking fast as she went. "I can't handle anything more tonight. I'm going to bed to try and get a good night's sleep." With a final, dismissive, "See you in the morning," she disappeared from view.

Smothering a yawn, Sherri Willett raked her fingers through her hair and struggled to stay awake. In each of the last two days she'd managed only three-and-a-half hours of sleep. She was running on nerves and caffeine.

In the dispatch room of the Carrabassett County sheriff's office at the county jail at two o'clock in the morning, Sherri was three hours into her eight-hour shift. The job was mind-numbing when they weren't busy and this particular night in late July had been completely uneventful. With a murder investigation going on, she'd have thought the phone would be ringing off the hook. No such luck.

Sherri shifted in the ergonomic chair at her console and wondered what evidence had convinced the state police that Liss MacCrimmon should be their prime suspect. So far, three people had told her that—a Fallstown police officer, a deputy, and the cleaning lady.

After getting up to refill her coffee cup, Sherri made another check of the security cameras and light panel. A second corrections officer was on duty inside the jail's cellblock. A third was assigned to intake, the booking of prisoners, and other assorted paperwork. Given her choice, Sherri supposed she preferred dispatching duties. At night, corrections officers, who were also sworn in as deputies in the county sheriff's department, handled 911 calls to local police departments, as well as those coming in to the S.O. Sherri had toyed with the idea of applying for a patrol job, but so far hadn't done anything about it. The risks were greater, and she did have her son to think of. On the other hand, it wasn't quite the dead-end job this one was.

She glanced through a window made of bulletproof

glass in time to see Craig LaVerdiere crossing the small lobby at the entrance to the jail. Sherri watched him for a moment, wondering how she could ever have thought he was attractive. She had terrible taste in men, that was how! Poor judgment. She'd made one mistake with her son's father and another, just about a year ago, after the annual law enforcement picnic, with the then newly-assigned state police officer.

Reluctantly, she pushed the necessary button on her console to buzz him in through the first of two security doors. During the slight delay while he removed his gun and left it in the weapons locker, Sherri resumed her seat and braced herself for what was sure to be an unpleasant encounter. Not only had Craig LaVerdiere never called her again, he'd taken to looking down his nose at her every time their paths crossed. He seemed to think he'd lowered himself to sleep with her. She'd been the one slumming, Sherri decided, but that conviction didn't make it any easier to deal with LaVerdiere's haughty attitude and snide remarks.

Once through the second heavy, reinforced steel door, LaVerdiere ignored Sherri and ambled over to the coffee pot.

"Hello to you, too," she muttered.

"You say something, princess?"

"Obviously not." She glared at his back.

To her surprise, he glanced over his shoulder. "I need to talk to you." LaVerdiere stirred his coffee, took a tentative sip, grimaced, and added more sugar. "About Liss Mac-Crimmon."

"What about her?"

He straddled one of several straight-back chairs scattered around the dispatch center and took a small, spiral-bound notebook out of a pocket. "You were with her most of the day on Saturday, right?"

So this was a formal interview. About time somebody got around to it. "That's right. *All* day."

"Till when?"

"Around six-fifteen, maybe six-thirty. I left first. I don't know how long she stayed. We didn't know Liss would need an alibi at the time," she added with a touch of asperity.

"Okay. Now go back a few hours. The victim paid a visit to your booth at the fair."

"Highland Games. Yes."

"You talk to her?"

"No." Sherri realized she'd been swiveling the chair, using her toes to move it back and forth. With exaggerated care, she dropped both heels to the floor and willed herself to stillness. No need to signal her nervousness to the enemy.

"You overhear what Amanda Norris and Ms. Mac-Crimmon said to each other?" LaVerdiere asked.

"No, but I can tell you one thing. Liss MacCrimmon wouldn't hurt a fly."

"You've known her what? About two days? You don't have a clue what she's capable of."

Seething, Sherri glared at him. "And you do?"

"I go by the evidence. I'll have this case all wrapped up in a couple of days. Your buddy Liss will be behind bars. Convenient, huh? You can visit her in jail every time you come to work."

"Bull. You just latched on to the first likely candidate and you're too lazy to look for others. Sloppy police work, don't you think?"

To her chagrin, he laughed. "Watch it, princess. You'll hurt my feelings."

"You don't have—" What would have been a childish retort was mercifully cut short by the phone. Sherri grabbed it on the second ring. "Carrabassett County Sheriff's Department, Officer Willett speaking."

By the time she finished dealing with old Mr. Higginbotham, who thought alien beings were stealing his goats, Craig LaVerdiere had left the building.

Liss and Dan met the next morning at breakfast. Liss was up at six, refreshed by a surprisingly good night's rest. She'd fed the cat and made a pot of coffee by the time Dan stumbled into the kitchen.

"I've been thinking," she said.

"Please. Coffee first."

She took a seat at the kitchen table and waited, sipping from a delicate china cup, while Dan poured some of the dark, fragrant brew into an oversized ceramic mug with "Ruskin Construction" emblazoned on the outside. He was dressed, but had not yet shaved or combed his hair. The look of him, tousled and sleepy-eyed, reminded Liss of the dream she'd had about him during the night. Aware he was watching her as he downed half the contents of his mug, she suppressed a grin.

"Okay. Go ahead. The brain is now marginally functional."

"I've been thinking that unless there is some forensic evidence the lab can trace to a single suspect, Detective LaVerdiere is never going to find out anything."

"So much for hoping you'd give up playing girl detective."

"I thought you agreed to help me."

"I did. I just—. I did." He drained the mug and turned away to refill it.

"I admit I was torqued last night. Well, babbling, actually. Okay—acting like an over-stimulated twelve-year-old." She winced when she remembered flipping Dan onto the sofa, her one and only self-defense move. "But I haven't

changed my mind about taking a hand in the investigation."

If she didn't prove herself innocent, who would? She
couldn't see waiting around, hoping LaVerdiere would
come to his senses.

"So, this morning we talk to the neighbors." Dan did
not sound enthusiastic. "Okay if I finish waking up first?"

"Go for it. In the meantime, I want to run another idea
past you. I can't imagine Mrs. Norris as a blackmailer, but
I have been thinking about the records LaVerdiere said he
found in her house. 'Evidence,' he said. She had 'compromising information about a number of people.' Do you
think he meant diaries or journals of some sort? There
could be a perfectly innocent reason for her to write things
down."

Dan brought his coffee to the table and sat down opposite her. "There was a looseleaf in her library. Lumpkin
knocked it down when Pete and I were chasing him. It fell
open and some pages scattered." A pucker appeared in his
brow. "I just glanced at them, but I thought I recognized a
couple of names. The thing is, I'm not sure why they seemed
familiar. They weren't townspeople." He shrugged. "Maybe
Mrs. Norris was into recording celebrity gossip."

"That can't be what LaVerdiere was talking about. If
they were famous names, surely one of the officers would
have recognized them. Besides, he implied she had dirt on
the locals." She considered that for a moment. LaVerdiere
wasn't local. "Maybe he didn't recognize any of the names
either. Can you remember the ones you saw?"

Dan closed his eyes and rubbed the bridge of his nose.
He looked tired, Liss thought, as if his night had been full
of bad dreams.

"One was Pitt," he said at last. "And not Brad Pitt.

Thomas Pitt. Do I know him? I'm pretty sure there's no one in Moosetookalook with that name."

"Thomas . . . Pitt? I know who he is, but that makes no sense. Can you remember anyone else?"

"There was a woman's name."

"Charlotte?" Liss guessed.

"No, it was . . . Emily?"

"Well, yes, I suppose. Charlotte and Emily are—"

"No. Not Emily. Amelia. And the last name was Peabody. A good New England name, and I thought it sounded familiar, but I can't think where I know her from." He hesitated, giving Liss a wary look. Her own face was likely a study in confusion. "The page I saw said the two of them were planning a clandestine meeting, that Amelia wanted to keep her association with Pitt secret from her husband."

Liss checked her jaw to make sure it hadn't dropped. "Whew! Talk about not making any sense!"

"You know who they are?"

"Sort of." She stared at the dregs of her coffee and wondered what on earth Mrs. Norris had been up to.

Dan reached across the table and waved a hand in front of her face. "Earth to Liss."

"Sorry. This is my befuddled look."

"Clue me in here, Liss. Who is Thomas Pitt?"

"He's the detective in a series of books by Anne Perry. A fictional character. He does his sleuthing in Victorian London."

"And Amelia Peabody?"

"Also fictional. She's the protagonist in a series of historical mysteries written by Elizabeth Peters. Same time period, more or less."

Liss read a lot, often mysteries Mrs. Norris had recommended. There hadn't been much else to do, except sleep or play cards, while traveling from one gig to the next in the company bus.

"I don't get it," Dan said. "What were the names of fictional characters doing in that looseleaf?"

"I don't suppose you remember any other names from the page you saw?"

"Sorry, no. I just got a glimpse, and the impression that the notes meant that the two of them were having an affair. I assumed they were real people and I figured what they got up to was none of my business."

Liss felt the coffee she'd just consumed turn to acid in her stomach. "What if they are? Maybe she used fictional names to hide their real identities." At Dan's snort, she felt compelled to defend the theory. "What? It makes sense. Sort of."

"Only if LaVerdiere is right, and no way in hell was Amanda Norris a blackmailer!"

Chapter Eight

The sudden flash of anger in Dan's dark eyes surprised Liss. His hands curled into fists on the tabletop, he glared at her.

"I'd like to keep thinking Mrs. Norris was just a nice old lady, too, but it's me LaVerdiere wants to arrest. I can't afford to overlook any possibility."

After a moment of heavy silence, Dan's jaw unclenched. Liss watched in fascination as, muscle by muscle, he seemed to will himself back into calmness. She admired his self-mastery. At the same time, seeing it in action made her a little uneasy. Did he ever lose control completely? She didn't think she wanted to be around to see it if he did.

"She was a good woman."

"Yes, she was, and I'm sorry she's dead, sorry she's being slandered, but none of that changes the facts. Here's the sad truth: what we want and what *is* aren't always the same thing. I want to be dancing in Chicago with *Strathspey*. We have a three-day gig at a real theater there. Guaranteed publicity. Enthusiastic audiences. But I'm here and you're here and if we're going to find out who really killed Mrs. Norris and why, we need to keep our minds open . . . about everything."

Gesturing with both hands, Liss nearly sent her coffee

cup flying. Dan reached out to steady it. He didn't look happy, but he nodded.

"You're right. We can't rule anything out. And it makes sense to talk to the neighbors. How much do you want to tell them?"

"Probably not a good plan to say the police suspect me of murder," Liss quipped. She rinsed her cup and Dan's mug and put them in the dishwasher.

"You've got that right. You've been gone ten years. Most of them don't know you."

She turned, resting her backside against the kitchen counter, and was surprised to find he was only a foot away from her. "What do you suggest?"

"A variation on the old welcome wagon. You're back. You'd like to reconnect with people here."

"And then we just segue into the fact that I found Mrs. Norris's body? I don't think so. What if we go door-to-door to solicit ideas on how to honor her life? She had no kin. Maybe the neighborhood could hold a memorial service."

"That's a good idea. And it doesn't have to be a ploy. We should do . . . something."

"I agree. She was a big part of our lives." Feeling suddenly restless, Liss shoved away from the counter, brushing past Dan as she went to stand at the kitchen window and stare out at the backyard.

The swing her father had attached to the high branch of a maple tree no longer hung there, but she found herself remembering how it used to sway gently in a morning breeze.

Dan came up behind her, putting his hands on her shoulders. "What's wrong?"

"I can't help thinking that if I hadn't decided to bring

some of Aunt Margaret's merchandise home with me from the fairgrounds, I might have been back in time to save her."

"It's not your fault Mrs. Norris is dead. Don't ever think that."

For just a moment, Liss let herself lean back into Dan's strength, his warmth. Their reflections in the window glass gazed back at them, a couple who looked as if they belonged together.

Abruptly, she straightened. "Time's a wasting."

He stepped away from her, releasing his grip on her shoulders. She pretended she didn't miss the contact.

"Give me a few minutes to call the construction site and we'll get started."

Liss opened her mouth to protest that he shouldn't cut work, then closed it again. Selfishly, she wanted him with her. His presence would make talking to the neighbors much easier. They'd open up to him more than they would to her. He'd been right earlier. She'd gone away. She was one of them by birth, but now a stranger.

While Dan went off to shave and call his father, Liss changed into one of her more conservative outfits, a light summer dress that swirled to mid-calf. The colors were a mix of dark reds, browns, and greens—not exactly mourning, but as close as she could be comfortable wearing.

"All set," Dan said they met in the entry hall. "I've got the morning free. After that, I'll have to put in a few hours. Dad's shorthanded because he had to let one of the carpenters go." He shepherded her out onto the porch.

"Okay. Let's get started then . . . with you." She seated herself on the glider. "You were here all day, right? What did *you* see?"

"Not a heck of a lot." He leaned against the railing, arms folded across his chest. "I was in the workshop. That's the old carriage house. I converted it so I could do wood-working in my spare time. I stopped for lunch around noon. Your cousin stopped by."

"What did Ned want?" She set the glider in motion, but the soothing rhythm failed to relax her. She thought again, with real longing, of the backyard swing.

"To annoy me?" Dan cracked a smile.

"When was he here?"

"I didn't look at my watch. Mid-afternoon. He'd had time to take your aunt to the airport and drive back."

"Before or after 3:30?"

"Could have been either. I don't know. Why 3:30?"

Liss watched as a maintenance worker drove his riding lawnmower back and forth across the peaceful town square. The drone of the engine was no more than a low background hum but the smell of newly mown grass hung in the sultry morning air. Liss sighed. Instead of being able to enjoy the sounds and smells of summer, she had to keep her mind on murder.

"I read crime novels, okay? And I saw Mrs. Norris's body. She wasn't stiff yet."

He lifted an eyebrow at her irritable tone but didn't comment on it. "And that means?"

"Apparently there's no way to pin down the exact time someone dies unless there's a witness. They make guesses based on . . . things that happen to the body." She grimaced. "To tell you the truth, I usually skip over those passages in a book, but some of it must have stuck because I know that if rigor mortis hadn't yet set in, then she couldn't have died much more than four hours before I found her. If I got home at 7:30—"

"It was closer to eight. Just before sunset."

"Okay, then move the time up to four. Did you notice

anything or anyone unusual between four and eight that day?"

"No, and after about 6:30 I was keeping an eye out for you. I wasn't watching constantly, but if anyone had parked and gone into the Emporium, I think I'd have noticed."

"The killer might not have come by car. And you can't see Aunt Margaret's back door from here. It's on the other side of the building."

"Then let's hope one of the other neighbors saw something." He pushed away from the railing and offered her his hand.

Dan's next-door neighbor to the east, on the corner of Birch and Main, was John Farley, an accountant who specialized in preparing income taxes. He used two rooms on the first floor of his house as an office but this was the wrong season for him to be in it much. He agreed Mrs. Norris should be given a memorial service and promised to attend, but he hadn't been open on Saturday. He hadn't even been home.

"The wife and I went to her sister's for the day. When we got back, there were about a dozen police cars over at the Emporium." He shook his head. "Damned shame. Amanda Norris was a good woman. Interrupted a robbery, you think?"

"The police aren't saying," Dan said.

Patsy's Coffee House stood just across Main Street. Inside, a small seating area flanked the sales counter. Chalkboards advertised coffee blends by the cup and by the pound, ground to order, along with homemade donuts and pastries. It was a far cry from Starbucks, but it had a certain homey charm and it smelled wonderful. Dan requested "the usual," which turned out to be coffee and two Boston Creme donuts.

"How about you, Liss?" asked Patsy, the pale, thin fifty-something owner, who did all the baking. "The sticky buns are wicked good."

Liss couldn't help but smile. She hadn't heard that expression since she'd left Maine. "Wicked good, are they? Then I guess I can't resist."

"Sit a spell, Patsy," Dan invited when she brought their order. For the moment, there were no other customers.

Unfortunately, the only unusual event she'd noticed on Saturday had been Jeff Thibodeau's headlong dash across the town square.

The municipal building was next door to Patsy's. "Everything was closed on Saturday except the police station, and that's at the back of the building. Jeff wouldn't have seen a thing."

"Onward, then." She checked at a sign that read "Angie's Books" on the porch of the house at the corner of Main and Ash. "That used to be Cecil Morgan's place."

"He moved away about five years back. The bookstore will be closed, since this is Monday, but Angie will be home. Angie Hogencamp. She's got two young kids."

"What does she do with them when the shop is open?"

"They 'help' her with the business." Dan grinned. "As long she keeps everything that's breakable on high shelves, it works out fine."

Liss got only a glimpse of the shop on the lower level of the house as Angie, who lived upstairs with her family, led them through to the kitchen. The former living and dining rooms had been turned into a new and used bookstore crammed with bookshelves and knick-knacks that were also for sale.

"Coffee?" she asked. "I just put on a fresh pot."

Liss accepted to be courteous but passed on the coffee

cake. Dan devoured both. The man seemed to have a hollow leg. She didn't know where else the food could be going.

"Such a shame about Mrs. Norris." Angie's eyes were the big brown variety that always looked a little sad, but she seemed sincere in her sentiments. "She was an old busybody, but she was nice about it," she added with a self-conscious little laugh. "I mean, you knew she was prying into things that were none of her business, but she was so sweet about it, so sympathetic when sympathy was called for, that before you knew it you were telling her your deepest, darkest secrets."

"You didn't worry about her repeating things you told her?"

"Oh, no. She'd gossip, sure, but she never passed on anything that really mattered." A frown creased her brow. "She'd hint, once in awhile. Like she knew something really juicy but she wasn't going to tell." Her expression cleared. "Well, she was old. I suppose she had to have something to amuse herself with."

Liss and Dan exchanged a look, but neither made any comment.

After a moment, during which Liss could hear the quiet murmur of children's voices from another room, Angie started talking on her own. "It was such a quiet day on Saturday, or so everyone says. It seems impossible that some stranger could have walked into the Emporium and committed murder."

"You didn't notice anything unusual? No one hanging around Aunt Margaret's shop?"

"No. Not that I was looking. It wasn't just a quiet day, it was dead." She flushed as she realized what she'd said. "Slow, I mean. My son took a nap that lasted most of the afternoon and I spent the time restocking shelves. I don't suppose I glanced through the window more than once or twice."

"And you didn't see anyone?"

"Well, there was old Lenny Peet, walking his dog. I swear, that dog's got to be as old as he is, but they're out there every day, taking their exercise."

"Regular schedule, huh?" Liss asked, hoping she sounded casual. "Like clockwork?"

"Well, no, he's not quite that much a creature of habit, but close. Early morning. Late afternoon. Speaking of clocks." She turned her attention on Dan. "You willing to make a few more and put them in here on consignment? We did pretty well on them last leaf-peeper season."

"You make clocks?" Liss asked.

"Oh, he makes wonderful clocks. Haven't you seen them?" Angie started to get up from the kitchen table but Dan stopped her.

"I'll show her the ones in the shop."

"Well, alright. I've only got one of the little picture-frame clocks left anyway. I want another big Shaker-style, and at least two more with picture frames, and . . . well, surprise me." She turned to Liss again. "He makes the most interesting shapes and sizes. I sold one that looked like a boat, and a couple made from cherry burl. The customers love it when I can tell them he knew the tree personally." She chuckled.

Dan just looked embarrassed. "I'll get some to you before the leaves turn. Right now, though, we should get going."

"Yes, of course. Let me know when the services for Mrs. Norris are. I'll close up the shop if need be."

"She seems nice," Liss said when they were out on the sidewalk again.

"She is nice."

"A real fan of yours, too."

A band of red crept up his neck and into his face. "Angie got a little carried away."

"Don't be modest. And don't think you're going to get out of showing me your workshop later, either."

Ash Street went east to west along one side of the town square, but just beyond the corner of Main and Ash was another cross street, Elm. Next door to the bookstore, on the corner of Main and Elm, was Locke Insurance. Liss checked the line of sight. In spite of the gazebo and the trees in the square, the front windows had a pretty clear view of Moosetookalook Scottish Emporium, and on the side with the entrance to the stockroom, too. "Should we stop in there?"

"They were closed Saturday. And the upstairs apartment is vacant right now."

"Figures. What's next, then . . . ?" Her voice trailed off as she took a good look at the building on the corner opposite Angie's Books. It was, and always had been, Preston's Mortuary.

Douglas Preston was a refined gentleman of indeterminate age who offered them tea and sympathy and informed them that Mrs. Norris had made her own pre-arrangements for burial. After a moment's thought, however, he decided that a memorial service arranged by her neighbors would not conflict with what she'd wanted for herself. "She said no fuss, but how could she object to something that will give closure to her friends?"

How could she object, indeed, Liss thought cynically. She wasn't around to stop it, and Preston had no qualms about making a few extra bucks.

He wasn't any help otherwise, however. He'd been busy "out back" all afternoon on Saturday. Liss decided not to inquire into exactly what had occupied his time.

Alden's Small Appliance Repair came next. Like the other businesses, it occupied part of the ground floor of what had once been a one-family house. Moosetookalook had been extraordinarily fortunate. No "great fire" had destroyed the many homes built during the late nineteenth and early twentieth centuries by bankers and ministers, merchants, and professional men. Nowadays, for the most part, the owner of each store lived above the premises. Only in one or two cases were the upstairs apartments rented out to strangers.

Warren Alden was in his seventies, lived alone, and opened his shop when he felt like it. Saturday afternoon, like Angie's toddler, he'd taken a long nap in his living quarters. If anybody had come by wanting his services, they hadn't bothered to ring the bell.

"It's a good loud one," he informed them. "I'd have heard it if it rung."

"I'm beginning to get discouraged," Liss said. "For a small town, these folks sure do mind their own business."

Dan chuckled. "Just wait. The fact that you and I are making the rounds together will have all of Moosetookalook buzzing by nightfall."

"What an appalling thought."

"Hey! I think I'm insulted."

She ignored him and pushed open the door to the next building on the west side of the square. The Clip and Curl occupied the back of the house, with no view of the square or of Aunt Margaret's shop. The proprietor, Betsy Twining, lived in the rooms above, but she'd have been busy doing hair on Saturday afternoon. Liss and Dan popped in only to tell her about the memorial service. The front half of the building, completely separate from the Clip and Curl, was the Moosetookalook Post Office.

Liss didn't know the postmaster, a husky brunette about

her own age, but the woman recognized her on sight. "You're Margaret's niece!" she exclaimed in a loud, nasal voice. "Nice to meet you. How'd Margaret take the news about Amanda? She coming back early?"

"I doubt it. She has a commitment to the tour company."

"Well, I guess that makes sense." She checked the old-style mailboxes as she chattered, pulling out both Aunt Margaret's mail and Dan's from her side and passing it over the counter. "And a package." She took back the yellow card. "Hold on." She was back a moment later. "Something from Klockit. More clock parts, huh?"

"So, Julie," Dan said, leaning on the counter and giving her his best smile. Liss was surprised to feel a twinge of jealousy at the overt flirtation. "You miss all the excitement Saturday?" The post office closed at noon.

"I guess. Terrible thing. I mean, you can see Mrs. Norris's house plain as can be from here." She gestured at the front window. The post office was on the northeast corner of Ash and Pine. Mrs. Norris's house was on the southwest corner.

"Had she come home before you left?" Liss asked. "She was at the Highland Games earlier in the day."

"No idea. She picked her mail up right after I opened up. She always does. Did." Her face twisted as she tried to fight off tears. "I really liked her, y'know?"

"Everyone did." Dan said as they beat a hasty retreat.

"She's not from around here, is she?" Liss asked.

"New Yorker by birth. She married local, though. You remember Will Simpson?"

"Simple Simpson?" Liss glanced back at the post office, trying to imagine the shy, gawky high school kid she'd known, romantically involved with the rather brassy woman she'd just met. Apparently opposites did attract.

Mrs. Norris's house still had yellow crime-scene tape over the doors, as did Moosetookalook Scottish Emporium. They continued along Pine Street to the next house, another white clapboard Victorian but with a difference. The shutters were painted bright purple and there was a life-size skier on the sign mounted on the roof of the front porch.

Stu's Ski Shop had been in that location for years. Inside it hadn't changed much, nor had Stu Burroughs, the proprietor. "Well, well, if it isn't little Amaryllis MacCrimmon." He reached up, intending to pinch her cheek, but she took evasive action in the nick of time. She was wise to his moves.

"Never little, Stu," she reminded him. She'd towered over his five feet two inches by the time she was twelve.

There followed the usual exchange. Sadness over Mrs. Norris's death. Plans for a memorial service. Aunt Margaret's obligations in Scotland. Nothing out of the ordinary to report on Saturday afternoon or evening.

"Last one," Dan said as they stepped off the porch of the ski shop, crossed Pine Street to the southwest corner of the town square and looked across Birch at the three houses in the block between Pine and Main. When Liss had lived at 4 Birch Street, the one in the middle, number six had belonged to old Mrs. Crowl. She'd gotten birthday wishes on *The Today Show* during Liss's senior year for living to be a hundred.

"She's dead, right?" Liss asked. "I mean she looked like a corpse ten years ago."

Dan snorted a laugh. "Yeah. You're safe."

"She used to yell at me for cutting across her yard. And she didn't much like my folks, either. Because of her, Dad had to soundproof the spare bedroom so he and I could practice on the bagpipe without getting cited for disturbing the peace."

"I wondered about that. Warmest spot in the house. Anyway, a couple from Waycross Springs bought Mrs. Crowl's house a few years back. They put a consignment store in the downstairs. Sell used clothing and accessories. Surprisingly nice stuff. They'd probably do better in Fallstown, with all the college kids there, but they seem to be making a go of it."

Liss liked Marcia Katz from the start. The visit was another repeat of their previous stops, but Liss stayed on and chatted a bit, admiring the stock and promising to come back when she had more time to browse. The line between thrift shop and vintage clothing store was very thin.

"Oh, I almost forgot," Marcia said as they were leaving. "I got a sale thanks to the Emporium being closed on Saturday. Guess I should thank you for that. A couple came in. Asked if I had a key to Margaret's shop because they wanted to look around in there. When I told them I didn't—well, I wouldn't have let them in even if I did have one—they spent some time in here and the woman bought a nice designer scarf that was just as good as new. Priced like it too," she added with a grin.

Liss felt her heart speed up as she stepped back into the shop. "What did they look like?"

"Well, let me see. I'm not so good at remembering faces. The guy was real pushy. You know the type? Wants what he wants when he wants it?"

"Big nose? Thin lips? Late thirties or early forties?"

"Could be. I didn't look at him that closely. The woman with him was a blonde. I remember that."

"Strawberry blonde?"

"Yeah." Marcia's face cleared. "And she wore it in a

bun of some sort. She was the classy type, except for her perfume. Strong, you know?"

"Jason Graye and Barbara. I don't know her last name."

"Couldn't prove it by me," Marcia said.

"Do you remember what time this was?"

"Afternoon sometime. Sorry, that's the best I can do. Is it important?"

"Probably not. They were at the fairgrounds earlier and I told them the Emporium was closed. They must not have wanted to take my word for it."

"That goes with this guy's attitude. Don't you hate customers like that?"

Liss waited until she and Dan were outside and on their way next door to his house to comment further on Jason Graye. "Do you think he could have tried to get in the back door after he found out Marcia didn't have a key?"

"Even if he did, even if he found the key over the door and went in, why would he kill Mrs. Norris? If she'd caught him, he'd have been embarrassed, but that would just have made him bluster at her. All sound and fury—"

"Signifying nothing. Nice quote, but I'm not sure it's accurate. I wish we knew when he was here. It must have been sometime between one and two when Barbara looked at kilts in the booth. Do they both live in Moosetookalook?"

"He does. Over on Lowe Street near my dad's house. I don't know about her." Dan glanced at his watch as they climbed the steps to his front porch. "We've got time enough to put together some sandwiches for lunch. Then I've got to get to the construction site. What are you going to do this afternoon?"

Liss turned to look at the square and the buildings surrounding it. Her gaze returned a second time to the municipal building. "I'm going to stop by the police station and find out when I can get back into Aunt Margaret's."

Chapter Nine

"How soon can I move back into my aunt's apart-ment?"

Jeff Thibodeau shrugged. "Coffee?" he offered, waving her toward an uncomfortable-looking plastic chair.

"No thanks. Just information."

Liss had never visited the police department before and was surprised at how small it was. Stuck at the back of the municipal building, the whole shebang consisted of a re-ception area, presently unoccupied, an office with two desks, and a tiny holding cell, also empty, in a connecting room. Since that door stood open, she had a clear view of a space not much bigger than a closet.

Perched on the edge of her chair, Liss clasped her hands over her knees and waited until Officer Thibodeau was seated behind the desk facing her. Then she repeated her question.

Thibodeau had been on the Moosetookalook Police Force—three full-timers and a handful of part-timers—as long as Liss could remember. He'd been "Officer Friendly" for school programs and done annual safety inspections on all the kids' bicycles. It didn't occur to her to be wary of him. She couldn't lump him in the same category as Detective LaVerdiere any more than she could put Sherri or Pete there.

Smoothing down the few wispy strands of hair that surrounded a nearly bald head, Thibodeau hemmed and hawed
a bit before finally admitting he didn't have an answer to
give her. "Local police get pushed pretty well out of an investigation like this, unless they happen to know something that's useful. Not that I'm complaining. I wouldn't
want the responsibility. Tricky thing, murder."

"Do you suppose you could find out for me?" Liss gave
him her most winning smile. "If I could get back in tonight, I might still be able to open the shop on schedule tomorrow."

He shifted his big body in the oversized desk chair and
began to fiddle with a pencil. "I'll see what I can do, if
you're sure you want to open."

"Why wouldn't I?"

"Bound to draw rubberneckers. Just like the scene of a
traffic accident. Everybody's got to slow down and take a
look, even though they know it would be better if they just
kept on driving."

"I don't mean to sound heartless, nor do I approve of
that kind of curiosity, but since I can't do anything to control other people's habits, I'd just as soon Aunt Margaret
got the advantage of them. If they want to come in and
gawk, let them buy souvenirs."

Thibodeau grinned. "Hey—you could sell tickets for a
peek at the stockroom."

"That's cop humor, right?"

"Pretty sick, huh? Still, there's nothing wrong with turning lemons into lemonade. I'll find out when you can take
the crime-scene tape down. You going to be at Dan's house
all day?"

It didn't surprise Liss that he knew where she was staying, but she was relieved to hear no censure in his voice.

"I'll be there until I can get back into Aunt Margaret's apartment."

"He's a good kid, that Dan."

"Not such a kid these days."

"Well, yeah, but I gave him his first speeding ticket. That's what I remember. Haven't had a bit of trouble with him since."

"That's good to know." She hesitated, then asked about something else that had been bothering her. "Any problems lately with Ernie Willett?"

"You're thinking of that incident at the Emporium? That was a fluke." He made a dismissive gesture with his free hand—the other was still toying with a pencil, flipping it over and over between his fingers. "Ernie's usually got better control of his temper than that. Oh, we were out to his place on domestic disputes a time or two, but let me tell you something—Ida Willett's got a temper too. Had to arrest her once for beating on him. He didn't press charges, though."

TMI, Liss thought. Or was it? "Ernie doesn't seem to like my aunt."

"He knows how to carry a grudge, I'll give you that, but last time I saw him and Margaret together—at a pot-luck supper at the church—they seemed to be friendly enough."

"How did he get along with Mrs. Norris?"

"Same as everybody. Tolerated her. Mostly liked her." A wary look came into Thibodeau's eyes. The pencil abruptly stilled. "What are you getting at, Liss?"

"Detective LaVerdiere has some wild theory that Mrs. Norris was a blackmailer," Liss blurted.

The pencil snapped in half. Very carefully, Thibodeau tossed both pieces into the wastepaper basket. "First I've heard it. You sure?"

Liss nodded.

"Naw. Makes no sense. Nice old lady like her?"

"She did . . . keep an eye on things. That bay window of hers has a great view of the neighborhood."

"Well, sure. She was a champion gossip collector. But she didn't have a mean bone in her body." He sounded as if he were trying to convince himself as well as Liss. "Besides, everybody knew she'd be watching. Nobody would be so foolish as to get caught doing something they shouldn't with her looking on."

He had a point, but the tension radiating from him in palpable waves made her wonder if he was as confident of that as he wanted her to believe.

Carpentry was hard, sweaty work, but as Dan stepped back from the house the crew had been framing, reaching for the water bottle attached to his tool belt, he felt a deep sense of satisfaction. For the most part, he enjoyed construction work, especially the kind the Ruskins did. No high-rises in Moosetookalook. Not even many condominiums. Ruskin Construction built houses, raised barns, put on additions to people's homes and businesses, and did renovations.

He'd taken the morning to help Liss—he'd felt uneasy leaving her on her own, though he couldn't say for certain why—but with the crew shorthanded, he'd felt a responsibility to his father, too. It had ended up being just Dan, Sam, and Joe Ruskin on this job. Dan's father came up beside him as Dan took another swig of water.

"Ought to be finished by next weekend if the weather holds."

"It would go faster if you'd hire another carpenter," Dan said.

"I'm being careful this time. I should have done a background check on Ralph before I put him on the crew. Then I'd have known about his criminal record."

"You'd still have given him a chance."

"If he'd been honest with me about his past, yeah."

"And you'd still have caught him if he tried to steal from you."

"Yeah."

"And you'd still have decided not to press charges. Face it, Dad, you give everybody the benefit of the doubt."

"Maybe I shouldn't. Maybe you shouldn't, either. I hear you've got a house guest." Joe Ruskin took a swig from his own plastic water bottle.

Dan gave him a level stare. "Just helping out a neighbor."

"Good-looking girl, as I recall. Kinda skinny, though."

Dan took a few more swallows, then capped the container. "You got a point to make here, Dad?"

"There's talk."

"Big surprise. Moosetookalook thrives on gossip."

"I don't suppose she cares. She's not likely to stick around long."

"Maybe she would if folks made her feel she belonged here. She'd be a credit to the community if she moved back permanently. And she didn't murder Mrs. Norris."

"Who said anything about murder? It's her morals the old biddies are yammering about. And I can't say they don't have reason. After all, she moved in with a single man her second day back." Although he shook his head in mock disapproval, his eyes twinkled with humor. "You want to be careful of that girl's reputation, son."

Dan felt the back of his neck turn red. This was not a discussion he wanted to have with his father. Or with anybody else, for that matter. "This isn't the 1950s, Dad. What Liss and I do is our business and nobody else's."

"If you believe that, you're number than a pounded thumb." Joe waited a beat. "So who thinks it was Liss killed Amanda Norris and what are you going to do about it?"

Ernie Willett stood behind the counter in his small store, one hand resting on the cash register as if to protect it and its contents. Liss wondered who guarded it when he had to go out and fill gas tanks. She was surprised he hadn't gone to self-service. She supposed it was because he didn't trust people to come in and pay for what they pumped.

One other customer roamed the aisles, preventing Liss from speaking privately with Sherri's father. To kill time, she did a little browsing herself, amused to find that she'd been right. Willett's Store did carry mousetraps as well as milk. He also stocked canned goods, paper products, pet food, soft drinks, and a selection of the blaze-orange vests and caps folks were well-advised to wear during hunting season to keep from being mistaken for a deer.

When she heard the cheerful jingle of the bell over the door announce the other customer's departure, Liss grabbed a candy bar from the rack and approached the counter. Ernie Willett ignored her at first. He'd taken a feather duster to the overhead cigarette racks and that apparently required all his concentration.

Tapping one foot, she waited. She had time to inventory everything else behind the sturdy wooden sales counter before he finally acknowledged her presence. She noted in particular the high, padded stool, the upholstery mended with a strip of duct tape, and the microwave on top of a set of shelves that held rolls of cash register tape and several small, unmarked boxes. The warning sign on the wall, reading "Microwave in Use," was so sun-faded it was nearly impossible to decipher. Ernie no longer offered to sell hot sandwiches or English-muffin pizzas to his customers. Liss imagined that bit of courtesy had vanished at the same time Mrs. Willett decamped.

Willett glanced at the candy bar, rang up the sale, and accepted her money.

Suddenly tongue-tied, Liss realized she didn't know how to begin. "Mr. Willett, can we talk?" Oh, that was lame! She'd have to do better if she expected to get answers.

"I'm a busy man."

"I can see that." She let the sarcasm register and met his dark-eyed glower with an unblinking stare. "It's important."

"I got nothing to say to you."

"Something's been bothering me, Mr. Willett. You came to the fairgrounds yesterday after you heard about Mrs. Norris's death. You said you were worried about Sherri. I want to know why."

The incident had been relegated to the back of her mind by other events, but after she left the police station, Liss had found herself remembering how Ernie Willett had behaved. That he had a temper was no surprise, but she didn't understand what had set it off.

"Don't want to talk about it." The surly voice and mulish expression would have discouraged most people, but she had him trapped behind his sales counter. He wouldn't bolt, not when it would mean abandoning his cash register.

Liss leaned in until she was eye to eye with him. "You didn't make a whole lot of sense yesterday, Mr. Willett, but on reflection it seemed to me that you made three distinct claims during your diatribe."

He retreated a step, scowling. "Well ain't you the one for la-de-dah big words."

"You claimed it was dangerous for Sherri to go on working at the Emporium. Why?"

"I got no time for this." His thin lips flattened into a line no wider than a hair's breadth.

"Make time. You also claimed you weren't surprised that Mrs. Norris got herself killed. And you flat out said it should have been Aunt Margaret who was murdered, almost as if you thought—or knew—that the killer mistook Mrs. Norris for my aunt."

"I never—"

"You did."

"Then I mispoke. Do that sometimes when I lose my temper."

"You were angry at my aunt when she hired Sherri. You broke up the place."

"She betrayed me."

"Sherri?"

Liss thought she saw a flash of surprise in his eyes, but it was gone so quickly that she couldn't be sure. "Yeah. Sherri. Who else?"

"Your wife? She left you."

"Good riddance to bad rubbish. And that's all I've got to say on the subject. You'd best run along, missy, before I lose my temper. You wouldn't like me if I lost my temper."

"I don't like you much now."

Eyes locked, they exchanged another glare. He looked away first, those thin lips twitching. A nervous tic, she decided. He couldn't possibly find this confrontation funny.

"I believe you were worried about your daughter. You said you were when you came to the fairgrounds yesterday and she wasn't buying it, but it has to be true. You'd have to have been worried to close this store for an hour or more, or leave it in an employee's hands, in order to make the trip to Fallstown."

And that same reasoning, she realized, made it unlikely he'd killed Mrs. Norris. Didn't it?

"She's my daughter. I got a right to be concerned for her safety."

"But why did you think *Sherri* was in danger? Or was that just an excuse to get her to quit and leave my aunt in the lurch?"

"Whole country's going to hell," he muttered. "Crime. Violence. No respect for your elders."

"Well, that's the pot calling the kettle black! The way I hear it, you nearly destroyed my aunt's store. Went on a rampage."

"Exaggeration. If it had been that bad, she'd have pressed charges."

"And Mrs. Norris? Why did you say you weren't surprised someone killed her? What did she have on you?" Once again Liss leaned over the counter, into his space, close enough to catch the faint smell of Old Spice aftershave.

A look of befuddlement momentarily replaced the hostility on his deeply-lined face. "What are you babbling about, missy?"

"Mrs. Norris. You said she was a busybody."

"Hell, yes. Everybody knew that. Always spying on people from her window. Built that special, she did, so she could see half the neighborhood."

"And what did she do with what she learned?"

"Do? Didn't do anything. Just liked to snoop."

"And you think someone killed her for that?"

"I don't have a clue why she was killed. Don't give a tinker's dam, either."

"And Sherri? Do you think she's in danger?"

"What I think is that she shouldn't be working in that shop. She shouldn't be working for the sheriff. She should be here, working for me."

Contradictory old coot! "Why did you say it should have been Aunt Margaret who was killed? Do you hate her that much? She gave Sherri a job to help her out and not to hurt you. You can't know Aunt Margaret very well if you think that."

"Hah! Known Margaret MacCrimmon longer than you've been alive. She ain't no saint. You ask her about her business dealings sometime. Besides, all I meant was that she's the one who would usually have been in the store alone."

"Business dealings? What business dealings?" *Did he mean the hotel?*

"There's been some shady characters come into that shop."

Startled, Liss stared at him. "Shady characters?"

"You gonna repeat everything I say?"

"Mobsters? Smugglers? Government agents?" The conversation was growing more absurd, more melodramatic, by the minute.

"Don't know. Don't care."

"Mr. Willett, you—"

A car pulled in at the gas pumps and Willett shot out from behind the sales counter. "Time for you to go, missy. You got your candy bar. That's all you're going to get."

"But, I—"

He jerked the door open, making the bell jangle discordantly. "On your way. Git."

Liss got.

The public library hadn't changed much since Liss's last visit. The first-floor entrance, set between the firehouse door and the big windows of the town office, opened on a hallway with a wide flight of stairs to the left. Unable to resist, Liss stopped at the downstairs drinking fountain before she went up. As she'd remembered, it offered the coldest, best-tasting water in the world.

The second-floor library consisted of two large rooms filled with floor-to-ceiling bookshelves and long tables. The librarian's desk stood opposite the door, in front of a bank of windows that had once been much larger but had been made smaller with wooden insets and insulation to conserve energy. The retrofitting looked decidedly odd enclosed by late nineteenth-century window frames.

Dolores Mayfield, the librarian, had the air of a queen holding court. She adjusted her glasses to look down a long, thin nose, examining Liss as if she suspected her of plotting to steal a book. "Yes?"

"Good afternoon, Mrs. Mayfield. Do you remember me? I'm Liss MacCrimmon."

"Oh. Oh!" Her eyes widened, suggesting she'd heard something very recently about Liss—perhaps that morning. "What do you want? You can't check out books. You don't live here anymore."

Swallowing a mixture of hurt feelings and irritation, Liss kept smiling. "I'd like to take a look at some back issues of the *Carrabassett County Clarion*."

Moosetookalook had always been too small a place to have its own newspaper. The *Clarion*, published twice weekly in Fallstown, reported local news and events for both towns, as well as covering Waycross Springs, Wade's Corners, and several other smaller communities in Carrabassett County.

"How far back?" Mrs. Mayfield asked. "Issues from 1883 to 1995 are on microfilm. More recent years have been electronically scanned and can be accessed from a zip disk."

A few minutes later, Liss was settled at one of the library's computers, rapidly scrolling through several years worth of newspapers. Fortunately, no issue was more than eight pages. It didn't take long to find the item about Ernie Willett.

The headline read: LOCAL MAN GOES BERSERK.
Willett must have loved that! She read on.

> *Local businessman Ernest Willett was arrested*
> *Friday on vandalism charges after he did approxi-*
> *mately three-hundred dollars worth of damage in*
> *Moosetookalook Scottish Emporium, a shop*
> *owned by Margaret Boyd. Mrs. Boyd called po-*
> *lice after her disgruntled customer started smash-*
> *ing figurines and hurling books across the room.*
> *Neither Mr. Willett nor Mrs. Boyd could be*
> *reached for comment but according to police*
> *Mrs. Boyd will not be pressing charges. Willett*
> *was released after a brief stay in the Moosetook-*
> *alook lock-up.*

Unable to believe that was it, Liss went back through
the issues covering the two weeks after Willett's arrest,
hoping for some follow-up, but nothing more had been
written about the incident.

She wasn't entirely sure why she was pursuing the matter. Ernie Willett was clearly delusional. Shady characters?
That sounded like a conspiracy theory to her.

But did she dare discount everything he'd said just because it sounded far-fetched? She'd believed Willett when
he said he'd known Margaret Boyd longer than Liss had
been alive. But he hadn't said Margaret *Boyd*. He'd called
her Margaret MacCrimmon. That probably meant they'd
grown up together in Moosetookalook. The MacCrimmons
had been in the area for several generations. No doubt the
Willetts had, too.

But what if there was more to it than that? The thought
nagged at her until she left the computer and requested the

reel of microfilm containing issues of the *Clarion* for the years 1970 to 1980.

"What is it you're looking for?" Dolores Mayfield asked when she handed it over.

"Family history." It was almost true.

"I'd think you'd be too busy to have time to spend on genealogy."

"Busy?" Liss looked up from threading the film into the library's ancient, hand-cranked microfilm reader, a question in her eyes.

"You've got some cleaning up to do and no mistake."

"I'm not sure I know what you mean."

"There will be fingerprint powder on everything." Mrs. Mayfield gave a decisive nod of the head for emphasis. "Almost impossible to clean off. Be careful you don't get the surfaces wet or you'll have a real mess on your hands."

"Thanks for the advice. Unfortunately, I can't do anything about it until they let me back into the shop."

"Good thing you're closed on Mondays."

"Yes, isn't it?"

Liss toyed with the idea of trying to pry information out of Mrs. Mayfield but decided against it on two counts. For one, she wasn't sure what to ask. For another, she could hardly ask direct questions about Ernie Willett, Mrs. Norris, or her aunt without contributing to the local gossip mill. Several other library patrons had been there and gone while she'd sat at the computer. One had given her a suspicious look, another a glare that was downright hostile. Liss had the feeling they knew she'd been questioned about Mrs. Norris's murder and thought the worst.

"Thanks for your help, Mrs. Mayfield," she said in a dismissive tone, and began skimming pages. The librarian took the hint and went back to her desk.

Hoping she'd know what she was looking for when she saw it, Liss scanned reports on school plays and sporting events, municipal elections and traffic accidents, only peripherally aware that there were other patrons in the library. She advanced the film bit by bit, moving through the years, growing steadily more discouraged. There did not seem to be a single mention of any Willett or MacCrimmon or Boyd. By the time her eyes blurred and she had to stop what she was doing to blink and stretch, she was ready to quit. She lifted her hand to rewind the microfilm but froze at the sound of her own name.

"Why would the MacCrimmon girl kill Amanda Norris?"

"Maybe Amanda knew about her hot affair with Dan Ruskin."

Two men, elderly by the sound of their voices, stood just on the other side of a set of bookshelves, talking in low but carrying tones. Liss couldn't have stopped listening if her life depended upon it.

"What affair? She's only been in town a couple of days."

"Pretty obvious to me that something has been going on for awhile. Either that or she's awful free with her favors. Look how quick she moved in with him."

They moved away, their voices fading. Liss pressed both hands to her burning cheeks. She knew she shouldn't be surprised. She shouldn't even be offended, let alone embarrassed. Gossip was a part of life in a small town.

But she wasn't about to leave the shelter of the microfilm reader until those two men left the building. Why subject herself to the awkwardness of coming face to face with them?

Her hand shook a little as she gave the crank another turn. She stared at the page, unseeing, then turned again. She'd almost wound the microfilm right past the picture when something about one of the faces caught her attention. She blinked, then had to bite back a gasp of surprise.

The photograph was centered under the heading "VALENTINE'S DAY SWEETHEARTS." The caption identified the subjects standing inside a gigantic heart, not that Liss was in any doubt about who they were. The man on the right was a young, thin Moose Mayfield, whose real first name turned out to be Roger. Next to him was Dorothy Heston, now Dorothy Mayfield. Beside her was a beaming Margaret MacCrimmon. And on Margaret's other side, his arm around her waist and an adoring look on his face, was Ernie Willett. Thirty-five years ago, they'd been a couple.

Chapter Ten

The municipal building was directly across the town square from Moosetookalook Scottish Emporium. Emerging into the bright afternoon sunshine, Liss squinted against the glare. Trees blocked part of the view, but she could see enough to tell that yellow police tape was still in place. Two state police cars were parked in front of Mrs. Norris's house.

She debated cutting across the green to confront whoever was there now and demand access to the shop and apartment. After what she'd overheard in the library, staying longer than she had to with Dan was probably a bad idea. Not that she cared what other people thought. It wasn't as if she was planning to stay in Moosetookalook. *And if you believe that, I've got a bridge I'd like to sell you!*

The taunt from her inner voice brought a wry, self-mocking smile to Liss's face as she stepped off the curb and crossed the street to the strip of sidewalk surrounding the town square. She'd taken only a few steps onto the grass before she changed her mind. If Detective LaVerdiere wasn't on the scene, whoever was would probably just tell her she'd have to wait and talk to him. And if he *was* there . . . nope! Call it cowardly, but she just didn't feel like putting up with him or his cockamamie suspicions just now.

She walked briskly toward Dan's house instead. A cold drink and a cool shower, she thought. And maybe, if she was in the mood, she'd offer to fix supper.

She'd barely gone inside and turned up the air conditioner, relishing the blast of cold air on her overheated skin, when she saw a familiar truck pull up to the curb. Moments later, Sherri was pounding on the front door.

"I thought you were going to spend the day catching up on sleep. What's wrong?" The dark circles under Sherri's eyes were proof enough she hadn't gotten much rest. Then again, she wore no makeup and had simply pulled her hair back into a queue and secured it with a scrunchie.

"You try napping with a five-year-old in the next room." Sherri's expression softened at the thought of her son, but the next moment she looked grim again. "We need to talk."

Liss gestured toward the kitchen. She found a pitcher of lemonade in the refrigerator and filled two glasses, adding a couple of ice cubes to each. "So what's up?" She took a sip but it was sweeter than she liked. She set the glass aside and looked expectantly at Sherri.

"I saw LaVerdiere at work last night. He interrogated me." Sherri gulped down too much lemonade and started to cough. Liss waited impatiently until she recovered and was able to continue. "Sorry. It's just that the more I think about him the madder I get. I woke up angry. He thinks *you* killed Mrs. Norris, Liss."

"Yeah. I got that impression." But it was discouraging to hear it confirmed. So much for the faint hope she and Dan had been mistaken about LaVerdiere's conclusions.

"That's crazy. *He's* crazy." Sherri sucked down more lemonade.

"Crazy or not, he's the one in charge of the investigation. What did he ask you?"

"He wanted to know if I overheard what you and Mrs. Norris talked about. If I did, I don't remember any of it. And I could only say when I left the games, not when you did."

"Don't worry about it, Sherri. I didn't expect you to provide me with an alibi."

"No, but I could have found out what else he's got. I should have asked him flat out why he thinks you did it." With an irritated slurp, she drained the glass.

"I appreciate the sentiment, but there's no sense putting your job at risk. Besides, I already know what he believes my motive was." As concisely as she could, Liss told Sherri about the looseleaf Dan had seen. "We think that's why LaVerdiere has decided Mrs. Norris was a blackmailer."

"She was writing down juicy gossip about *fictional* characters?"

"Maybe. Or she was using those names to hide real people's identities." Liss had been mulling that question over, on and off, all day. "Keep in mind that Dan only saw one page and he didn't remember everything that was on it."

"Maybe I can find out more."

"Sherri, your job—"

"Well we can't just sit around doing nothing till he comes to arrest you! Besides, I'd love a chance to spike LaVerdiere's guns."

Liss hesitated, wondering why Sherri seemed so eager to help. It wasn't as if they were lifelong best friends. Until Saturday, they hadn't seen each other for more than ten years. Liss didn't know anything about Sherri Willett. Not really. Except that she was Ernie Willett's daughter.

Sherri's grin faded. She dropped her gaze and began to tug at a loose thread on the bottom of her cut-offs. "Guess it's none of my business. And I suppose LaVerdiere will have to see he's wrong eventually."

Liss sighed. "I wish I could believe that." She collected the glasses and carried them to the sink. Her back to Sherri, she tried to think how to broach the subject delicately and decided it was impossible. "I paid a visit to your father earlier today."

"What for?"

"I wanted to know why he made that scene at the fairgrounds. And why he broke up Aunt Margaret's shop."

The visit was still fresh in her mind and she'd been brooding about what Ernie Willett had said to her . . . and what he'd left unsaid.

"I think he was really worried about you, Sherri. He heard someone had been murdered in the shop where you work and he got to thinking how easily it could have been you. That's why he gave in to the impulse to go to the fairgrounds. He had to see for himself that you were okay. And then, probably embarrassed to be seen showing fatherly concern, he started yelling to cover up his real feelings."

"That's just crazy."

"Maybe, but there's more to all of this than we thought. After I talked to him, I went to the library. I found a picture in an old newspaper, a picture of my aunt and your father."

"Doing what? Trying to kill each other?"

Remembering the look the camera had caught on both their faces, Liss shook her head. She turned to face Sherri, bracing one hand against the counter on each side of her for support as she dropped her bombshell. "More like planning to spend the next week in a hotel room somewhere."

"What?" Sherri started to laugh, then caught sight of Liss's face. "You're serious? They were . . . together?"

"The library doesn't own the kind of microfilm reader

that makes copies, but I wrote down the date and page number. You can see for yourself."

"Thanks, but imagining it is bad enough."

"They were younger than we are now at the time. Young and in love by the look of that photograph."

Sherri looked reluctantly intrigued. "I wonder what happened."

"And I wonder what that long-ago relationship has to do with the way your father feels about Aunt Margaret today."

Sherri sucked in a sharp breath. "Whoa. Wait a minute. I know my father has a temper, but you can't be thinking that *he* killed Mrs. Norris. What, by mistake for Margaret Boyd? Not likely." She came to her feet in a rush, hands curled into fists at her sides.

"I never said—"

"You didn't have to!" Petite and blonde, Sherri looked like an enraged pixie, but Liss wasn't fool enough to underestimate the smaller woman.

"Will you calm down! I've already said I thought your father was checking to make sure you were okay. If he'd killed Mrs. Norris, he'd know that already."

Sherri blinked at her and then, to Liss's immense relief, gave a short bark of laughter. "You're right. Sorry I overreacted. Don't know why I did. It's not like there's any love lost between my father and me. It's just that . . . well, sometimes I get sick and tired of everybody thinking he's the bad guy. My mother—" She waved the thought away. "Never mind. That's neither here nor there."

There was more of her father in Sherri than Liss had realized. Disconcerted by the perception, she attempted to get the conversation back on track. "Your father is no longer on my suspect list, but just about everyone else is."

"You're collecting suspects?"

"Do I have any choice? You said it yourself. If LaVerdiere is set on me as his murderer, then we can't just sit around waiting for him to arrest me. I have to do some investigating on my own. That means I have to consider everybody." She forced a weak smile. "Even you, Sherri."

"Me? Why am I a suspect?"

"Least likely to have done it? If this were a mystery novel, you'd be a shoo-in."

"Yeah. Right. Okay, I'll go along. I leave you at the fairgrounds, drive up here and let myself in—with my own key, by the way—and I'm helping myself to . . . what? Not much to steal. The cash was all with you." She shrugged. "Whatever. Mrs. Norris is spying on the neighborhood, as per usual, and spots somebody moving around in there and goes to investigate." Sherri frowned. "At seven o'clock or so, wouldn't she just assume it was you?"

"You'd think. That suggests she was murdered earlier in the afternoon. It makes more sense that she'd have gone over to investigate if she'd seen someone then."

"The results of the autopsy ought to be available by the time I go on shift tonight. I'll see if I can find out what the M.E. put down for time of death. It will only be a ballpark figure. You know that, right?"

"I know. Anything will help. Maybe it will turn out that I got home too late in the day to have killed her."

"So, have we ruled me out yet?"

"You're in the clear . . . unless Mrs. Norris knew some deep, dark secret that you didn't want her to reveal."

Liss meant the comment as a joke. She expected Sherri to laugh, or else confess to some minor, humorous-in-hindsight sin similar to Liss's own teenage venture into crime.

Sherri looked stricken.

The slam of a vehicle door sounded loud in the awkward silence.

Liss cleared her throat. "Dan's home."

"You're right," Sherri blurted. "Everyone has secrets. You should suspect everyone, even me, but I've got an alibi. I was with you until I left the fairgrounds. I drove straight home. My mother and my son can verify that I fell into bed and slept from about five minutes after I arrived until I had to get up to go to work." She moved closer to Liss and lowered her voice. "You're right to suspect everybody," she said again. "Dan Ruskin, too."

"Sherri, I don't think—"

"Look at the facts, Liss. He was on the spot awfully quickly. He was around all day. I know you like him, but good-looking men usually turn out to be rats. Trust me on this . . . and watch your back."

That she spoke from her own experience was so obvious that Liss took the warning with a grain of salt. She squeezed Sherri's hand and promised to be careful. By then, Dan was coming through the kitchen door.

"Hey—two beautiful women waiting for me. What more could a man ask?"

"Oh, I don't know," Liss drawled. "A hot meal on the table? You'll notice that neither one of us is waiting with your slippers and your newspaper."

He chuckled. "That's okay. I'm a twenty-first century kind of guy. I'll settle for a welcome home kiss." Hauling Liss into his arms, he planted a big wet one on her.

Sputtering, she pounded on his chest—lightly, because she hadn't really minded. He ignored the ineffectual protest and zeroed in on her lips for a second try. This time he did it right. Way too right. It wasn't until she heard Sherri loudly clearing her throat that she surfaced and pulled away.

Their eyes held a moment longer, his full of promises, hers full of questions.

"Hot meal on the table, huh?" Sherri asked, *sotto voce*.

"Okay. That did it. Dash of cold water." Liss felt her face flame as she fumbled for the chair she'd been sitting in earlier and sank gratefully into it before her knees gave way. "Stop kidding around, Dan. We've got serious stuff to talk about here."

Sherri had taken the lemonade pitcher out of the refrigerator, retrieved their glasses from the sink and added a third from the cupboard, and poured generous portions into each while Liss and Dan had been preoccupied with each other. Now the two women brought him up to speed.

"So we're back to that damned looseleaf." Dan didn't look happy.

Sherri stared into her lemonade glass as if fascinated by the movement of the ice cubes. "Obviously there was more that you didn't see. We need to know what else was in it. I'm pretty sure I can find out what LaVerdiere took away from her house. They'll have made a list."

"Sherri, your job—"

"I'm not letting that jerk railroad you! I can help, Liss. Let me help."

"Only if you promise to be careful."

"I still think there has to be some explanation *other* than blackmail," Dan insisted. "If Mrs. Norris had been hitting people up for money, it would have gotten out. And any secrets she knew about, you can bet other people did too. Maybe . . . maybe she was writing a novel."

"Wouldn't she have made up her own names for characters?"

"Maybe she hadn't gotten around to it. Maybe it was a what-do-you-call-it? Like *Peyton Place*. You know—real place and people but disguised so she couldn't be sued."

"*Roman à clef*," Liss supplied. "Possible, I guess. Unless she also wrote down her reasons for leaving a record, we may never know for certain. In the meantime, I guess it's time for me to do some writing."

Dan leaned back in his chair until he could reach a nearby drawer and extracted a notepad and pencil. "Suspect list?"

"Suspect list. We've pretty much eliminated Ernie Willett, and Aunt Margaret was on a plane over the Atlantic, so that lets her out of the running. Dan and I talked to the neighbors this morning, Sherri. No one saw anything suspicious, but one woman did describe a couple who wanted to know if she had a key to the Emporium. It sounded like Jason Graye and his lady friend. What if he helped himself to the spare above the door?"

Sherri frowned. "And he'd kill Mrs. Norris because . . . ?"

"She caught him someplace he shouldn't be?"

"Why wouldn't he just tell her to mind her own business and leave?" Dan asked.

"It was the bolt of tartan cloth he was interested in that fell on top of Mrs. Norris's body," Liss reminded him.

"Coincidence."

"Maybe."

"He hasn't lived here all that long. He probably doesn't know that most people keep spare keys hidden near their back doors." Dan frowned. "We don't know if Margaret's key is missing or not. LaVerdiere didn't say."

"Maybe I can find out." Sherri grinned. "I need to start a list of my own."

Dan tore the memo pad in half. While he fished for another pencil in the drawer behind him, Liss grabbed the one he'd been using and wrote down Graye's name. She tapped the eraser end against her chin. "Graye lives on Lowe Street. That's not too far away. He could have walked back later. Sherri, do you know Barbara's last name?"

"Zathros. She rents from Mrs. Biggs over on Maple."

"Also an easy walk." She wrote down Barbara's name. "Who else was around that afternoon?"

"Ned," Dan said.

"Yes. Earlier. But why suspect him? Aside from the fact that you don't like him."

"I thought you said we should suspect everybody? Anyway, I don't know where he went when he left my workshop. I don't think I saw his car, but then again, like everyone else on the list, he doesn't live all that far away. Let's keep open the possibility that he went into his mother's shop that afternoon."

"He could have, but why would Mrs. Norris go in after him? If she recognized my cousin, she'd assume he had a perfect right to be there. He *would* have a perfect right to be there."

"Write him down," Dan said. "Hey, if you can include Graye just because he's obnoxious and was in the area, I can add Ned to the list."

She complied, then listed all the neighbors: John Farley, Patsy, Angie, Douglas Preston, Warren Alden, Betsy Twining, Julie Simpson, Stu Burroughs, and Marcia Katz.

"Don't forget Lenny Peet and his dog," Dan said.

Liss tossed the pad aside. "This is hopeless!"

Dan picked it up and added Peet.

Sherri glanced at her watch. "I really have to head home. I'll call you in the morning and let you know what I find out at work tonight."

Liss walked her to her truck, warning her once again not to risk her job trying to get access to privileged information.

"And don't you get too trusting with Dan," Sherri whispered. "I notice he didn't put his own name on that list."

"Sherri, Dan's been nothing but helpful. And he was as upset as I was when we found Mrs. Norris's body."

"Suspect everybody, remember? Why did he really go into Mrs. Norris's house before the police searched it? Was it just to get Lumpkin, or did he have another purpose in mind? Maybe he saw that page in the looseleaf because he was looking for whatever Mrs. Norris had on him. Maybe he removed a page or two before he left."

Liss shook her head. "If he did that, why would he even mention the looseleaf? Go home, Sherri. Try to get some more sleep before you have to go to work. I think you need it."

"You two aren't lovers are you?"

"No." *Not yet.*

"Good. Sex screws up common sense." And with that parting shot, Sherri drove away.

Equally disturbed by Sherri's suspicions of Dan Ruskin and her own confused feelings toward him, Liss hurried back into the house. She didn't realize Dan was waiting for her just inside the front door until she slammed into him.

He grunted and caught her arms to keep them both upright. "Geez, Liss. Have a heart. You've already proved you can knock me on my keister. You don't have to make a habit of it."

"I'm sorry. I didn't expect—"

Instead of letting go, he cradled her in his arms. "Do you know how often I've thought about you today? How often I've imagined holding you like this?"

"Dan!" She smacked him on the shoulder. "Your timing still stinks."

He was getting serious way too fast. Trouble was, she kind of liked the idea. She seized on the first excuse she could think of to distract them both. "The answering machine light is blinking."

It sat on a pie-shaped table just inside the living room. She hadn't noticed it when she'd come through earlier with Sherri.

"Let it blink."

"Jeff Thibodeau said he'd call if I could move back to Aunt Margaret's." Before Dan could stop her, she'd freed herself and pressed the play button.

The first three messages were from reporters. Liss deleted each one as soon as she'd listened to it. The next one was from Dan's sister, Mary.

"Call me. I'm hearing strange stories about you."

Liss sent a questioning look in Dan's direction.

He shrugged. "Just erase them all. Then we'll disconnect the phone and the answering machine and not leave the house again till Christmas."

She ignored the suggestion, frowning as the next caller identified himself as Edmund Carrier III. He left a phone number and address, then stated that he was Amanda Norris's attorney. "I am calling for Ms. Amaryllis Rosalie MacCrimmon," the message continued. "I am reliably informed that she can be reached at this number. I do not think it wise to go into details of my business with her over the telephone, but it is to her advantage to meet with me. Shall we say at my office in Fallstown at ten o'clock tomorrow morning?"

Chapter Eleven

Sherri racked her brain for a way to get information that would put Liss's mind at rest. She was coming up empty. It wasn't as if the state cops regularly stopped by to gossip with corrections officers. Most of the time, they didn't want anything to do with local law enforcement. They operated out of a van at the crime scene initially and, as soon as humanly possible, high-tailed it back to Augusta, the state capitol, where the crime lab was located. For such activities as questioning the neighbors, they commuted. Only LaVerdiere actually lived in Carrabassett County.

The rumor mill was up to speed, but it didn't have access to the M.E.'s office or any other forensic information. The only thing she could find out was that a trooper named Bud Murdoch was going to be conducting interviews in Moosetookalook the next day.

"Murdoch from around here?" she asked Larry Granby, who'd left intake during a lull to refill his coffee cup.

"Damariscotta," Granby told her, naming a town on the coast that was a good two-hour drive from Moosetookalook. "I tipped him off about the donuts at Patsy's, though."

"That was nice of you." And convenient.

Sherri drove right past her trailer park the next morning

after work and at twenty past seven was in line at Patsy's for a donut of her own. That and a large orange juice in hand, she sauntered over to the obvious cop in the room.

"Murdoch, right?" She sat down at his table without waiting for an invitation. Her brown deputy sheriff's uniform was enough to break through the first barrier.

"No coffee?" he asked.

"I'm coming off shift. Sleep is on the agenda, hopefully in the not-too-distant future. So how's the case going?"

He shrugged.

Sherri leaned closer and lowered her voice. "Thing is, I have a vested interest. If Margaret Boyd did it, I'm out of my part-time job."

"Thought she was out of the country."

"She's supposed to be, but who knows. Suspect everybody, right?"

Softened up by Patsy's "wicked good" donuts and excellent coffee, and perhaps by Sherri's gentle flirting, Murdoch wasn't as circumspect as he should have been. Unfortunately, most of what he knew about the murder was negative. The only clear fingerprints they'd gotten from the scene had belonged to people who had innocent reasons to be in the stock room: Liss, Margaret, Ned, and Sherri herself.

"Thought I'd heard of you somewhere before," Murdoch said with a nod at the name badge she wore above her shirt pocket.

The autopsy report had verified that Mrs. Norris died from a blow to the head and they'd matched the wound to the edge of one of the projecting brackets on the shelving. No question but that she'd been pushed hard, but it had been a fluke that she'd struck that piece of metal at just the right angle to kill her. The murder wasn't likely pre-meditated. It might even have been classed as manslaughter, if the person who'd pushed her had come forward at once and confessed.

"What about timing?" Sherri asked. "Liss MacCrimmon says she was only home a few minutes before she found the body. How long had Mrs. Norris been dead?"

"Hard to say. The M.E. gave us a four-hour window. The MacCrimmon woman could have done it, but it would have been at the upper end of the time frame and only if she was there more than the few minutes she claims. If she's telling the truth, then the victim could have been dead for anything from four-and-a-half hours to a half-hour before Ms. MacCrimmon got there."

Nothing new, Sherri thought. Liss had figured out that much on her own.

"LaVerdiere's convinced she did it," Murdoch volunteered. "Can't prove it, though."

"I heard he thinks Mrs. Norris was blackmailing Liss," Sherri admitted, "but I just can't believe that Mrs. Norris was an extortionist. She was such a sweet woman." She gave a little laugh and indicated Murdoch's now-empty plate. "Always baking treats for people she liked."

"Oh, that blackmail stuff turned out to be bogus." Murdoch sent her a conspiratorial smile. "LaVerdiere screwed up. He thought the Norris woman was collecting information to extort money from her neighbors, but when the forensics guys went into her computer it turned out there weren't any real names in the files LaVerdiere thought were for blackmail. Looks like she was just making notes to herself about characters in books."

"Gee, what a concept—LaVerdiere looking like a fool." *Computer?* Sherri wondered if she should risk mentioning the looseleaf.

"Yeah. He found a sheaf of printouts and jumped to

conclusions about what they meant. I don't know any details, but whatever was in the actual files shot his theory all to hell."

"So he's got to look for another suspect?"

"Maybe. Maybe not. I heard something before I headed up here this morning about him having found another motive for Ms. MacCrimmon to have rubbed out the old lady."

"Are you even looking at anyone else? I mean, anyone could have gotten into the stockroom with the key over the back door."

Murdoch looked startled by her display of temper and Sherri could almost see the barriers go up. "We know how to do our jobs."

"I'm sure you do." *Oh, what the hell*, she thought. *He already knows I'm after information.* "What about that back door key? Did you find it?"

"And just why," asked Craig LaVerdiere from behind her, "do you want to know?"

Liss stole a glance at Dan as she dug into scrambled eggs and ham. He'd made breakfast while she was on the phone with Sherri. Definitely a handy man to have around the house.

For once, Liss refused to consider the damage eating like this could do to waistline, hips, and cholesterol levels. She needed fuel this morning. Real food, not just a breakfast bar or a vitamin drink. And she was heartily sick of yogurt. She wondered what would happen if she simply forgot about counting calories and found a good recipe for scones. Would Dan still be interested in her after she passed the two-hundred-pound mark?

He'd been a perfect gentleman all evening. He'd made no further reference to his feelings for her and if he'd heard gossip about their relationship, he was ignoring it. She hadn't gone near that subject either. Instead, they'd reminisced. He'd brought her up to date on what various classmates were doing these days, and she'd told him a few stories about life on the road with *Strathspey*. She'd called it a night first, going up to bed, alone, at a little past eleven. The faint sounds of a late-night local news show, issuing from the television in the living room, had lulled her to sleep.

"So what did Sherri find out?" he asked as he took the chair opposite her and inhaled his second mug of coffee.

Liss filled him in on what Sherri had just told her, including the fact that she'd discovered most of it within the last half-hour and less than a block away from where they were sitting. "She called from her cell phone. Didn't dare come over here with LaVerdiere watching. Besides, she said she needed to get home and get some sleep. She sounded exhausted."

"So you're not off the hook, but she doesn't know why."

"They clammed up about that part. I hope she knows what she's doing. I'd never forgive myself if she lost her job over this."

The lawyer's office in Fallstown was a throwback, something out of the late-nineteenth century. Big leather chairs furnished the waiting room, together with ornately carved, marble-topped tables and a curio cabinet filled with knick-knacks. Edmund Carrier III had apparently declined to change anything from the days of the first Edmund. Inhaling, Liss smelled only furniture polish, but she could almost imagine the days when the aroma of pipe tobacco and the tang of brandy lingered in the air. Here Carrabassett County's elite—all men, of course—might once have met to discuss the future of their community.

Carrier himself was less formal than his surroundings,

though he did wear a suit and tie. Ruddy-cheeked, big-bellied, and smiling, he was somewhere in his mid-fifties. If he'd had white hair and a long white beard, he'd have been a ringer for Santa Claus.

"Thank you for coming, Ms. MacCrimmon. I wasn't sure you'd get my message." He waved her into the chair across from his desk.

Liss sank down onto butter-soft leather, but no matter how comfortable the furniture, she couldn't relax. "Your office was closed for the evening by the time I listened to the answering machine, so I just came along as requested. What's this about, Mr. Carrier?"

"I thought you might already know, since you talked to Mr. Preston about a memorial service."

He didn't sound quite so stiff in person as he had on the phone. In fact, if Liss hadn't known better, she'd have said he was uncertain what to make of her. He took a document from one of the folders scattered across the top of his enormous mahogany desk—a will. Liss's eyes widened.

"I am Mrs. Norris's executor, Ms. MacCrimmon. She didn't want a funeral, and burial will have to be postponed until the police, er, finish doing their job, but I saw no reason to put off probate."

"I don't understand what that has to do with me." But she was beginning to have an inkling.

"Everything, Ms. MacCrimmon. You are her only heir."

"I'm her—? Her only—? That's crazy!"

"Not really. You see, Amanda Norris, having no relatives by blood or marriage, liked to keep track of former students. From time to time, when one of them had a run of bad luck, she'd change her will so that this person would benefit should she die. Over the years, she made at least a dozen wills. The most recent was drawn up about two months ago, shortly after she heard about your injury."

Fingers clenched so tightly on the arms of her chair that she left little pockmarks in the leather, Liss struggled to take in what the lawyer was saying. The sum of money he mentioned had her jaw sagging in disbelief.

"That's in various certificates of deposit and money-market accounts. Then there is the house, free and clear. No mortgage. The contents are included, along with whatever animals are currently in residence. She stipulated that they be cared for, although she did not make it a condition of inheritance."

A bubble of hysterical laughter surfaced. "I get Lumpkin! Oh, joy!"

Carrier gave her a hard look, put down the document he'd been reading from, and went to the sideboard. A pitcher of ice water and some glasses were already set out. He poured and brought the glass over to Liss. "Here. Drink this."

She obediently sipped the water, wishing it were something stronger. Her earlier flight of fancy came back to her and she managed a faint smile. "You really ought to keep brandy on hand to revive fainting damsels."

With a dry laugh he opened a cabinet to reveal a fully stocked bar. "Name your poison."

"Thanks, but no. I think I'd better keep a level head. Will you start over, please? I think I can take it in now."

"In simple terms, it's all yours. You really had no suspicion? When I heard you wanted to arrange a memorial—"

"No, I really didn't. That was just something Dan Ruskin and I thought of because, well because a lot of people in town would like to pay their respects." She repeated the cover story with a twinge of conscience. It was true, but it hadn't been the primary reason they'd talked to the neighbors.

"Then by all means go ahead with your plans. You understand, though, that she left her own instructions. Mr. Preston is to see she's cremated."

"And the ashes? I don't inherit them, do I?" Appalled, she clapped both hands over her mouth. "I wasn't being flippant. I just—"

She shook her head. She couldn't believe she'd come right out and asked such a thing. At the same time, she waited nervously for his answer. The idea that she might be expected to keep Mrs. Norris on the mantlepiece gave her the willies.

"I have orders to scatter her ashes along a particular cross-country trail at one of our better known winter resorts. Apparently she was quite an avid skier in her younger days."

The emotional roller-coaster ride continued. Liss had a sudden mental picture of the dignified lawyer creeping through the snow-covered landscape, urn in hand, determined to fulfill the promise he'd made to his client. It would have to be by stealth. Liss didn't kid herself that any of the ski areas would grant permission to scatter human remains on their property. If the story got out, they might lose business over it. They'd never take the chance that they might lose a single tourist dollar.

Mr. Carrier folded the will and returned it to its file. "Do you have any questions?"

Only about a million of them! Liss thought for a moment before she replied. She was both pleased and humbled that Mrs. Norris had thought so well of her, but she could scarcely take in the extent of her changed circumstances.

Good luck? Certainly not for Mrs. Norris. She hadn't expected to die when she did. If she'd lived, Liss would never have known about the will. Mrs. Norris would have changed it again once she saw for herself that Liss's injury hadn't crippled her. "What about the others?"

"What others?"

"The ones who were beneficiaries of earlier wills. Are they all right now? Did they ever know they were her heirs?" *And did any of them still need financial help?*

"Both Mrs. Norris and I agreed that information should be kept confidential, but I can assure you that she never changed her will unless she was convinced that the new heir needed her estate more than the previous one did."

The reality of it was at last sinking in. She owned a house. And a cat.

Mr. Carrier cleared his throat. "Unfortunately, there is one problem Mrs. Norris did not anticipate. Given the circumstances of her death, it will not be possible for you to take possession of the house until the police clear it." Avoiding her eyes, he studied his blotter. "And it was necessary that I share details of the will with the state police detective in charge of the case. He was quite interested to learn that you would inherit."

"I'll bet he was." The thought of LaVerdiere's reaction destroyed any happiness Liss had derived from the news of her good fortune. She closed her eyes and tried to gather the energy to get up out of Mr. Carrier's chair. "I suppose he wants to talk to me again?"

When she got no answer, she opened her eyes just enough to peek at the lawyer from beneath her lashes. He was studying her with a disconcerting intensity. "Do you want to tell me about it?"

"Do you handle criminal cases, Mr. Carrier? You see, Detective LaVerdiere thinks I killed Mrs. Norris. At first it was just because I found the body. Then he decided she'd been blackmailing me. And now, I suppose, he thinks I knew about the will and murdered her to get her money."

Two hours after leaving the lawyer's office, Liss sat in a much less comfortable chair—plastic—in much less pleasant surroundings. LaVerdiere had commandeered an interview room in the Carrabassett County jail in which to question Liss. With Mr. Carrier at her side, she sat across from the detective at a heavy wooden table that took up most of the space. A tape recorder sat between them on its scarred surface.

They'd already gone over everything twice. LaVerdiere's annoyance ratcheted up a notch with each repetition. "How could you not know you were in line to inherit that much money?"

Mr. Carrier spoke before Liss could. "She did not know because no one told her. She wasn't in the area until a few days ago, and I know Mrs. Norris had no intention of mentioning the matter to anyone. Why should she? She might well have decided to make someone else her heir once Ms. MacCrimmon recovered completely from her injury and found new employment."

"She looks pretty fit to me. Maybe Mrs. Norris was already looking for a new heir."

"Groundless speculation, as was your earlier supposition that Mrs. Norris acquired her fortune by illegal means." Carrier abruptly stood, making Liss scramble to follow suit. "Detective LaVerdiere, I have had enough of this nonsense. Do you plan to charge Ms. MacCrimmon?"

Santa Claus had morphed into Perry Mason. Liss felt like letting out a cheer.

LaVerdiere glowered at him. "Not at this time."

"Good. Have you finished with Mrs. Norris's house?"

He got a curt nod in response.

"And my aunt's building?" Liss chimed in.

"Yes. We have all we need. But you haven't seen the last of me, Ms. MacCrimmon."

Carrier put a hand on Liss's arm to keep her from saying anything more. He'd already opened the door for her when he turned back to speak to LaVerdiere. "One more thing, Detective. About Mrs. Norris's effects? I assume you have a list of what you took away as evidence. There was a computer, I believe?"

Liss held her breath, hoping LaVerdiere wouldn't guess that her lawyer only knew that because she'd passed on what Sherri had told her.

"Ongoing investigation. I don't discuss—"

"We'd like a receipt for everything you confiscated. I'll expect to have it in hand by this time tomorrow."

The door closed with a quiet snick right in LaVerdiere's face. Liss had to stifle a laugh.

Yup—Perry Mason, all right. As played by Raymond Burr. With a dash of Peter Falk's Columbo thrown in for good measure.

In spite of LaVerdiere's continued suspicions, Liss felt much more optimistic as she drove back toward Moose-tookalook. Her route took her past the trailer park where Sherri lived with her mother and son. On impulse, she stopped. Sherri might still be sleeping, but if she wasn't, Liss could share her news.

Most of the trailers were neat and well-kept, the single exception an old wreck at the back near the woods. The Willetts lived in a blue and white double-wide with a picket fence around its small yard. Flowers had been planted next to the trailer but the rest of the space was a grassy playground containing a swing set and a sandbox. Mrs. Willett looked up at the sound of a car stopping. Her young charge, a small, towheaded boy who could only be Sherri's son, Adam, paid no attention to Liss's arrival.

Liss didn't have much experience with children. Some

parents brought their offspring to *Strathspey* but they were usually older than this. "Good morning, Mrs. Willett. I don't know if you remember me, but—"

"You're Liss MacCrimmon. You take after your mother."

Liss was surprised by the observation. Most people said she looked like the MacCrimmon side of the family. "Is Sherri up yet?"

"No, and I'm not going to wake her." Sherri got her size from Ida Willett. Hands on thin hips, the woman looked as if a good gust of wind could blow her away, but Liss didn't doubt her determination for a minute. Sherri had inherited that from her mother, too.

"That's good. That's fine. I just took a chance stopping by." She wondered if Sherri had told her mother anything about the investigation.

"Nana? Who's she?"

The high piping voice of Adam Willett served to remind Liss that anything they said would be overheard by an impressionable child and probably repeated at the most inconvenient time to someone who didn't need to know what they'd talked about. So much for asking Ida questions.

"This is your mama's friend Liss," Mrs. Willett said. "Say hello and shake her hand, Adam."

Liss took the small, rather dirty hand in hers and solemnly shook. "Good morning, Adam. Is that your sandbox?"

He nodded earnestly. Then, suddenly shy, he sidled behind his grandmother's legs, clinging to her knees.

"Go make a sand castle," she told him. "I'll be right here watching." She moved a little farther away and motioned for Liss to follow.

Assuming Sherri had filled her mother in on some of what had been happening, or that at the least she'd have read about Mrs. Norris's death in the newspaper, Liss expected her to make some comment on the murder.

Instead she hissed a warning: "Leave us out of your troubles, Liss MacCrimmon."

Sherri *had* gotten into trouble over this. Liss started to ask what had happened at the jail last night, but Mrs. Willett was still talking.

"You've got no business snooping around in the past."

The *past*? "Mrs. Willett, my only goal is to find out who might have broken into my aunt's shop and killed Mrs. Norris."

"I know what you're thinking—if the intruder wasn't a thief, then maybe it was someone who wanted to hurt Margaret Boyd's business, someone who had a personal grudge against her."

"Like your ex-husband?" Liss's gaze shifted to Adam, who was industriously scooping sand into his bucket and piling it in towers. When she glanced from the boy to the street beyond, she was not surprised to see several neighbors taking an interest in her presence.

"Like Ernie," Ida Willett agreed.

"The police didn't find his fingerprints. Besides, his absence from his store would have been noticed and remarked upon. Since it wasn't—as far as I know—then the odds are good that he never left the premises that day, let alone had time to drive to the Emporium, get inside, murder Mrs. Norris, and get back to his own place."

"So you've got no reason to tell anyone, then? About the picture you found?"

Belatedly, Liss caught on. "Not unless he *does* have a personal grudge against Aunt Margaret."

"I'm the one with the grudge," Mrs. Willett snapped. "Your aunt ruined my marriage."

Liss stared at her. Did she really expect anyone to believe Ernie Willett was suffering from a broken heart? That the origin of his anger—and Ida's—might go back thirty-five years boggled the mind. Granted, if he'd never gotten over losing his first love, that would have been hard on the woman he later married, but for Ida to have been jealous of Margaret Boyd all this time . . .

"I'm only interested in finding out who killed Mrs. Norris," Liss repeated. "Unless *you* did it—"

"I was here, with my grandson, all afternoon. And if I was going to kill anyone, it wouldn't have been Amanda Norris."

Chapter Twelve

Liss made one more stop before going back to Dan's house. She wanted to talk to her aunt, but first she needed to know how Aunt Margaret had reacted to the news of Mrs. Norris's death. Certain Ned had been able to reach her in Scotland by now, Liss drove one more block instead of turning right off Main Street onto Birch, and hung a left onto High Street. Ned lived in one of two apartments above the grocery store.

She parked and was halfway across the small lot before she remembered she still had all the merchandise left over from the Highland Games stored in her car. She fished in her bag for her keys and pressed the lock button. The horn beeped once, startling her. She really had to get in the habit of locking up before she slammed the car door. Much quieter. But she hadn't even gotten used to owning a car yet. With a cab, or the company's tour bus, all she'd had to do was get out and go.

Liss didn't expect her cousin to be home and had planned to leave him a note telling him that she was moving back into Aunt Margaret's apartment, at least temporarily. It didn't seem right to move into Mrs. Norris's house while things were so unsettled. But when she reached Ned's door, it was open. Ned himself lounged against the doorsill.

"Saw you coming through the window. Coffee? Cocktail?" He gestured toward the small kitchen directly across from the inside hallway.

"Nothing. I'm good. What are you doing home in the middle of the afternoon?"

"I took a vacation day."

Hence the ratty jeans and sweatshirt. And it was beer she smelled on his breath, not coffee. Liss hadn't visited Ned's apartment before and was struck by how oddly arranged the rooms were. They had to cross Ned's bedroom to reach the pocket doors that separated it from the living room. As Liss threaded her way through the mess in her cousin's wake, she couldn't help noticing that his bed was unmade and that discarded clothing lay scattered about in disorderly piles. The living room wasn't much better. The furniture looked both new and expensive, but Ned's carelessly strewn possessions, from magazines and DVDs to crushed beer cans and dirty socks, completely spoiled the effect.

"Did you talk to your mother?"

"Yeah. I called her." He picked up the can of beer he'd left on the coffee table and took a long swallow. "I said I would, didn't I?"

"How did she take the news?" Liss shoved a pile of newspapers aside so that she could perch on the end of the couch.

"She was upset, but she's not coming home early. You know Mom. She committed to the three weeks, so she'll stick it out. No reason for her to come home really. Nothing she could do." Still carrying his beer, he settled into the recliner and elevated the footrest.

"I need to talk to her."

"What for? You'll just make her feel bad that she can't be here to help out. Probably mess up her concentration so she won't do a good job over there. I'm pretty sure she wants to be asked back. Don't go screwing things up for her."

Torn, Liss leaned forward, hands clasped on her knees. It wasn't just that she had questions for Aunt Margaret. She needed a dose of her aunt's common sense. A little affectionate consoling wouldn't be amiss either.

Ned regarded her through bleary, slightly bloodshot eyes. "Give Mom a break, Liss. Don't bug her about stuff she can't do anything about. Besides, she's going to be moving around a lot. She said it would be easier for her to call me than for me to catch up with her again."

Liss frowned. That didn't sound right. Margaret had given her a copy of her itinerary, complete with phone numbers. "But, Ned—"

"Let her enjoy herself, for God's sake!" He came halfway out of his chair and tossed the now empty beer can across the room for emphasis.

"Okay. Okay, I won't try to phone her. But she's going to call you?"

"That's what she said."

"When she does, please let her know that I'm moving back into the apartment tonight and I'll reopen the shop tomorrow or the next day, depending on how long it takes to put things back in order."

"Mom said to tell you she trusts you to take care of everything."

"That's good to hear." But Liss couldn't quite shake the feeling that Ned was improvising, saying whatever it took to get her off his back.

"So, the cops are through with whatever they were doing in the shop?" Ned's eyes drifted closed. He looked relaxed enough to drop off to sleep at any moment.

"Yes. If it's not gone already, I'll be taking down the crime-scene tape as soon as I get back there."

"LaVerdiere arrest anybody yet?"

"No." She gave Ned a sharp look, wondering what rumors he'd heard. "He suspects me."

Her cousin's eyes popped open. "No way."

"Way." She sighed. "He's got a dilly of a motive now, too." Certain he'd hear about it soon anyway, Liss filled him in on Mrs. Norris's will. By the time she'd finished explaining, she stood in front of the big bay window that overlooked the street and Ned had left his chair to wander into the kitchen and get himself another beer.

"Well, I'll be damned." He toasted her with the can before he took the first gulp. "Here's to you, cuz. May you spend your fortune well, preferably on generous gifts to members of your immediate family."

His attitude irritated her. "Maybe I'll invest in The Spruces," she said in saccharine tones.

He choked on the second swallow. Glaring at her, he reached for a tissue and dabbed at his chin. "What is it about that place? Or is it the Ruskins?" He gave a short bark of laughter. "Must be pheromones or something. Mom falls under old Joe's spell; you're hot to trot with Dan."

"Hey!"

"Just saying—"

"Well, don't. Dan's a friend, that's all. And I was kidding about The Spruces." Probably. She'd have to look into the idea now that she'd thought of it. "Besides, I've still got to prove I didn't kill Mrs. Norris. Can't inherit if I'm the one who murdered her."

"Bummer."

"You could help me out, Ned. You stopped by Dan's workshop that afternoon. Did you see anyone hanging around the Emporium?"

"I came straight home."

"No need to sound defensive. No one saw anything. It's very discouraging."

"Ah, Liss, Liss. Have a little faith. If you're innocent, eventually you'll be cleared."

"In this decade? Sorry, but I'm too impatient to wait for the police to get their act together. I've got to at least *try* to find out who really killed Mrs. Norris on my own."

He considered that for a moment, contemplating the ceiling above his recliner. When he glanced at Liss again, he looked both sober and concerned. "You know, Liss, you go poking around, asking questions and acting suspicious, you might as well paint a big old target on your forehead. Whoever did kill her isn't going to want to be caught."

"I'll be careful."

"I hope so. You know what they say—it's always easier to kill the second time."

With her cousin's dire warning still fresh in her mind, Liss returned to Dan's house. There were messages on his answering machine. This time she didn't hesitate to play them.

Two were for her. Mr. Preston had set Mrs. Norris's memorial service for Saturday morning at ten. He promised to notify the newspapers and the radio station. And Liss's parents had called. They still had friends in Moosetookalook.

"Are you all right?" her father demanded. "What's going on there?"

On the extension, her mother's voice was more soothing. "Give us a call, darling, when you have a moment. We worry about you."

Liss stared at the phone. If they knew to call here, it was a good bet they'd heard an earful already about her "relationship" with Dan Ruskin. She reached for the phone.

It had a long cord. Liss stood at Dan's living-room window as she listened to the distant ringing. Looking out across the corner of the town square, she had a clear view of the two houses to which she now had keys.

Her mother answered and called for her father to pick up in his den. Liss cut short their anxious questions and gave them a garbled version of events. She didn't want them to know she was a suspect in a murder case.

"Are you shacked up with that Ruskin boy?" her father demanded.

"That's none of our business," Liss's mother chimed in. But Liss could tell from her tone of voice that she wanted to know what was going on every bit as much as Liss's father did.

On her second attempt, Liss managed to give a more lucid account, event by event, ending with the news of her unexpected inheritance.

"So it's just platonic between you and Dan?" Her mother sounded a trifle disappointed.

"What? I don't have enough complications in my life right now?"

"Leave the girl alone," her father said. "Do they have any idea who did it?"

"No. The only trouble Aunt Margaret's ever had in the shop before this was an incident with Ernie Willett a couple of years ago. Dad? Did you know they used to date?"

A long silence answered her.

"Dad?" Liss realized she was twisting the phone cord and forced herself to let go.

Violet MacCrimmon was the one who finally spoke. "They were engaged to be married once. I never heard exactly what happened, but there was a bitter quarrel and they didn't speak to each other for years afterward."

"I know what happened." Liss heard the reluctance in

her father's voice. "But it's Margaret's place to tell the story, not mine."

"Dad, it could be important." She was relieved when he didn't ask why. She didn't know the answer. She just had a feeling it might be.

After a bit more hesitation and a heavy sigh, he told her what he knew. "My sister was twenty-three. She'd been away to college but she came home after she graduated because our mother was ill. After Mama died, Margaret wanted to have a career of her own before she settled down and got married. Our father said she could take over the Emporium but she wanted to try something else, something away from Moosetookalook. Ernie didn't want to budge and he didn't want to wait. They quarreled something fierce over it."

"That's it? That's all there was to it?"

"It was a big deal to them. If you want to know anything else, you'll have to ask your aunt. Are you moving back into her apartment today?"

"As soon as I hang up." After a few more minutes of repeated reassurances, she said goodbye and broke the connection, but she continued to stand at the window, staring at the two houses, until Lumpkin appeared, twining himself around her ankles.

"Do you want to go home?" she asked him.

He gave her what her mother always referred to as "the hairy eyeball" and said nothing.

Mrs. Norris's house belongs to me now. The idea took some getting used to. Liss realized she could move in today if she liked, and take Lumpkin with her. Carried in her arms rather than confined to his carrier, she thought, remembering Dan's rueful account of Lumpkin's last journey.

"I'd better check on things first," she told the cat. "Who knows what kind of mess the police left behind."

She went upstairs to pack the few belongings she'd brought with her on Saturday. She'd be staying elsewhere tonight, so she might as well take her things. That would just leave Lumpkin for the next trip.

Mrs. Norris's front door opened easily with the key Mr. Carrier had given her, but she felt like an intruder when she stepped into the foyer. She was a teenager the last time she'd been in this house, lured by the promise of tart apple pie and spicy novels. Not only had Mrs. Norris offered a better selection of mystery novels than the library had in its collection, she'd also shared her favorite romances.

Walking quietly, beset by the sense she might disturb someone if she made too much noise, Liss stopped first in the living room. The furniture was overstuffed and comfortable, and largely catproofed. Up on high shelves were the breakables—a Royal Doulton figurine of a nineteenth-century lady, a crystal vase containing a silk rose, and a small collection of bisque animals.

The infamous window alcove contained a Canadian rocker, a knitting bag beside it. Liss didn't sit down, but she did observe the view. Lenny Peet was walking his dog in the park. Children played on the merry-go-round. Marcia Katz was out on her front porch, talking to Stu Burroughs.

"Better than television," Liss murmured, "but it looks G-rated to me."

In Mrs. Norris's library, old friends awaited her. She smiled a little as she recognized familiar titles and authors. This room showed signs of having been searched, but the disorder was not too bad. She could see where the computer had been—Mrs. Norris had always put dusting low on her list of priorities—and noted the absence of the stack of computer printouts Dan had mentioned. Remembering what he had said about the looseleaf notebook, she looked more closely at the bookcase nearest the desk. A blue binder lay on its side on the top shelf, its importance apparently dismissed by the police. Liss took it down and flipped through the neatly typed pages—no more than a couple of dozen in all.

Just as Dan had said, they contained a series of brief notes. Every entry she stopped to read contained the names of fictional characters from mystery novels. Liss set the binder on the desk and began to skim the shelves. Yes, there were Anne Perry's books and what looked to be the complete works of Elizabeth Peters right next to them. The novels were arranged alphabetically by author.

Mrs. Norris's collection of mysteries and romances had grown considerably in the ten years since Liss had last looked through it. To her surprise and secret amusement, a separate, smaller bookcase was now entirely devoted to something a little different. Liss pulled out a few of the titles and read the blurbs to confirm her first impression. She'd been right. The new section contained nothing but vampire novels. Vampire romances. Vampire mysteries. Vampire chick lit. Mrs. Norris had been a woman of eclectic taste. Liss browsed a bit more, then added *Dead Until Dark* to the duffle bag holding her clothes and toiletries—might as well expand her horizons! Tucking the looseleaf under her arm, she went next door to the Emporium.

The main room was in disarray, as if a great many very clumsy people had been in and out. Displays had been handled, and some moved around, and the sales counter and window frames looked dingy where fingerprint powder had been applied. Some of it had spilled onto the carpet in front of the door to the stockroom.

For the moment, Liss ignored the mess and went straight upstairs to the apartment. To her relief, the police appeared to have contented themselves with a simple search of the premises. She unpacked and changed into her oldest pair of jeans and a t-shirt before going back down to the shop.

A closer look confirmed that fingerprint powder, some gray, some black, coated a number of surfaces but had not been applied to Aunt Margaret's stock. Liss was grateful for small favors. She doubted she could have successfully removed it from the bag of a bagpipe or a stuffed toy.

Tentatively, she rubbed at the powder with one fingertip. That seemed to make matters worse. She toyed with the idea of going back up to the apartment and using the computer to Google "fingerprint powder." Surely the Internet would offer suggestions for cleaning it off. Then she remembered Dolores Mayfield.

The librarian was delighted to be of assistance. "Vacuum first," she instructed, "but be careful not to spread the powder around. Keep vacuuming even after you can't see any dust. Then use a little soapy water on one small section at a time. Very gently. Then wet a clean, white towel with lukewarm water and use that to blot the area before the soapy water can dry. Then use another clean white towel to pat the area dry."

"And that will take it out?"

"It should. Unless it's on antique furniture, of course." Her cheerful voice grated on Liss's nerves. "The varnish on antiques is porous. Absorbs the powder and ruins the piece."

Dan noticed the absence of the crime-scene tape on his way home and wasn't surprised to find Liss's note on the refrigerator, held in place by the magnet his mother had given him when he bought the house. Shaped like a sampler, it read: "You too can enjoy the great outdoors—just miss a few mortgage payments."

"I'm at the shop," Liss had written, "getting ready to reopen."

Lumpkin, standing by his food dish, made a rude remark but for once didn't attack Dan's ankles.

"Yeah. You got that right." He fed the cat and went upstairs.

The guest room closet was empty and Liss had changed the linens on the bed. Fifteen minutes later, hair still wet from a quick shower, Dan loped across the town square and into Moosetookalook Scottish Emporium.

Liss had left the front door unlocked. Dan didn't feel much sympathy for her when the jangle of the entry bell had her jumping up, eyes wild, to wave a stained white towel at him as if she thought she could somehow use it to defend herself.

Hastily lowering her arm, she gave a shaky laugh. "Hello. I guess I lost track of time."

"And common sense."

"That thing about criminals always returning to the scene is nonsense. Anyway, I left it open for you. I figured you'd come over when you got home. I've got a lot to tell you."

"Save it for a bit. Pete came by the work site today. He and Sherri are bringing Chinese, if that's okay with you. Sherri doesn't go to work until eleven. Pete's on day off."

"Pete and Sherri together? Oh. Well, that's good, I guess. And so is the idea of eating in." She looked down at herself and grimaced. Her t-shirt had almost as many dirty streaks as the white towel.

"So, you're not going to be staying with me any longer?" Dan tried to sound casual. There was no real reason for him to feel disappointed that she wouldn't be sleeping in his spare room. He ought to be happy for her. If she'd been allowed back into her aunt's place, that probably meant the police were moving forward with their investigation.

"I really appreciate your putting me up, but it doesn't make sense to stay any longer now that I've got other options." She grinned suddenly. "Boy, do I have options, but I may as well wait until I can tell all three of you at once."

"Something good happen? LaVerdiere find another suspect?"

Her face fell. "Not that good." Her gaze shifted toward the door to the stockroom and just as quickly away.

Dan wanted to push, to hear her "options," but her words were a forceful reminder that she still had him filed in the "old friends" category. No sense beating his head against a wall. "Things bad in there?"

"I don't know. I didn't dare look."

"No time like the present." He grinned and spoke in a poor imitation of John Wayne. "I'll protect you, little lady."

Liss stepped in front of him to take the lead. When she opened the door, Dan felt his jaw drop. The police had removed half the contents of the room. What remained was liberally coated with splotches of fingerprint powder.

"Oh, no," Liss wailed, heading straight for several bolts of fabric carelessly tossed onto the table Margaret used for packing and unpacking merchandise. "That horrible black powder is all along the edges. I'll never be able to wash it out. These are ruined."

The contents of boxes and bins appeared to be undamaged, although they had obviously been gone through, but there was more fingerprint powder on what remained of the shelving. One entire section, the one against which Mrs. Norris had struck her head, had been taken away, along with the tartan cloth that had fallen on top of her body.

"What a disaster area." Liss circled the room, careful to avoid stepping in the spill of powder on the wood floor. She shoved a box back into place, righted a wastepaper basket, and had started to straighten the oversized bulletin board her aunt used to keep track of orders due to arrive when she suddenly froze.

Dan was at her side in an instant. He saw at once what had startled her into stillness. "Well, I'll be damned. There's a wall safe behind there."

Chapter Thirteen

Over containers of cashew chicken, beef lo mein and fried rice, sitting on stools around Margaret Boyd's kitchen island, Liss gave Dan, Sherri, and Pete a quick summary of her day.

Sherri stopped chewing to gape at her. "Wow. I don't know which part amazes me more, the news of your inheritance, that LaVerdiere overlooked the looseleaf binder when he searched Mrs. Norris's house, or your discovery that Margaret was actually engaged to my father."

"Margaret Boyd and Ernie Willett." Pete shook his head. "Still waters run deep."

"What's that supposed to mean?" Sherri sent Pete a wary look.

"Only that I remember my Dad talking about Ernie in his younger days. He was quite a hell-raiser. He and Moose Mayfield used to get into all kinds of scrapes. And Margaret—well, she's always struck me as . . . I dunno . . . sophisticated, I guess."

Liss thought of her aunt—dyed red hair, decked out in the traditional Scottish clothing she sold in the shop, a little overweight but comfortable with it. Sophisticated? Hardly.

On the other hand, Liss had just as much difficulty imagining her with Ernie Willett as Pete did. Only if the old saw about opposites attracting was true could they possibly have made a go of it.

"Whatever we think about it, that old relationship could be the reason behind Ernie's actions three years ago. Now? Who knows?"

Sherri held up one hand. "Okay. Before this goes any further, I think you should know that my father doesn't have anyone working for him right now. If he left the store long enough to come here, kill Mrs. Norris, and return, someone would have noticed. They'd have seen the "Closed" sign or gone in to pay for gas and realized no one was there to take their money. We'd have heard about it by now. When he did close up on Sunday—when he came to the fairgrounds—at least a dozen people noticed, because all of them made sure my mother heard about it."

"Go, small town gossip," Liss murmured. "I'd already figured that out for myself," she reminded Sherri.

"Say what you will about the local grapevine; it comes in handy sometimes."

"What's the population of Moosetookalook? A thousand people in all? Only that many minus the four of us and Ernie Willett left to exonerate." Liss cleared the empty containers away, depositing them in the trash, and steered the others into the living room.

"Sure you want to rule the three of us out?" Dan asked.

"Better not," Sherri chimed in. "Better safe than sorry."

"Better to let the police handle things." Pete settled himself next to Sherri on the sofa as they moved into the living room.

"I can't." Liss spoke more sharply than she'd intended, but she was getting a little tired of receiving this particular bit of advice. "As long as the murder goes unsolved, the shadow of suspicion hangs over me and my aunt."

Sherri slanted a look at Pete. "Are you sure you should be here? Technically, you're on LaVerdiere's side."

"Bite your tongue. And the same goes for you."

"I don't like the way he's doing things. He's not even looking at anyone but Liss."

"You don't know that."

"Do you know he *is*?"

Pete glowered at her. Sherri glared back.

Liss fought a smile at the sparks flying between the two of them. She had a feeling Sherri's qualms about getting involved with another deputy weren't going to be enough to stop nature from taking its course.

"There's no reason I can't help out an old friend," Pete said through gritted teeth.

"We'll *both* help."

"Fine."

"Good."

"Ah, could we move on to the actually helping part?" Dan asked. "There's one thing Liss left out of her story. We found something in the stockroom."

"Did you know there was a wall safe behind that heavy corkboard?" Liss asked Sherri.

"Get out of here! Really?"

"Really. And from your reaction, you don't have any idea what the combination is, either." Liss had fiddled with the dial, trying various numbers, but Aunt Margaret's birthday hadn't worked, nor had Ned's, nor had Liss's father's. All she'd gotten for her trouble was fingerprint powder all over her hands.

"I didn't even know there was a safe there," Sherri said, "and I'm pretty sure I would have if your aunt used it regularly."

"It's probably completely irrelevant. Speaking of

which . . ." She brought out the looseleaf she'd brought from Mrs. Norris's house.

"That's the binder I saw," Dan said. "The police didn't take it?"

"Apparently not." Liss divided the pages among the four of them. "See what you think. Even though LaVerdiere has ruled out blackmail, we need to keep open minds about this. Ignore the names. See if anything rings a bell. We're looking for scandal in Moosetookalook."

Dan started to protest, then thought better of it. For the next few minutes the only sounds to break the silence were an occasional snort or giggle, the turning of pages, and the steady hum of the air conditioner. Finally Liss looked up. She'd recognized lots of names—all of them fictional characters in mystery novels—but she'd been unable to match the "dirt" with anything she knew about real people.

"This one reference might be to Moose Mayfield," Pete said, "but there just isn't enough to go on to be sure. I can't begin to guess at any of the others."

Sherri agreed. "Nothing leaps out at me, and I probably hear most of the local gossip. People repeat it to my mother and she tells me. Half the time it goes in one ear and out the other, but I think I'd remember the really scandalous stuff. She—" Sherri abruptly dropped her gaze. "Well, anyway, she doesn't miss much."

"I take it I'm the subject of gossip these days," Liss said, trying to pretend it didn't hurt. "So what's the betting? Did I do Mrs. Norris in for her money, or was I trying to rob my aunt's store when she caught me?"

"That's not what they're talking about." Sherri looked no less ill at ease, but at least she met Liss's eyes. "The old biddies in town, the ones who've forgotten that most of them were young in the sixties and seventies when things were considerably wilder than they are these days, are all stirred up because you moved in with Dan."

"Appalling lack of morals that MacCrimmon girl has!" Dan winked at her to take the sting out of his words.

Liss didn't like the idea that her personal life was gossip fodder, and liked it even less that the gossip was inaccurate, but if she had to be the subject of gossip, she'd much prefer the focus be on sex rather than murder.

"Okay, enough about me. Since we can't connect up anything in the looseleaf, let's go back to the suspect list. What more do we know about Jason Graye? All we came up with yesterday morning was that he lives within walking distance of the Emporium."

Pete perked up, recognizing the name. "He's had a couple of shady dealings in his real estate business."

"What kind?"

"Not enough to give cause for arrest, or even bad publicity. Houses that weren't all he'd claimed they were, except that none of it was in writing. It came down to him saying he told the buyer everything and the buyer insisting he left out a few details."

"I never asked if you'd met him before, Dan. Have you had dealings with him?"

"Only in passing. He didn't handle the sale of your house. I bought it directly from the guy your parents sold it to ten years ago."

"What about his girlfriend? Who is Barbara Zathros?"

"I think she's his secretary," Pete said.

"More than that if he's buying her expensive presents," Sherri put in. "Kilts don't come cheap."

"I need to contact her about that," Liss murmured. "The fabric was taken as evidence. I don't want to order more unless she's sure she still wants the kilt."

"Contact him, you mean," said Sherri.

"Contact them both."

"Hold on," Dan protested. "If you really think one of them killed Mrs. Norris, you don't want to do anything to arouse their suspicions."

"I have a perfectly legitimate reason to get in touch. And a perfect opportunity to fish for more information. I'll just tell Jason Graye I want to sell Mrs. Norris's house. Then he—"

The appalled look on Sherri's face stopped her. Dan's expression was almost as disconcerting—he looked disappointed.

"Do you know how bad that will look?" Sherri asked.

"I'm not really going to put it up for sale. At least not right away."

Selling the house made sense, but in her heart Liss knew she was far from ready to put it on the market. Foolish of her. It wasn't as if she could stay in Moosetookalook and live there. She might prove she never murdered anyone, but she'd still be the shameless hussy who'd moved in on Dan Ruskin. Small town life, small town gossip—that wasn't her style. She'd go back to a city, once she decided what she wanted to do with the rest of her life. Wouldn't she?

Shaking off the melancholy mood that threatened to overwhelm her, she tapped her list. "This Barbara. Aside from her poor taste in men, she's hardly a likely suspect, but if she and Graye were here that afternoon, she may have seen something. Oh, and I need to talk to Lenny Peet, too. He was out in the square that afternoon, walking his dog."

"Well, there's your murderer," Sherri said with a sly grin. "Weren't you the one who told me that the least likely suspect is always the person who dunit?"

"Most crimes are pretty straightforward," Pete said. "If

we put our minds to it, we should be able to figure out who'd profit most from Mrs. Norris's death."

"Besides me, you mean." Liss sighed. "I wish I knew who her previous heir was. Maybe he or she didn't know Mrs. Norris had changed her will."

"Long shot," Dan said.

"You're sure the police didn't find any fingerprints but ours?" Liss asked Sherri.

"I imagine they found lots of them, but they have to be able to match prints with those already on file to identify them."

"Can you find out—?"

"Not for a bit." Sherri held up a hand, palm out, to stop her question. "LaVerdiere turned up when I was . . . chatting with another state cop. I don't think he bought the story that I was just being friendly."

"Let me see what I can come up with," Pete offered.

Dan had picked up Liss's list of suspects. "What about Ned Boyd? He was around here earlier that afternoon and I don't know where he went after he left me."

"He went home," Liss said. "I stopped by his apartment when I got back from Fallstown. I was going to leave him a note but he was there. Took a vacation day."

Sherri cleared her throat. "Uh, Liss? He isn't on vacation. He got fired from his job at the call center in Fallstown a couple of months ago."

"Huh," Dan said. "Interesting. Just last week, Margaret was bragging that he'd been promoted to shift supervisor. To hear her tell it, he was all but running the place."

"Margaret doesn't know. Ned's been keeping it from her. The only reason I found out is that one of my neighbors works there. She told me all about it when it happened. I didn't say anything because I didn't think it was my place to rat him out to his family."

Liss plopped down on the arm of Dan's chair, her gaze fixed on Sherri. "Why was Ned let go?"

"Bad attitude. He pissed off the boss. That's what my neighbor said, anyway."

"I'll bet that's why he's so stirred up about the hotel deal," Dan said. "Margaret invested money that Ned could have used himself."

"Can't see how that would lead to him killing Mrs. Norris," Pete said.

Liss sent him a grateful smile. "Good point. If she'd seen Ned go into the building, she wouldn't have bothered to investigate. It's his mother's place, after all."

"And round and round we go." Sherri stood and stretched. "Sorry to break this up, but I need to go home, kiss my son goodnight, and get ready for work."

Pete went with her, leaving Liss alone with Dan.

"I don't like you staying here by yourself," he said.

Liss hadn't felt nervous before, but the worried look on his face had her wondering if it wouldn't be better to go next door to Mrs. Norris's house. "Nonsense," she said, as much to herself as to him. "I'll be fine. All the locks are dead bolts."

Before he could offer to stay with her for protection, Liss sent him a bright smile. *Keep it light*, she reminded herself. "I've got an idea. Go get Lumpkin. He's an excellent watch cat—goes straight for the ankles."

Sherri had barely settled in on her shift when Larry Granby shuffled into the dispatch center from intake. "Sheriff wants to talk to you, Sherri. What'd you do? Lassiter hardly ever stays this late."

"No idea," Sherri lied. By the time she walked the short distance to the administrative offices, she'd broken out in a cold sweat, convinced she was about to be fired.

"Come in, Sherri," the sheriff said in a low, throaty voice. "Haul up a chair."

"Yes, ma'am."

Penelope Lassiter was second-generation law enforcement. Her father had been sheriff of Carrabassett County in his day and she had won the office in the most recent election. She was not much bigger than Sherri, standing a little under 5'5" in stocking feet, and she had a small, up-tilted nose, a pointy little chin, and almond-shaped eyes that put you in mind of a pixie . . . until you spent a few minutes in her company. She made up for being "cute" with a forceful personality, formidable scores in every area of police training, and a dogged determination to make herself and her department the best in the state.

"I've been hearing things about you," she began.

Sherri started to speak, then thought better of it.

"You seem to be doing some investigating on your own initiative. You realize that's not part of your job description?"

"Yes, ma'am."

"Do you think you could unbend for a second?"

"Ma'am?"

"For God's sake, Sherri. You make me want to tear my hair out." She gave a yank at one short, straight, mud-brown strand. "I'm only a dozen or so years older than you are. See? No gray yet. Ten years ago, I was working your job. At least in private, will you please relax and call me Penny!"

"Yes, ma'—I—thank you, Penny."

"Better. Now, about your extracurricular activities. I can't say I think you're wise to pursue them, but as long as you don't break any laws I'm prepared to overlook your interest in Amanda Norris's murder." She tipped back in the desk chair, propping shoeless feet on the blotter. "I take it you don't think much of the way Detective LaVerdiere is handling the case?"

"He's on the wrong track. Liss MacCrimmon never killed anybody."

"Got any theories who did?"

"Well . . . no. Not really."

"I'd like to get rid of him, you know."

"LaVerdiere?"

She nodded, watching Sherri through half-closed but alert dark brown eyes. "God only knows if the next one will be any better, but this one's a dead loss. You didn't hear it from me, but LaVerdiere was transferred here because he screwed up his last assignment. They wanted to give him another chance. I don't know why, but Carrabassett County seems to be the dumping ground for incompetent officers. You should have seen the last one. Geoff Tooley. God, what a loser. Thought he was hot stuff, too. Even made a pass at me once."

Sherri felt warmth creep up her neck and into her cheeks and hoped Penny Lassiter wouldn't notice. The sheriff seemed to be lost in her own thoughts. Her gaze drifted to the ceiling as she rambled on.

"Bad apples. That's what they are. But instead of tossing them out, they send them here. I expect that's why he's so fixated on your friend. He needs a high-profile arrest to save his career."

Bad apples, Sherri thought. That about summed it up. She knew that all law enforcement agencies tried to screen applicants, but some misfits always managed to slip through. More often it was the overly aggressive type, bullies drawn to the power of the badge. They didn't last long. They overreached their authority and got canned for it. Poor interview skills and pigheadedness, on the other hand, were harder to use as grounds for dismissal.

The sheriff lowered her feet to the floor and sat studying Sherri's face. "I don't want to hear any more complaints about your interference and I don't want to hear that you're leaking information. I don't want to *hear* about it. You understand? And if you need to miss work, you take vacation time, not sick days."

"Yes, ma—Penny."

"Good. I'm glad we had this little chat. Get back to work."

Liss did not sleep well. Lumpkin was restless. Every time he jumped up onto her bed, Liss jerked awake. When the phone rang at a little past seven, she embarrassed herself by squeaking in alarm. One hand over her rapidly beating heart, she picked up before the instrument could shrill again, expecting Sherri to be on the other end of the line.

"Hope I didn't wake you," Aunt Margaret chirped, "but the day's half gone over here." It was a good connection. She sounded as if she were standing in the next room.

"I was just about to dress and go down to the shop," Liss told her. "You'll be glad to hear we can reopen tomorrow."

Today was earmarked for a trip to Fallstown to talk to Jason Graye. It might be foolish to think she could succeed where the police could not, but she didn't see any way around trying. Otherwise she might yet end up in jail.

Liss's announcement was greeted by a long pause on the other end of the line. "Excuse me?"

"You, ah, didn't know we were closed yesterday?"

"Amaryllis MacCrimmon, what is going on there?"

Standing in the kitchen doorway with the phone, Liss took a moment to turn and bump her forehead, none too gently, against the wall. She should have expected this. The minute she heard Ned had lied about his job, she should have realized he'd also lied about calling his mother.

"Aunt Margaret, you'd better sit down. I've got a lot to tell you."

Liss left out as much as she put into her account. She didn't want her aunt to worry. She had no need to hear that her niece was Detective LaVerdiere's prime suspect, or that her son had chickened out and put off calling her with the news of Mrs. Norris's murder. For the moment Liss also held back the story of her unexpected inheritance, although she had to admit that Lumpkin was in residence. Aunt Margaret heard him yowling in the background.

By the time Liss wound down, she felt as exhausted as if she'd lived through the last few days all over again. It took another ten minutes to convince her aunt to stay put in Scotland.

"There's no point in rushing back home," she repeated. "There's nothing you can do here."

"It's my store that was broken into."

"Do you have any idea why? I discovered a wall safe in the stockroom but I didn't have the combination. I don't know if anything was taken from it."

"The safe?" Aunt Margaret sounded surprised but not alarmed. "Mostly I use it to store documents, since it's fireproof. My passport, when I'm not using it. My birth and marriage certificates. My social security card. That sort of thing. Oh, and my diamond ring may be in there, the one your uncle gave me when we got engaged. It got too tight, so I stopped wearing it a few years back. Or did I leave that in my jewelry box? I don't remember. Do you have a pencil and paper? I'll give you the combination."

Liss wrote down the series of numbers Margaret gave her, then listened as her aunt rambled on. Should she mention stumbling upon Margaret's past relationship with Ernie Willett? It no longer seemed relevant. Willett might have an irrational streak when it came to his wife, his daughter, and his old girlfriend, but he also had an alibi.

"My God. Amanda Norris murdered. I just can't take it in. Is there anything I can do?"

"I don't think so, Aunt Margaret. Everything's under control here now. And we had two very good days at the Highland Games. Oh, and you may have a customer for a custom-made kilt. A woman named Barbara Zathros?"

"I remember her. Works for Jason Graye, doesn't she? What does she want with a kilt? Zathros isn't exactly a Scottish surname."

"Don't be such a snob," Liss teased. "She wants the Flower of Scotland tartan."

Too late, Liss realized she'd opened up a can of worms. She hadn't planned on mentioning the damage to the stock, but there was no way to avoid it now. "I'm going to have to order more cloth. The fingerprint powder made a terrible mess. I don't think it will clean out of the bolts of fabric." That the Flower of Scotland was unavailable because the police had taken it was something Liss chose not to share with her aunt.

In hindsight, it was easy to see that bolts of cloth should have been stored in their protective wrappings, but who could have imagined that the ordinarily spotless workspace where Aunt Margaret processed mail orders and unpacked newly arrived merchandise from her suppliers, would turn into a crime scene?

"Hold off on that," Aunt Margaret instructed.

"But the kilt—"

"She'll have to wait." She spoke sharply, cutting off Liss's protests, but with the next sentence had moderated her tone. "Now that I think about it, you'd better tell Ms. Zathros to go elsewhere for her kilt, or choose one off the rack. I've got a busy schedule when I get back. I won't have time for sewing."

Liss hated to lose the sale, but she didn't argue. After further assurances that both she and the shop could survive on their own until her aunt's scheduled return, Liss ended the call.

Five minutes later, Liss was in the stockroom, the slip of paper with the combination to the safe clutched in her hand. At least one mystery would be solved today.

Nothing seemed to have been disturbed. One by one, Liss took out the envelopes her aunt had stored there, checking the contents against the notations on the outside. Birth certificate. Marriage certificate. Uncle Noah's death certificate. Ned's birth certificate. Certificate of Deposit from the Carrabassett County Savings Bank—closed out two months ago. Liss frowned. When she checked the other envelopes with the bank's name on them she found similar evidence of recent withdrawals. Aunt Margaret's savings account was down to three-hundred dollars. She had even turned in her life insurance for the cash.

The last two envelopes in the safe held the explanation. One contained the agreement Margaret Boyd had signed with Joe Ruskin for a share in The Spruces. The other held documents relating to the bank's claim on the Emporium. Aunt Margaret had taken out a second mortgage to help finance her plans.

Considerably perturbed, Liss returned everything to the safe and locked it up again. It looked as if Ned had been right. His mother had risked more than she could afford on the renovation project. If the hotel failed and the shop had even the slightest setback, Aunt Margaret faced bankruptcy.

Chapter Fourteen

Liss spent the drive from Moosetookalook to Fallstown trying to think of ways to improve her aunt's bottom line. A slick mail-order catalog. Online sales. Liss was certain that if she put her mind to it they could generate more income. Even though she'd never before had occasion to use it, Liss did have a degree in business.

She almost steered off the road when she realized where her ideas for improving the Emporium were leading. Was she actually thinking of *staying* in Moosetookalook?

"Oh, no," she whispered. "Nonsense. Of course I'll move on after Aunt Margaret gets home."

There was nothing for her in a small rural town.

Just the shop. Family. Friends.

Dan?

Stop it!

It was a relief to pull into the tiny, secluded parking lot in back of Graye's Real Estate. The only emotion likely to be involved in dealing with Jason Graye was extreme irritation.

The real estate office was small and reeked of Barbara's trademark perfume, but was extremely well-appointed. The receptionist's desk in the outer room was equipped with all the latest gadgets and gizmos.

Liss made a mental note: *invest in upgrade for the Emporium's computer.* Aunt Margaret still relied on a five-year-old system with a printer that did nothing but print. Even Liss's secondhand laptop, which she'd bought to take on the road with her, was newer and faster.

Barbara Zathros turned from watering a fern and recognized Liss. "Ms. MacCrimmon. How can I help you?"

"I'd like to talk to Mr. Graye about selling some property, but I'm afraid I also have some bad news for you. I talked to my aunt this morning. I'm sorry, but she won't be able to make a kilt for you after all. Perhaps you'd like to come by the shop and take another look at what we have ready-made?"

"This is very disappointing, Ms. MacCrimmon." She frowned as she moved on to a spider plant. "And very unprofessional."

That stung, but Liss wasn't about to apologize again.

"Does this have something to do with that old lady getting killed?" Barbara stopped to pinch a dead leaf off an African violet, her back to Liss.

No, she was definitely not going to apologize, but she would offer an explanation, if only to forestall further complaints. "Fingerprint powder. Fabric. Not a good mix."

"Fingerprint—? Oh. Oh, dear, that's most distressing."

"Why? Did you and Mr. Graye leave prints when you stopped by?"

The raised watering can bobbled. For a moment Liss thought Barbara might drop it, but she recovered. When she spoke, her voice was bland and unconcerned. "What makes you think we were there?"

"The neighbors saw a couple peering through the front windows. I assumed it was you two."

"Oh. Oh, yes. We did take a peek. The store was locked up tight, of course. We were just curious, and it was on the way home." Abandoning her watering, she crossed to the desk and pushed the button on the intercom. "I'll just tell Mr. Graye you're here, shall I?"

"Wait. Did you see anyone else around the shop? Anyone who looked out of place?"

"How on earth would I know who was out of place and who wasn't?"

She had a point.

Five minutes later, Liss was seated in the inner office. She'd refused an offer of refreshments.

"Well, Ms. MacCrimmon, what can I do for you?" Graye was all charm this morning. Amazing what the scent of a commission could do for someone's personality. His attentive, encouraging expression did not alter once in the time it took Liss to explain about her unexpected inheritance and her supposed interest in selling Mrs. Norris's house.

"I don't want to put it on the market quite yet," she added. "I mean the poor woman hasn't even had her memorial service yet. But as soon as all the paperwork's done and it's decent to put a for-sale sign up. . . ."

"You're wise to plan ahead. I know the house, of course. Lovely old Victorian. I'd have to take another look. Make sure it's structurally sound and in good repair. I can stop by this evening."

"Better wait a few days." Liss didn't want him tramping around in Mrs. Norris's house at all, but she smiled encouragingly. "Anything before the memorial service and people will talk."

"As you wish." His smile was as phony as hers. "Next week, then?" He thumbed through an appointment book as if looking for a blank slot.

"Will you be attending the service? It's scheduled for Saturday morning."

"I think not. I never met her, you see. Terrible loss, of

course." He oozed counterfeit sympathy and waited only a beat before shifting the conversation back to business. "Now, then. Are you also thinking of selling the contents of the house? I can recommend an excellent firm that does estate auctions."

"I hadn't thought about it," Liss admitted. The idea of getting rid of Mrs. Norris's things left her feeling vaguely unsettled, but what else could she do with them? All those books! She'd have to buy another house just to keep the library.

Or stay in the one she already owned.

Keeping a smile in place took effort but Liss managed it. She reminded herself that she'd had a reason for coming here and it hadn't been to sell Mrs. Norris's house. "I'm afraid I'm still reeling from what happened Saturday," she confided, leaning forward to rest her elbows on the edge of his desk. She looked up into his eyes. "If only I'd done as you asked and gone back to the shop for that fabric. I might have been able to prevent what happened."

He seemed startled by her comment but reached across the desk to pat the back of her hand. "Now, you mustn't think that way. No point in blaming yourself."

Liss cringed inwardly at the contact but didn't let her reaction show. "I suppose you're right. And the police think she was probably killed later in the afternoon. Shortly after *you* were there."

"I beg your pardon?" He withdrew his touch with a jerk. His face closed and his shoulders went stiff.

"You *were* there, weren't you? One of the neighbors said—"

"Yes. Yes, certainly. We, uh, stopped by to look at the window display. Didn't go in, of course. The shop was closed."

Had she succeeded in rattling him? It was hard to tell,

and even harder to decide if he'd been momentarily thrown off stride because he'd killed Mrs. Norris or because he'd suddenly realized that he might have been standing outside the Emporium while murder was being done inside. Most likely the latter. She couldn't think of any reason why he'd have wanted Mrs. Norris dead. He hadn't even known her.

"It's so frustrating that the police can't discover anything about the crime," Liss said, keeping a close watch on his expression. "Did you happen to notice anything out of the ordinary while you were there?"

Graye considered for a moment, his face unrevealing. "Might have seen some dry rot in your aunt's porch."

Dry rot? He was thinking about dry rot when a woman had been murdered? The man's utter callousness pushed all of Liss's hot-buttons. Consumed by an overwhelming need to force him to think of Mrs. Norris as more than the former owner of a house he might put on the market, she blurted out the first thing that came into her head.

"She had secrets, you know."

"I beg your pardon?"

"Mrs. Norris. She had secrets. That being said, there are a few special items in her effects that I want to . . . sell separately."

"Oh?" He paused, pencil over yellow pad, waiting expectantly.

"Mrs. Norris collected . . . information." Liss hesitated. Graye's expression showed mild curiosity but not the slightest flicker of concern. "Uh—local history. She was working on a history of Moosetookalook and had a looseleaf full of details she'd accumulated. It would only be of value to someone who was in it. Or whose family was. If you see what I mean."

He didn't have a clue what she was talking about—for

that matter, neither did she—but Liss could tell he thought there might be money in it for him. She wondered if he was a partner in that auction house he'd mentioned. At the least, she expected he got a kickback on any business he sent their way.

"I'm sure I can find a buyer for anything you choose to sell." Graye produced two business cards from a drawer. One was his own, the other the auctioneer's. "We'll talk further when I come to take a look at the house."

Dan removed yet another window from the second floor of The Spruces and looked through the opening to see Liss's car pull into the parking lot. "Taking a break," he called to Sam.

He'd been thinking about Liss ever since they parted company the previous night—when he hadn't been obsessing about the contents of Mrs. Norris's looseleaf. After he'd dropped Lumpkin off with Liss, he'd taken it home with him to read all the way through. Maybe the cops had decided it wasn't important, but he was no longer so sure. Most of it had been incomprehensible, but there was that one passage . . . .

How had Mrs. Norris found out? And what had she planned to do with the information? He still couldn't picture her as a blackmailer, but if that wasn't the answer, why had she written what she had? Only a small portion of the entries seemed to refer to anything truly scandalous, and even fewer to anything potentially illegal. Some of them were benign in the extreme. But she'd kept that looseleaf for a reason. And she'd known. Somehow, she'd known.

Dan made it to the lobby just as Liss pushed through the main door and stopped to gape in astonishment at the interior.

"Wow!"

Her admiration momentarily banished darker thoughts. Dan was justifiably proud of his father's accomplishment. "Like it? We started the restoration in this area and used the results to get publicity for the project. Helps investors visualize how it will be."

"It's . . . it's incredible. I remember how it looked when we were kids, but this is so much more grand."

The check-in desk gleamed in the early morning sun, its rich woods polished to a high gloss. Dan ran a hand over the surface, proud of the job he'd done. He'd also restored the wall behind it, with its old-fashioned cubbyholes for guests' keys and messages.

Taking Liss's arm, he led her deeper into the lobby. The Ruskins had left the beautiful wood floors intact, although they planned to put down large, plush rugs in the seating areas. Pillars created small pockets of privacy. A huge fire-place no longer provided the only heat, but it looked very fine with its Victorian mantel and the mirror above. The ceiling, a carved wonder of animals and flowers, had been painstakingly cleaned and painted, returned to its former glory with hours of hard work.

"See that trim? I painted that, inch by picky inch." And he'd loved every minute of it.

The sound of a crowbar ripping into wood struck a discordant note. Then Liss turned to face him and he noticed the troubled look on her face.

"What's wrong?"

"Aunt Margaret phoned this morning. Ned never called her. I had to tell her about Amanda Norris's murder." Speaking rapidly, as if she wanted to get this over with, she summarized their trans-Atlantic conversation.

"You aren't going to go all weepy on me, are you?"

She managed a laugh. "No. I'd rather punch someone. Preferably my good-for-nothing cousin. But he wasn't home."

"So you came here instead?" He meant it as a joke, but she wasn't laughing.

"Dan, I checked the contents of the safe. I looked through my aunt's papers. I wasn't snooping, but . . . things look bad. She's nearly broke. If this hotel doesn't pay off, she could lose the Emporium."

Dan stared into the empty, tile-lined hearth, avoiding Liss's eyes. He couldn't brush off her concerns the way he had Ned's. "We're all in the same boat," he said at last. "If we go down—"

"You go down together?" Temper simmered beneath the question.

He shook his head. "We'll help each other stay afloat."

"Why don't I find that reassuring?"

A wolf whistle echoed across the lobby, cutting short their exchange. Sam Ruskin sauntered over, a big grin on his face. "Liss MacCrimmon, as I live and breathe. Aren't you a sight for sore eyes."

"Hello, Sam. It's good to see you again."

"So, did my little brother ask you the burning question yet?"

Dan's head snapped around and he stared at his brother. *What the—?*

Sam sniggered. "We've been trying to decide what color that car of yours is."

Dan breathed again. Liss actually smiled.

"The manual calls it 'light almond.'"

Sam shook his head. "Where do they come up with these names? House paint's going the same way. All 'big country blue' and 'festive orange' and, my personal favorite, 'funky fruit.'"

"He's been decorating his kid's toy box," Dan whispered in an aside.

That was Sam's cue to haul out pictures. When Liss had duly admired little Samantha in a dozen different poses, Sam switched to bragging about his other pride and joy, The Spruces.

"The roof's done. We've removed nearly thirty miles of old piping and replaced it with all new state-of-the-art plumbing. Ditto on the electrical and heating/cooling systems. Now we're working on the cedar siding. I don't even want to think how many miles of that needs to be restored, but I do know how many windows have to be taken out, sanded, painted, and reglazed: seven hundred and twenty-seven."

"So the renovation is going well?"

"The renovation is going great."

"Don't get him started on the wallpaper," Dan warned, *sotto voce*. They'd discovered eight layers of the stuff, all of which had to be removed from every bedroom.

"Everything will look as great as this lobby does when we're through," Sam predicted.

"And when will that be?" Liss asked.

The light in Sam's eyes dimmed. "Hard to say. Dad's still taking on other jobs, but we spend at least a couple of days a week here. After the roof, the first thing we did was reconfigure the guest rooms. There aren't as many now, only a hundred and forty, but the new ones are more spacious and comfortable and every one has a spectacular view."

"It's an expensive project." Liss's cautious tone should have been a warning to Sam, but he was a natural-born optimist.

"Well, yeah, but you can't scrimp and expect results."

"My aunt put a good deal of money into The Spruces."

Solemn, reproachful green-blue eyes shifted from Sam to Dan.

"No one twisted her arm to invest," Dan said carefully.

"I know that, but—"

Belatedly catching on, Sam barreled forward. "We can't tell you the hotel is a sure thing, Liss, but your aunt knew that going in. She believes in what we're trying to do here."

"We cut costs by doing the work ourselves," Dan reminded her.

Liss didn't seem to find that reassuring.

"When we open, rooms will go for $250 to $300 a night."

"I can do the math as well as you can, Sam. It will take a long, long time for The Spruces to start paying off for investors."

"What can I say? Our dad and your aunt think the risk is worthwhile. Margaret Boyd isn't the only one out on a limb. Dad went into hock up to his eyeballs to finance his dream."

Liss drew in a deep breath. "Okay. Okay, I get that. And . . . it is beautiful." She let her gaze rove over the luxurious lobby again. "But I can't help but worry about what might happen to Aunt Margaret."

"Money aside," Dan said quietly, "this place is part of our heritage. We're committed to preserving it."

Liss spent the evening brooding. It had been a mistake to visit the construction site. Nostalgia . . . or something . . . had gotten to her. She'd come within a heartbeat of offering to put a chunk of Mrs. Norris's estate into the hotel project.

Temporary insanity—there was no other explanation. The place . . . or the man . . . had cast a spell on her.

She certainly hadn't dropped in on Dan with investment

in mind. When she'd seen the state her aunt's finances were in, she'd been appalled. She'd started thinking about them again on the way back from Fallstown, prompting her to stop first at Ned's apartment and then at the construction site. Assuming she got Mrs. Norris's money—that she wasn't arrested for murder and barred from collecting her inheritance—the Emporium had priority. If she put any money into Moosetookalook's economy, it should be in her aunt's shop.

Liss went to bed late, exhausted, but her sleep was restless. The slightest sound woke her. A dog barking. A car with a faulty muffler. And the third time, an odd thunk, as if someone had bumped against a piece of furniture.

Groggy, Liss lay in the darkness staring at the ceiling. Straining to hear, she didn't move a muscle. At first her own quiet breathing, a little fast from being jolted awake, was the only sound in the stillness. Then she heard it—a soft footfall, then another. Someone was in the apartment.

A quick glance at the clock on the bedside table told her it was 3:35 in the morning. She kept a small travel flashlight on the night-stand, too, and closed her hand around it as she slid out of bed. There was no extension in the guest room but her cell phone was in her purse. Liss tried to remember where she'd left it and realized with a silent groan that it was in the living room next to the sofa. Damn!

Moving to the door, she put her ear against the wood and listened hard. She thought at first that she must have been mistaken, that she'd imagined the earlier sounds. Nothing seemed to be stirring beyond the barrier. She felt for the knob and slowly turned it, praying the door hinges wouldn't squeak. Inch by inch, perfectly silent, the portal swung inward and Liss peered out through the opening.

At first she could see nothing but a few pale streaks of

light from the streetlight. They slitted through the edges of the living-room drapes. Then she saw it, off to her right, the illumination from the screen on her laptop.

Only she distinctly remembered closing it before she went to bed.

Was someone still there? With as much stealth as she could manage, she started to move toward the kitchen then stopped. *Cliché much? "Our intrepid heroine, clad in filmy nighty, walks straight into the villain's clutches."*

No, thank you!

She prudently retreated, stopping only to feel around for her shoulder bag. She still had the small flashlight in her hand but she didn't dare use it. Her bag was not on the floor next to the sofa where she'd left it. It was *on* the sofa, and open. Someone, whoever was in the apartment, had rifled through it.

Liss didn't need the soft curse from the kitchen to spur her on. Grabbing the bag, she fled with it back to her room, locking the door behind her. A moment later, she had her cell phone out and had hit the speed-dial number she'd programmed into it only a few days earlier.

Dan picked up on the third ring. "Wha—? Hello? Who is this?"

"Dan, wake up. There's someone in my aunt's apartment." She sank down on the end of the bed, her legs too shaky to hold her any longer.

"You sure it's not just Lumpkin?"

He still sounded only half awake. Liss hoped he wasn't going to need two cups of coffee before he'd be coherent.

"Liss?" She heard a creak and a curse on his end and hoped that meant he'd gotten out of bed.

"I don't know where Lumpkin is, but I'm fairly certain he doesn't have the dexterity needed to search my purse. There's someone out there, and by now I'm pretty sure he's figured out that I've locked myself in my room because I know it."

"Stay put and call 911," Dan ordered, and broke the connection.

Liss had just finished talking to the emergency dispatcher when she heard an unearthly howl from the direction of the kitchen.

"Lumpkin!" Springing to her feet, Liss dropped the phone and unlocked the door.

Chapter Fifteen

Across the town square, Dan pulled on the jeans he'd left on the floor by the bed. He didn't bother with shoes or a shirt. He stopped only long enough to collect the heavy-duty flashlight he kept handy for power outages and was in such a rush that he left the door of his own house unlocked. Eyes glued to the windows above the Emporium, he sprinted across the green. There were no lights showing. He wasn't sure if that was a good sign or a bad one.

The sound of running footsteps behind him made him glance over his shoulder. He couldn't see who it was, but there was enough moonlight to show him that the figure was coming from the direction of the police station and was in uniform.

"I'll go around back," Dan shouted. "You take the front."

He didn't wait for agreement. Nor did he check his headlong pace until he realized that the rear entrance was wide open. His stomach in knots, Dan forced himself to go slow, shining the flashlight ahead of him, even though what he really wanted to do was run straight through and head up the stairs to Liss.

There was no one in the stockroom this time, dead or otherwise, but the door to the shop, ordinarily kept shut, was only halfway closed. He hauled it the rest of the way open and plunged through. Still no one. He headed for the front door, but as soon as he unlocked it, he made a bee-line for the sales counter and the stairs behind it.

He took them two at a time, calling Liss's name as he burst into the apartment. He almost collapsed with relief when he heard her answering shout. The beam of his flash-light caught her as she emerged from the kitchen wearing some kind of filmy negligée that had his eyes popping. He had only time enough to flick on the overhead light before she flung herself straight into his arms.

"He's gone," she whispered. "I heard him go."

"You're trembling." He wrapped his arms more tightly around her but it didn't help. Not when he was shaking, too.

Heavy footsteps and the sound of labored breathing an-nounced the arrival of Jeff Thibodeau. He had his gun out when he came through the door, but he quickly holstered it when he recognized them.

"She says he's gone."

"Better make sure." He headed for the bedrooms.

"I've got to find Lumpkin." Liss freed herself from Dan's embrace and got down on hands and knees beside the sofa to peer underneath it. "There you are, my brave boy. My hero."

A low growl greeted this overture.

"Liss, why were you in the kitchen?" It had taken him a moment to realize she hadn't stayed safely locked in the guest room but had come out into the apartment, possibly while the intruder was still on the premises.

"I was looking for Lumpkin."

"Christ, Liss! That cat isn't worth—" He broke off when he saw the look on her face. He wanted to shake some sense into her. He wanted to lock her away somewhere she'd be safe. He wanted . . . too damn much. He settled for offering her a hand to help her to her feet.

Thibodeau returned to the living room. "All clear. You want to take a look around, Liss? See if anything is missing?"

A short time later, Liss had checked all the rooms in the apartment. Her face wore a puzzled expression. "The only thing I'm sure is gone is a looseleaf with a blue cover. I can't find it any—"

"I've got it," Dan cut in. "I, uh, took it home with me the other night to have another look at it."

After a considering glance in Thibodeau's direction, Liss let the subject drop. "Then it doesn't appear that the thief took anything, but someone was definitely here and he did go through my purse."

As she told them about her foray into the living room to fetch her cell phone, Dan's heart almost stopped all over again. He understood why she'd taken the risk, but he wasn't happy about it.

"And I'd left my laptop closed," Liss added. The three of them congregated around the kitchen counter on which the notebook computer rested. "It's open now."

"You protect your files with a password?" Thibodeau asked.

"It never seemed worth the bother. Mostly I use it to surf the Web and send email."

There was a pad of paper and a pencil next to the laptop. Dan moved closer. She'd made several notations. It was easy enough to see what she'd been researching. She'd found the website of a hotel over in New Hampshire. Like The Spruces, it had been closed for awhile before someone bought it and fixed it up. It had reopened as a resort and spa in 2002 in a town no bigger than Moosetookalook.

From everything Dan had heard, the place was doing okay. But the figure Liss had written down and underlined twice was $20,000,000—the total cost of the renovations.

"Could you tell if the intruder was a man or a woman?" Thibodeau asked.

"No, but you might try looking for someone with a bite on the ankle." She gave a shaky laugh and pointed to a tuft of fur on the kitchen floor. "That's why Lumpkin let out such an ungodly howl. Whoever was in here stepped on his tail."

"And you came charging out to rescue him. Geez, Liss, where's your common sense?"

She lifted an eyebrow, her gaze moving from Dan's bare chest to his bare feet. Then she ignored him to take a can of tuna out of the cupboard and open it. The sound of the can opener combined with the smell of fish was enough to lure Lumpkin out from beneath the sofa.

"I'd better check downstairs," Liss said when she'd finished making much of the damned cat.

Both men went with her while she walked through the displays and inspected the stockroom.

"No sign the lock on this door has been tampered with," Thibodeau said.

"Did the state police find Margaret's back-door key? The one she used to leave over the door?" Sherri had said she couldn't find out if they had it or not, that the troopers had clammed up on her when she asked.

"No idea," Jeff said.

"Damn. If the person who killed Mrs. Norris used that key to get in and took it with him—"

"Then tonight's intruder may have been her killer." Liss's face lost color with alarming speed. She turned wide, frightened eyes to Dan.

All he could think of to do was take one of her small,

soft hands in his own big, work-hardened paw and give it a reassuring squeeze.

"Get the locks changed first thing in the morning," Thibodeau advised.

"And tonight?" Her voice shook.

"I doubt he'll show up again tonight. For one thing, there's not that much night left."

"But why did he come back at all? That makes no sense."

"Call in the state police," Dan said. "Let them figure it out."

"No!"

"Liss, be reasonable. They—"

"They'll send LaVerdiere. I don't want to have to deal with him again."

"Jeff, talk to her."

Jeff cleared his throat. "I'm gonna leave this up to Liss. Gotta say there's no evidence to connect this to the murder. And nothing was taken."

"The back door was wide open when I got here," Dan reminded him.

"If you want, I can do the whole fingerprint-powder thing—"

"Oh, no! Not again."

Jeff talked right over Liss's interruption. "—but it probably wouldn't help. If there was someone in here, he was most likely smart enough to wear gloves. Everybody watches crime shows these days. And even if there are unidentified prints, that's just what they'll be—unidentified."

"So you're saying you aren't going to do anything?" Dan felt his temper spark.

"I'm saying it's up to Liss."

"Let it go, Dan. I'm scheduled to reopen the shop in less than six hours. Aunt Margaret can't afford another delay."

She couldn't be swayed in her decision, but after Thibodeau left, Dan pushed a heavy worktable in front of the back door. Then he followed Liss back up to the apartment.

"I'm sticking around till dawn."

"Fine. Coffee or bed?"

"Is that a variant on 'coffee, tea, or me?'"

She made a face at him. "Your timing continues to stink, Ruskin."

"Yeah, I know." But when he tugged her into his arms, she didn't resist, and there followed a pleasant interlude that he knew he would treasure for the rest of his life.

Just after sunrise, Dan went home. It wasn't until he opened his front door that he remembered he'd left the place unlocked when he went haring off to rescue Liss.

The first thing he saw when he walked into his living room was the looseleaf binder Liss had taken from Mrs. Norris's house. If he hadn't borrowed it, it would have been in the apartment. Was the looseleaf what the intruder had been looking for?

Picking it up, Dan flipped through the pages. He couldn't tell if any had been removed. The sheets weren't numbered. It didn't look as if anyone had come into this house while he'd been gone, but if someone had, they'd have found the blue binder in plain sight. If only one page went missing, Dan thought, no one would ever know the difference.

For the first hour after Moosetookalook Scottish Emporium was open, not a single customer came through the door. Liss found herself wishing some of the "ghouls" Jeff Thibodeau had predicted would show up. At least a few of them might have bought something.

The locksmith did put in an appearance. In short order

Liss had brand new locks and a shockingly large bill to pay.

The quiet after he left soon had her yawning. Between the excitement of the break-in and the shamelessly romantic interlude with Dan Ruskin that had followed, she had not gotten much sleep the previous night.

"Don't go there," she muttered, unsure herself which part of her early-morning adventures she meant.

She attempted to distract herself by rearranging stock, but after she'd twice tried out new ways to display kilt hose, flashes, and buckles and ended up going back to the original arrangement, she abandoned the effort and returned to the sales counter.

Everything was in order there as well, from the packages of McVitie's Rich Tea Biscuits and jars of Scottish Blossom Honey to a stack of the mail-order flyers Aunt Margaret sent out twice a year.

Liss frowned as she studied one of the latter. It was nothing more than a list of items and prices. No pictures of the merchandise. No Web address for easy ordering. There was an email listed, but only for questions. She really had to bring Moosetookalook Scottish Emporium into the twenty-first century. Aunt Margaret didn't use her computer for more than a fraction of the things it could do in connection with the store.

Liss's associate's degree in business hadn't gotten much use in the eight years since she earned it, but she hadn't forgotten a thing she'd learned about promotion. And while she'd been with *Strathspey*, she'd helped design and maintain the company's website. She flexed her fingers, literally itching to get started, but at that moment the bell over the shop door jingled to announce, at last, the arrival of a customer.

"They told me I'd find you here," a familiar voice caroled.

"Gina?" Liss was off her stool and across the shop in a flash. After an exchange of hugs they just grinned at each other. "What are you doing in town?" Her best friend from high school had gone on to get a degree in law and had joined a prestigious firm based in Chicago.

"Taking a few days off so I could attend our reunion, what else?" Gina had the slick and sophisticated look that went with big-city success. She wore her dark hair in a short, sleek cap that made her eyes seem enormous.

"Ohmigod! It completely slipped my mind."

"You? Forget something? Amazing!" Gina stepped back to take a quick survey of the shop. "Does anything ever change in here? I swear it's exactly the same as when you used to work here as a teenager. God, even you look the same, right down to the Scottish outfit!"

Liss had dressed in store merchandise—a hostess skirt and sash in the Royal Stewart tartan and a long-sleeved white-blouse with a jabot. "Hey, I could have worn a Billie skirt and boots." Her aunt listed Billie skirts as "fashion minis" and they certainly were short!

"Oh, I've missed you. You and your Scottish stuff. And you ended up going pro with your dancing. All those competitions really paid off for you, huh?"

"I could say the same to you."

That they'd been such fast friends during high school could only be explained by the fact that they had both been involved in odd extra-curricular activities. While Liss had competed in dance at Scottish festivals, Gina had entered beauty pageants. She'd used her not-inconsiderable earnings from winning so many of them to pay for college and law school.

"Did you really forget about our tenth reunion? It's only two days away."

"Saturday," Liss murmured. Had it only been five days ago that she and Sherri had talked about brazening it out? She hadn't given reunion a thought since, not even when she'd agreed to hold Mrs. Norris's memorial service on the same day.

"I gather you've had a few distractions lately," Gina said.

Now blessing the lack of customers, Liss steered Gina to what her aunt called her cozy corner, a section of the shop that displayed Scottish-themed books—everything from cookbooks to mystery novels set in Scotland—and boasted two reasonably comfortable chairs. "Sit. Tell me every-thing you've heard."

After kicking off her shoes and curling her legs beneath her, Gina ticked each item off on her fingers. "Your aunt is in Scotland. Her next-door neighbor was murdered. The police don't have a clue who did it."

"That's it? That's *all* you've heard?"

"What else is there? I only know what I've read in the newspaper. My folks live in Fallstown, remember? They're not on the Moosetookalook grapevine." She peered more closely at Liss's face. "How much worse is it?"

"I found the body." She was surprised Gina's parents hadn't heard that tidbit, even way off in Fallstown. According to Dan, details of her discovery had reached the scone lady in Waycross Springs by the morning after the murder.

"Oh, Liss. I'm so sorry. It must have been horrible for you." A wave of sympathy flowed toward Liss, warming her.

"The worst part is not knowing who did it. And Gina . . . because I found her, the police suspect me."

"Ridiculous."

"Well, yes." Her friend's immediate certainty had an even more heartening effect. It wasn't as if they'd stayed in close touch over the last few years. As far as Gina knew, Liss could have turned into a drug-crazed mass murderer in the interim. "But the suspicion will be there, hanging over me, until someone else is arrested."

She gave Gina the basics of the situation—the motive LaVerdiere thought she had and her certainty that he wasn't looking at any other suspects.

Gina tapped beautifully manicured nails on the arm of her chair. "I bet you're thinking of staying home Saturday night, aren't you? Don't deny it. I know you. Well, you can't. You've got to attend and you've got to make sure everyone there ends up knowing you were just an innocent bystander. Then they'll tell their friends and families and popular opinion will be on your side no matter what happens next. Simple."

"Simple," Liss echoed. But not easy. The idea of repeating even part of the story over and over again for the benefit of curious classmates made her stomach churn.

"Can you recommend a good criminal lawyer, just in case?" Liss meant the question in jest, but sobered fast when her old friend took it seriously. By the time Gina left the shop, Liss had three names and phone numbers and the sinking feeling that her old friend thought she was going to need them.

A short time later, Liss picked up the phone, but the number she punched was that of Dan's cell. "Are you going to reunion?" she asked when he answered.

"Liss, this isn't a good time." His voice sounded strained and she could hear traffic noise in the background.

"Okay. I know it's not safe to drive and talk. Call me back when you have a minute."

Her phone rang an interminable quarter of an hour later.

"I can't talk long," Dan said, barely giving her time to say hello. "My sister is in labor. I'm at the hospital in Fallstown. No cell phones allowed inside."

"Mary's having her baby? That's great!"

"Not really. It's too early. Look, I can't talk now. Did the locksmith come?"

"Yes. I'm all set. But—"

"Good. I'll be by when I can but it's looking like a long haul. Watch your back."

He disconnected abruptly. Liss cradled the phone, letting her fingers rest lightly on the hard, smooth plastic of the receiver.

All of a sudden the shop seemed too quiet and empty. She'd never minded solitude before. In fact, she'd relished what little privacy she'd been able to find when she was on tour. Now she was aware only of being alone. Abandoned.

"Oh, stop the pity party," she muttered.

But she jumped when the bell over the door sounded.

"How's it goin'?" Jeff Thibodeau asked. "Thought you'd like to know we're going to keep an extra close eye on this place tonight. Just in case."

By closing time, Liss had heard from Dan again, but the news was not good. Mary and her two-month-premature son were both in critical condition. Everyone in the Ruskin clan was staying put at the hospital.

"Will you be okay?" he asked.

"Oh, sure. The entire Moosetookalook Police Department is keeping an eye on me."

They both knew how little coverage that really was. Moosetookalook had been a much larger town in the hotel's heyday and it was then that the municipal building and police station had been built. Now the force was down to three full-time men, one for each shift, and one patrol car. Some of the more frugal townspeople were reportedly lobbying to do away with the department entirely and let the county handle law enforcement.

With a long evening stretching ahead of her, Liss considered calling Gina. She decided against it. When she stopped and thought about it, she and Gina didn't have much in common anymore. They'd lost touch over the ten years since high school. It was all well and good to meet again and renew old acquaintances, but Liss didn't expect to generate a lasting friendship with any of her former classmates.

Not even Dan.

She spent a little time cleaning up after Lumpkin—he'd knocked the basil off the windowsill and a ceramic spoon holder off the stove, breaking the latter into a dozen pieces. After a light early supper, Liss spent considerably more time going over her aunt's books.

Business had picked up in the afternoon, but not by much. Apparently murder wasn't even a nine-day's wonder these days. The ledgers increased Liss's pessimism about her aunt's financial prospects. She began to think she should just go ahead and sell Mrs. Norris's house. The money from the sale, added to the rest of her inheritance, should be enough to bail out the Emporium and still leave a bit for Liss to invest in her own future.

Tossing her pencil aside, Liss collected Lumpkin and headed for the house next door. She had almost an hour of daylight left, time enough to explore a bit. She hadn't done more than take a quick look around on her last visit. She hadn't even gone upstairs.

They started in the kitchen, where Lumpkin took the lead and made sure she found his supply of cat food.

"What am I going to do with you when I leave here?" she asked him.

He was too busy scarfing down kibble to acknowledge that she'd spoken.

Liss wandered into the living room. As a toddler, she'd come here with her mother. She'd sat, quietly fascinated, watching Mrs. Norris knit and chat with Violet Mac-Crimmon. Only years later had Liss discovered Mrs. Norris's library and their mutual love of reading.

It occurred to her now that she didn't know much more than that about Amanda Norris. Mrs. Norris had taught school. She'd knitted. She'd baked. She'd taken an interest in her neighbors. And she'd been an avid reader. But Liss had only known her in her later years. What had she been like as a young woman? And what had happened to *Mr.* Norris? He'd been out of the picture by the time Liss first met his widow.

She left the living room and went upstairs, where five doors made a rough circle around a large central hall. Liss opened the one at the top of the stairs to discover a huge bath. It had probably been a bedroom once, she decided, before the house had indoor plumbing.

The next door led to a guest room, in which Mrs. Norris had placed three more Royal Doulton figurines—a shepherdess, a woman with a bouquet of flowers, and a Scottish dancer. Liss smiled at the latter and inspected the roomy closet—empty—and another door that led to a small balcony. She was careful to close the hall door when she left. She had a feeling this room was off-limits to Lumpkin. If he got in, the delicate and expensive figurines were likely to go the way of Aunt Margaret's spoon holder.

The next door opened to reveal the stairs leading to the attic. A quick look at her watch told Liss she didn't have time to investigate up there today. Instead she moved on to the master bedroom.

Mrs. Norris's room occupied the front corner of the house and had the same view as the bay window in the living room. Liss surveyed the neighborhood, her gaze drawn first to her old house. Dan's house. There was no truck in the driveway. No lights had come on inside. He wasn't home.

She looked quickly away. It was ridiculous to start imagining that she could stay on in Moosetookalook. She couldn't support herself here. She wasn't even sure she could adjust to being in one place all the time. She'd liked being on the road, savored the constant change, the constant challenge of travel.

Liss's eyes were on the town square, but her thoughts tumbled round and round, refusing to settle. For some moments, she didn't register what she was seeing—an elderly man walking his equally ancient dog.

Liss sprinted down the stairs and out onto the porch. She caught up with Lenny Peet and his arthritic hound just as they were about to leave the square.

Ten minutes later, she was back in Mrs. Norris's kitchen. Just like all the others, Lenny had been minding his own business on the Saturday Mrs. Norris was killed. He'd seen nothing out of the ordinary, noticed no one in the vicinity of Moosetookalook Scottish Emporium.

With a wary glance at the setting sun, Liss looked around for Lumpkin. She called his name. She opened one of the little, expensive cans of cat food. Nothing worked. Lumpkin did not intend to be removed twice from his home. After nearly a quarter hour of futile searching, by which time darkness had fallen in earnest, Liss gave up trying to locate him. She made sure he had plenty of water to go with his food, left a night light plugged in, and went back to her aunt's apartment alone.

Chapter Sixteen

The evening was quiet. Too quiet. By the time Jeff stopped by to check on her, she was desperate for company. She made coffee and peppered him with questions while he drank it.

"It's just so frustrating," she confided. "I want to do something to help clear myself but I can't think what else I *can* do. I've talked to everyone I could think of. No one saw anything. It's possible one of them is lying, but I can't tell who, and that blackmail thing turned out to be a dead end."

"You know I don't have a clue what you're talking about, right?"

"Shouldn't you be involved in the investigation?"

"State police handle murders almost everywhere in the state, certainly in all the rural areas. They have the experience and training—I don't. Neither do you. You're just going to have to be patient, Liss. Good police work takes time."

"It would be easier if I thought I was getting good police work. What I've *got* is Craig LaVerdiere."

"I understand your concern," Jeff said patiently, "but he has a whole team of people working the case with him. Good people. Let them do their jobs."

"Do they always get it right? Do they even come up with the solution every time?"

"Well, no. But they never close the books on murder until they make an arrest."

"That is *not* reassuring. Not when I'm the prime suspect."

After Jeff left, she called Sherri, but Sherri was too distracted to talk. Her son had an earache. Ned didn't answer his phone, and she heard nothing further from Dan.

Liss shook her head at her own foolishness. It wasn't like her to need someone around every minute. Oh, it was understandable that she'd be nervous after the break-in, but she'd changed the locks and Jeff was right across the town square. She had nothing to worry about. She watched television for awhile and went to bed early, but sleep eluded her.

She found herself wondering why Dan had taken Mrs. Norris's blue looseleaf. What had he expected to find in its pages that the rest of them had missed? He must have been looking for something specific. Otherwise, he'd have told her he was borrowing it. They'd dismissed the idea that Mrs. Norris was writing down gossip about real people, hadn't they? And Dan had been the one who'd argued most fiercely against suspecting her of being an extortionist. No explanation had presented itself before she drifted into an uneasy doze.

She dreamed of being locked in a cell—*Prison Break* had given her an all-too-vivid picture of what life in jail was like. She woke before dawn, rose with the sun, and by nine, an hour before the shop was due to open, had consumed enough coffee to make her jittery as an ingenue with stage fright.

Friday at the Emporium started out as a repeat of Thursday. The dearth of customers gave Liss more time to think—the last thing she needed.

The bell over the door jangled, just as it had the previous day when Gina Snowe turned up. This morning, however, the former classmate entering the Emporium was not an old friend. Karen Cloutier, Dan's high school sweetheart, stopped just inside the door to give the shop a cursory once-over. With a disdainful sniff, she fingered a brass door knocker in the shape of a bagpiper.

"People actually pay money for this?"

"Some do." Liss came out from behind the sales counter, hackles rising as Karen continued to touch merchandise she had no intention of buying.

She picked up a tiny stuffed Loch Ness monster, carelessly tossing it aside to inspect a piece of thistle glassware. Once it was well smudged with fingerprints, she put it back on the shelf. Liss winced as it struck the adjacent glass with a loud clink.

"Something I can do for you, Karen?"

She looked good for a woman who'd been married and had produced two kids. The dark hair and snapping blue eyes were unchanged. "I hear you mooched off Dan for a couple of nights." Like Gina, Karen was from Fallstown, but someone had apparently filled her in on at least one bit of Moosetookalook gossip.

"I wouldn't put it quite that way." Liss waited for the other shoe to drop.

"I can't say I'm surprised." Karen abandoned the pretense of being interested in what the Emporium had to offer. "I had to watch him every minute back in the day and he always had a yen for you."

Liss felt her eyebrows shoot up. If Dan had been interested in her in high school he'd sure had a funny way of showing it. She couldn't remember that he'd said more than two words to her in public after they graduated from Moosetookalook Elementary School and matriculated at the regional high school in Fallstown.

"Of course he only strayed in his thoughts, and even they came right back to me. Every time." A particularly smug smile appeared on her face and she practically purred her next comment. "It was so nice being with him again last night. He hasn't lost a bit of his old fire."

The implication gave Liss a nasty jolt. Dan *had* stayed in Fallstown overnight. Just the possibility that he'd spent part of that time cozied up to his old flame hurt like hell. *Consider the source*, she reminded herself.

"I understand you have two children, Karen," she said. "Did you bring them with you?"

Karen scowled—not a flattering expression on her. Before she could manage a comeback, the shop door opened again.

Saved by the bell! Liss turned to greet the new customer, but her automatic smile faded as soon as she recognized Craig LaVerdiere.

"Ms. MacCrimmon, a word with you?"

"Certainly. Just as soon as I'm through with this customer."

Karen looked from Liss to the newcomer and back again. "Oh, I think I'll just browse a bit. Please, don't let me keep you from business."

Liss couldn't tell if Karen knew LaVerdiere was a cop or if she thought his business with her was personal and romantic. Either way, it was clear the other woman didn't intend to miss the chance to eavesdrop. Liss toyed with the idea of leaving her alone in the shop while she talked with LaVerdiere in the privacy of the stockroom, but decided the effort would be a waste of time. Karen would just use one of the thistle glasses to listen through the door.

Leaving Dan's old girlfriend to fiddle with a display of sporrans, Liss led LaVerdiere to the cozy corner and waved him into a chair. "What can I do for you, detective?" She kept her voice low and her tone neutral.

"I brought you your statement to be signed," LaVerdiere announced, indicating the manila folder he'd placed on the small table between the chairs. "Unless you'd like to change your story."

"Not a chance." She opened the folder and skimmed the typescript. She scarcely had to read it to know what it said. She'd answered the same questions so many times that she knew the contents by heart.

"I'm surprised you're not asking about the investigation," LaVerdiere remarked.

She lifted a brow at him as she signed her name. "Would you tell me anything if I did?"

"I don't mind having you know some things."

His sudden amiability made Liss wary. "So, how is the investigation going?"

"We still haven't found anyone to verify exactly when you returned here that evening."

Which meant she was still a suspect. *Big surprise.*

"And although motive isn't really as important in finding a killer as fictional detectives think it is, no one has a better one than you do. Seems to me you must have known she left everything to you, Ms. MacCrimmon. What else but the promise of a fortune would make you hightail it back to a dinky little burg like this one?"

"Career-ending knee injury? Desire to help my aunt run her business?" She forced herself to settle back in her chair and feign casual unconcern. *Never let them see you sweat.*

"You stayed in touch with Mrs. Norris after you left Moosetookalook."

"She stayed in touch with me. She stayed in touch with a lot of people."

LaVerdiere picked up the folder she'd returned to the table, checked her signature, and stood. "So you say, Ms. MacCrimmon. So you say."

Liss opened her mouth and closed it again. Since no argument she could make would convince him she was innocent, why bother?

LaVerdiere headed for the door. Karen Cloutier, looking as pleased as Lumpkin after a saucer of cream, timed her exit to coincide with his. She was flirting outrageously with the detective as they went out together. Liss wished her luck. She doubted LaVerdiere would tell her anything. Unfortunately, she'd already gotten an earful.

"This just keeps getting better and better," Liss grumbled.

There were no more customers after Karen left. Once again Liss had too much time to think. She doodled a to-do list.

1. Clear name by identifying real killer
2. Solve Aunt Margaret's financial problems
3. Find new career

Only with the last item did she have much hope of success. Liss started another list, this one of possibilities for future employment.

1. Teach dancing?

Liss made a face. Not her thing and never had been. She didn't want to teach what she could no longer do. Besides, children made her uncomfortable.

2. Management position with *Strathspey*?

That would only work if such a job were available: it wasn't. If she returned to the company, the best she could hope for would be work in some menial backstage capacity. *Not appealing!*

Liss hesitated, then wrote:

3. Stay in Moosetookalook.

She could buy into the Emporium, if Aunt Margaret wasn't averse to the idea, but would that be a wise investment? The business was dangerously close to failure. She could lose her entire inheritance from Mrs. Norris in a futile attempt to save it.

Then there was The Spruces. If it ever opened, she supposed there would be jobs. She could even put money into the renovation project. But there, too, the prospect of disaster loomed. A year or two down the road, she might end up worse off than when she'd started.

You don't have control of your inheritance yet, she reminded herself. And if Detective LaVerdiere had his way, she never would. Liss repressed a shudder. She wouldn't have to worry about her future if she was in jail.

By the time Liss started to close up at five, she was feeling a bit more upbeat. For one thing, Dan had phoned to say that Mary was out of the woods. Her newborn, now named Jason, was doing better, too. And Dan was on his way home. They were going to have supper together after she paid a return visit to Mrs. Norris's house.

She was just taping a notice to the inside of the door when she heard someone come up onto the porch. Her hand was halfway to the new deadbolt before she recognized her cousin. She jerked the door open instead.

"Where have you been?" She hadn't been able to track

him down since she discovered he'd lied to her about calling his mother.

"Never mind me. What's the meaning of this?" He gestured angrily at the sign, which said she wouldn't be opening until noon the next day. "Can't be bothered to keep the place open? Need to sleep in on Saturday?"

"I need to attend Mrs. Norris's memorial service."

"Oh." Although he took a step back, he looked more chagrined than contrite. "I'd forgotten about that."

"You're going, right?" She stepped out onto the porch and shut the door behind her.

He shrugged. "I guess." He watched her lock up, frowning. "There's something different—you changed the locks? Why? We can't afford—"

"If you want to talk to me, about locks or anything else, you'll have to tag along while I go check on Lumpkin." Too impatient to wait for a response, she headed across the lawn toward Mrs. Norris's house.

Ned trailed after her. "I hate that damned cat. He bites, you know."

"You deserve to be bitten," Liss said, unlocking Mrs. Norris's kitchen door. "You lied to me. You never called your mother."

"Oh. Yeah. Sorry about that." He followed her into the house.

"You should be." Lumpkin was waiting, sitting next to an upside-down water dish. With a sigh, Liss grabbed a towel and started mopping up the spill. Ned, mindful of the cat's bad habits, prudently stayed out of the way.

"You also lied about being on vacation," Liss said as she straightened up with the soaked towel in her hands. "You were fired from your last job."

"How the hell—?"

"Is it true?"

"Well, yeah, but it wasn't my fault."

Liss dumped the towel in the sink, disgusted with both man and cat. She should have known better than to expect Ned to accept responsibility for anything. Even as a kid, he'd been an expert at shifting blame. He'd been even better at not getting caught.

Ned maintained a sulky silence, one shoulder propped against the wall, while Liss refilled Lumpkin's food and water dishes and cleaned his litter box.

"Was there a reason you came looking for me?"

"Can't a guy just stop by to see how his cousin's doing?"

"After you've been avoiding me for days?" She headed for the hallway and the stairs, intending to take a look at the one room on the second floor that she hadn't yet inspected.

By the time Ned caught up with her, Liss had let herself into the third, much smaller bedroom and had opened the hope chest she found there. It appeared to be full of memorabilia.

"What are you doing?"

"I have to give a eulogy tomorrow and I think I just found what I need to inspire me."

He watched her burrow through the chest's contents for a few minutes before asking again about the new locks.

"Someone broke into the apartment the other night. Nothing was taken, but we're pretty sure it was the same person who killed Mrs. Norris."

"Pretty sure? Not positive?"

"Unless the state police have Aunt Margaret's spare key, that's the logical conclusion. If it was someone else, then that means there's another key floating around somewhere. Did you have one?"

"No. I always use the one over the doorsill if I need to get in and Mom isn't home."

"I'll have a copy of the new key made for you. In this day and age it's too dangerous to leave a spare over the door." She pulled an old photograph album out of the hope chest and started to go through it, ignoring Ned as he left her to wander through the other upstairs rooms.

He was back a short time later. "Nice old place. I haven't been in here for years and I don't think I was ever allowed upstairs."

"Mmmm." Engrossed in her discoveries about Mrs. Norris's past, Liss only half-listened.

"Liss? You still trying to find the killer on your own?"

Carefully, she set aside the papers she'd been reading and looked up at Ned from her perch on the floor beside the hope chest. "I'm still a suspect, if that's what you're asking."

"So what are you doing about it?"

"Worried about me, cuz?"

"Not really. I don't figure you're much of a detective." He made a rude noise. "Not that the real ones are doing such a bang-up job."

Irrationally irritated—not an unusual occurance around her cousin—Liss glowered at him and spoke with a bravado she was far from feeling. "I'll figure things out eventually, Ned. My own survival depends on it." She shrugged with assumed nonchalance. "It's just a matter of asking the right question of the right person. Then all the pieces will fall into place."

"What question?"

She had no idea, but she wasn't about to tell Ned that. "Wouldn't you like to know."

"Yeah, I would, actually." He left the doorway and moved toward her, taking up a surprising amount of space in the small room. "I—"

"Liss? Where are you?" Dan's voice boomed through the house, making Ned jump.

"We're up here!" A moment later she heard him on the stairs.

"I should go." Ned passed Dan in the hallway. They didn't speak.

"What was he doing here?" Dan demanded the moment he entered the room.

"Hello to you, too."

"Sorry." He leaned down and caught her by the elbows, pulling her to her feet and straight into his arms. "Missed you."

A short, satisfying interlude later, Liss went back to sorting through the contents of the hope chest while Dan told her, in more detail than she really wanted to hear, about the trials and tribulations of birthing a premature baby.

"More excitement than I've had here," she told him. "Sadly, that applies to the Emporium, too. I can count the number of customers on one hand and only two of them bought anything."

"Have you talked to Sherri since the break-in?"

"Only very short conversations. Her son has an ear infection. I filled her in on the details, such as they are." She hesitated. "We talked a little more about the contents of that blue binder, trying to figure out why Mrs. Norris made those notes. Why did you take it home with you?"

"I just wanted to read the whole thing. Sorry I haven't gotten it back to you, but I didn't figure there was any rush. There's nothing in it."

Liss paused in the act of removing a photograph from a frame, struck by the fact that Dan had turned away from her . . . as if he wanted to make sure he avoided meeting her eyes.

"I ran into Pete in Fallstown."

And now he was changing the subject.

"He wasn't able to find out anything more from the cops but he did tell me he's taking Sherri to our reunion. I thought we'd make it a foursome, if that's okay with you?"

"Misery loves company?"

"Something like that." At ease again, he grinned at her. "I wasn't planning to go, but I guess I can stand to play 'do you remember' if you're there with me."

Liss returned the last of the items she'd been looking through to the hope chest and closed the lid. She stared at her hands where they rested on the highly polished wood. "Did you happen to see Karen Cloutier while you were in Fallstown?"

"Oh, hell! I didn't know she was coming." There was too much dismay in his voice to be anything but sincere. "Can I change my mind about reunion?"

"Not a chance."

Sherri wore her one professional-looking suit and high heels to Mrs. Norris's memorial service. She was glad the shoes pinched. That was the only thing keeping her awake. If she didn't catch some sleep sometime between now and this evening she'd be doing a good imitation of a zombie for her former classmates.

Hiding a yawn behind her hand, she scoped out the other mourners. The funeral parlor's largest room was filled to capacity and the overflow had spilled out into the vestibule. That was where Craig LaVerdiere had ended up, nose in the air, eyes suspicious. Sherri was a little surprised to see him. If he was convinced Liss was the killer, why would he need to attend? Maybe he had doubts after all. She hoped so.

Liss and Dan were off in a corner, engaged in intense conversation. Sherri wasn't the only one watching them and speculating. They practically sparked when they were together.

So much for warning Liss not to get involved. Not that Sherri had anything personal against Dan Ruskin. He was a nice enough guy, but he wasn't telling Liss everything.

Talk about the pot calling the kettle black, she thought with a wry grimace. She was keeping a few things from Liss herself. And not all men were untrustworthy. Pete seemed to be—. She cut off that line of thought. Why on earth had she let him talk her into allowing him to escort her to the reunion? It wasn't even his class.

Maybe she'd figure that out tonight. *After* she got some sleep.

"Sherri, isn't it?" a soft voice asked. "Is this seat taken?"

"Hello, Mrs. Biggs. Please sit down." She'd been saving it for Pete, she realized, but he hadn't turned up yet. His loss.

Hermione Biggs was close to Mrs. Norris's age. Sherri imagined they'd known each other all their lives. She was also Barbara Zathros's landlady.

Sherri took another look around. She recognized most of the Moosetookalook residents. Even though it had been awhile since she'd actually lived in this little town, she'd worked at the Emporium since her return. She'd met everyone in the neighborhood at least once. Absentees were easy to spot. There was no sign of Lenny Peet or Ned Boyd. Jason Graye hadn't shown up and neither had his lady friend.

At precisely ten o'clock, Liss mounted the podium to begin her tribute to their late neighbor. She had found a good photograph of Mrs. Norris and had it mounted on a stand beside her.

"I don't think most of us knew Amanda Norris as well

as we thought we did," Liss said with a glance at the likeness. She shuffled the note cards in front of her, but she didn't need to look at them. "She was born in 1925 and married young. Her husband was killed fighting in World War II. Afterward, she moved into the house on Pine Street, which at that time belonged to her mother-in-law, and commuted to classes at what is now the Fallstown branch of the University of Maine. Back then it was a teacher's college, one of the best around, and when she graduated she took a job right here in Moosetookalook. After her mother-in-law died, she inherited the house and continued to live there until her own death. She kept teaching until she was seventy."

After a few more words, centering on Mrs. Norris's love of reading, Liss invited other neighbors to take the podium. Hermione Biggs was the first to comply.

"Amanda discovered the Internet about five years ago. She joined all kinds of groups to talk about the things that interested her. Her favorite was the fanfic group, filled with other people who loved to read mysteries. And then there were the on-line auctions. She had a ball buying and selling online. Her mother-in-law left behind a collection of Hummels. Amanda always hated them. She preferred Royal Doulton figurines. She found good homes for the Hummels and bought several of what she called her 'little ladies' with the proceeds."

Another of Mrs. Norris's former students reminisced about the way she'd taught spelling. She'd made up stories incorporating each week's list of words. Sherri remembered being featured in one of those tales himself. It had been a science-fiction saga, she recalled. When she misspelled a word, Mrs. Norris had banished her to a planet where the inhabitants had nothing but spinach to eat.

Chapter Seventeen

The Student Center at the Fallstown branch of the University of Maine had a large function room available for gatherings such as class reunions. School banners had been hung on the walls and bunches of balloons in team colors formed centerpieces at the tables, but otherwise the decor was not particularly festive. Neither was Dan Ruskin's mood.

Liss eyed her escort warily, wondering what he wasn't telling her. His sister was indeed on the road to recovery. Liss had talked to Mary on the phone herself. That left local gossip to worry about . . . and Karen Cloutier.

"Liss! Over here!" Gina Snowe's voice carried easily across the room as she gestured for them to join her at the table where she was holding court. There was no other word for it, Liss thought with a smile as they made their way over. No fewer than five of their male classmates were gathered around the ex-beauty queen in the bright red dress, vying for her attention.

Unfortunately, only two chairs remained empty. "Sorry, Gina. There are four of us." Liss indicated Sherri and Pete.

For a moment, Gina looked startled. "Hello, Sherri."

"Gina." Sherri gave the other woman such a cool nod that Liss found herself scrambling to remember what their relationship had been like ten years earlier. She couldn't think of anything to explain the sudden chill in the air. Then again, as a high school student, she'd been pretty oblivious to everything outside her own interests.

They found a table with four places free toward the back of the room, claimed the chairs with the programs handed out at the door and their evening bags, and put on their name tags, ready to mingle. Dan looked as if he was on his way to an execution and Sherri's attitude wasn't much better.

"Drinks for everyone?" Pete suggested.

Forty minutes later, Liss was bracing herself for the next "do you remember when?" encounter when she recognized Karen Cloutier's voice behind her and a little to the left. "I heard she not only sleeps around, she does it for money."

The malicious words fell into a momentary lull in other conversations.

Liss closed her eyes and prayed for fortitude. *It isn't worth confronting her over*, she lectured herself. Karen had clearly been imbibing heavily and she'd never been particularly discreet. Liss had already heard that Karen had been spreading the word that Liss was a suspect in Mrs. Norris's murder. *Let her say whatever she wants about me. Sticks and stones and all that.*

But the voice that answered Karen belonged to Gina. "Maybe years ago, but surely not now."

Liss choked back an outraged cry of protest at this betrayal by her "best friend." Liss hadn't even had a serious boyfriend in high school and Gina knew it.

"What, you think she got law-abiding just because she put on a uniform?"

Not me. Sherri.

Liss was ashamed of the relief she felt. Had Sherri overheard? The noise of dozens of people all chattering at the
same time should have covered the exchange between Karen
and Gina. But Dan had heard. His grip on Liss's arm tightened. He tried to tug her out of earshot, but it was too
late.

Liss heard Gina chuckle. "You're probably right. I
wouldn't put it past her. I ran into her once before she
came back to Maine to live, and let me tell you, she wasn't
exactly law-abiding then."

"Ooooh—details!"

Karen's delighted trill of laughter grated on Liss's nerves.
Without taking the time to consider consequences, she
pushed her way through the classmates separating her from
the two gossiping women and confronted them. Outrage
made her voice louder than she intended. "This isn't high
school any more, ladies. And trashing someone's reputation isn't a joke."

Karen gave her a cat-after-cream smile. "Trashy is as
trashy does. My mother *saw* her. Last summer. Flashy car.
Flashy man. Cheap motel room."

Suddenly aware they had an avidly listening audience,
Liss felt herself flush with anger and embarrassment. She
looked around for an escape route only to have her gaze
collide with Sherri's.

Time seemed to stop. It was all there to read in the horrified expression in Sherri's eyes. She knew Karen and Gina
had been talking about her. Worse, at least some of what
they'd said was true.

Liss swung back to Karen, fists clenched at her sides.
"Drunk or sober, you haven't changed a bit in ten years.
You're still a petty, small-minded troublemaker."

It occurred to Liss that several of her own long-forgotten

high school humiliations could probably be laid at Karen's door. Naïve as she'd been then, she'd never made the connection.

She leaned in close, so that only Karen could hear. "Dan *always* liked me best."

It was a childish remark but damn, it felt good to have something with which to pay Karen back. Then her old nemesis ruined the moment by bursting into tears.

"Oh, hell. I didn't mean to make her cry."

"Why not?" Sherri asked as she and Pete came up beside Liss and Dan. "I can't think of anyone who deserves a few minutes of misery more. Don't worry, it won't last. She'll be back to normal by the end of the evening."

"And inventing new lies." Dan had been silent till then. "I don't know about you three, but I've had enough of Old Home Week. How about we skip the banquet and go out for pizza?"

"No way," Sherri objected. "Who knows what stories she'll invent if she thinks her lies drove us away."

The brave front crumbled as soon as Dan and Pete left them in a secluded corner to fetch refills of their drinks. Sherri looked as if she, too, was about to turn on the waterworks.

"I just made things worse," Liss lamented. "I didn't mean to draw attention to Karen's comments."

Sherri blinked back the incipient tears and squared her shoulders. "Not your fault. And, sadly, neither Gina nor Karen was lying. Gina and I crossed paths when I was at a pretty low point in my life. And what Karen's mother saw? I'm afraid that was true, too. I guess I should be grateful she didn't know who I was with that night." Color flamed into Sherri's face and she shifted her gaze to a spot on the floor. "It was LaVerdiere, Liss. I was fool enough to sleep with Craig LaVerdiere."

Struggling to hide her shock, Liss put her hand on Sherri's forearm and squeezed. "He . . . ah . . . well, he is kind of good-looking. Till he opens his mouth."

Sherri managed a chuckle. "It was back when he first got to the area. I was lonely. He was sexy. We met at the annual law enforcement picnic and there was chemistry. I figured, what the heck? This could work out. We have the job in common. But afterward he made it clear he hadn't been interested in anything more than a one-night stand. Made me feel cheap. Worse, made me feel like an idiot."

"I've had a stupid moment or two myself."

"I've had more than one."

"And I'll bet you Karen has had dozens."

"There is that." Sherri caught sight of Pete and Dan returning and spoke quickly. "Time to change the subject. Do you have Mrs. Norris's looseleaf?"

"Not yet. Dan's giving it back to me in the morning."

"Can I come over around noon tomorrow and take a look at it? I heard something earlier tonight that sounded an awful lot like one of the entries."

Liss hastily agreed. She wondered why Sherri didn't want Dan and Pete to overhear her request, but she didn't ask questions. She figured she'd find out soon enough. *If they survived the rest of the evening.*

Liss slept in on Sunday and woke up to find a note from Dan pushed under the stockroom door. She was not expecting anything romantic. He hadn't even hinted that he'd like to sleep anywhere but in his own house the previous night. He'd checked the apartment for intruders before having her let him out the front door of the Emporium, but he'd contented himself with an almost chaste kiss. Liss didn't know what to make of the way he was pulling back from her.

The note simply said that he'd gone out to The Spruces and that she'd find the looseleaf at his place if she wanted it before he returned. She'd asked about it again during the drive home from reunion.

Liss duly retrieved it—she'd not yet returned the spare key Dan had given her when she was staying with him— after she'd stopped at Mrs. Norris's house to refill Lumpkin's food and water dishes.

She was making a hearty brunch when Sherri arrived. She had sausages keeping warm, waffle batter ready to go, and a second pot of coffee perking.

"What, no scones?"

"They're harder to make than I expected. My first try would have made a rock seem light and flaky in comparison."

"Waffles will do," Sherri decided. "Oh, good. You got the looseleaf." It didn't take her long to find the section she'd read when they'd divided up the pages. She skimmed through it again while Liss poured coffee. "Ah, here it is! She's using fictional character names again, I assume. Joe Morelli?"

Liss couldn't help grinning as she poured batter into the waffle iron. "Sexy cop in Janet Evanovich's Stephanie Plum novels."

"Well, sexy or not, here he's defrauding people out of their homes so he can tear them down and build high-rise condos."

A reference to construction work? Liss's concentration slipped and she brushed too close to the hot waffle iron with her hand. Jerking away from the heat, she stared at Sherri. "What did you hear last night that made you remember that entry?"

"That Jason Graye bid on The Spruces. He drove up the

price, then dropped out leaving Joe Ruskin as high bidder. Word is that Graye planned to tear down the hotel." She held up a hand to forestall Liss's protest. "I know. It's a stretch, but Graye and defraud just seemed to go together. I'll bet he uses substandard construction, too." She sighed. "Do you think I'm trying too hard to find suspects?" She sounded discouraged.

"I don't know. I do know that I hate being so suspicious of everyone all the time."

But Liss was also relieved that Sherri hadn't thought "Joe Morelli" might be Joe Ruskin. Sherri had assumed Mrs. Norris meant Jason Graye. She might even be right, but that didn't mean Graye was a murderer. *Did it?*

"Pete said there had been some complaints about Graye," Liss added in a thoughtful voice.

Sherri's expression brightened. "That's right. And it was Gracie Lomax I talked to last night. She works at one of the banks in Fallstown. She's a solid source."

Liss moved the looseleaf aside to serve brunch. They talked of other things while they ate. Not all the memories of the previous night's gathering were bad ones. It wasn't until they were clearing the table that she noticed a tiny bit of paper clinging to one of the rings of the blue binder. It looked as if someone had ripped out a page.

Dan? Or Pete or Sherri before Dan took the looseleaf home with him? Or someone else? Was this what her intruder had been looking for? And had he gone on to search Dan's house after leaving here? Dan had mentioned leaving his front door unlocked.

Liss didn't like any of those possibilities, but they forced her to reconsider why Mrs. Norris had been making her odd notes in the first place. "Everybody has secrets," she murmured.

Sherri paused in the act of putting the maple syrup away to give Liss a curious look. "You already know mine. Feel free to share yours."

Liss told her.

"In theory, both of those incidents should be in this loose-leaf, with the names changed to protect the not-so-innocent."

"I didn't spot anything last time."

"You only read a quarter of the entries." Liss divided the pages in half and started reading. "It's not in here," she announced a short time later.

"Yours or mine?"

"Neither."

"Nothing here either," Sherri said after another few minutes. She sounded relieved. "Not on you. Not on me. And nothing I can connect to Dan or Pete or your family, unless Margaret is Agatha Christie's Miss Marple and Ned is Miss Marple's nephew."

Liss glanced at the entry Sherri indicated. It suggested that the nephew had hatched a "nefarious plot" to augment his income. "Well, that could be Ned, I suppose, but it's hardly a secret worth killing over."

"He didn't come to the memorial service."

"No, he didn't, but I doubt that means anything. It's not as if he was close to Mrs. Norris. He told me the other day that he hadn't been inside her house in years."

She pondered another entry, this one involving an unlikely combination of fictional characters—Joan Hess's Claire Malloy, an Arkansas bookseller, and Aaron Elkin's "skeleton detective," Gideon Oliver—and a plan to smuggle prescription drugs into the U.S. from Canada. "I wonder. . . ."

"What?"

"Your father said there were some 'shady characters' hanging around the Emporium. Do you have any idea who he might have meant?" She ran water to wash the few dishes they'd used and Sherri automatically reached for a dishtowel.

"Not a clue. Dad's not the most reliable witness when it comes to your aunt," she added after a bit. "Maybe he just made that up."

"Maybe. I certainly can't see Aunt Margaret in league with smugglers."

Sherri giggled. "Oh, I don't know. She does import all kinds of things. Maybe there's something hidden under the stitching at the top of the kilts. Diamonds? A small one would just about fit inside each pleat."

"Naw. Got to be microchips." The silliness relieved the tension and Liss was glad of it, but she couldn't quite shake the feeling that they'd overlooked something important. "There's a page missing from the looseleaf."

Sherri sobered as Liss showed her the torn bit of paper. "Maybe someone *does* think Mrs. Norris was writing down local gossip."

"You said Graye dropped out of the bidding on the hotel." Liss let the soapy water drain away while Sherri hung her dishtowel over a rack to dry. "I wonder why?"

"You think Mrs. Norris put pressure on him to give up his plan for The Spruces, thus making sure Joe Ruskin got the winning bid?"

"Far-fetched, huh?"

"Very. *Maybe* she recorded gossip. But *blackmail*? Sorry, Liss. Doesn't compute."

"Well, then, maybe Jason Graye is one of your father's 'shady characters.'"

But Sherri shook her head. "Wishful thinking, Liss. It's not that I don't believe Graye's shady, but Dad said 'characters,' right? More than one. And that missing page? Face facts—the logical person to have removed it is Dan Ruskin."

* * *

Late Sunday afternoon, when Liss saw that Dan's truck was back in his driveway, she headed across the town square. She'd been steeling herself to face him ever since Sherri left.

He was in the carriage house he'd converted into a workshop. The sight of all those woodworking tools took her aback. She'd had no idea he had such a professional setup at home. She supposed she shouldn't be surprised. About some things, Dan Ruskin was a perfectionist.

"Hey, Liss," he greeted her. "I was going to come over in a bit. I have to make a run to Portland tomorrow afternoon to pick up a special order coming in by air. I won't be back here till late."

"No problem." She really did not want to suspect this man of hiding something. He was so open, so genuine. Or *seemed* to be. "Nice place you've got here." She managed not to wince at how lame that sounded.

His pride in the pieces he'd created was evident in his tone of voice and in the expression on his face as he gave her a quick tour. He felt every bit as strongly about the fruits of his labor as she had about her performances with *Strathspey*. For a little while longer, Liss put off what she had to ask him and let her senses revel in the moment.

The workshop had its own special smell. She didn't know what the components were, but the result appealed to her. She ran her fingertips over the satiny surface of a small clock, delighting in the feel of it and in the look of the wood. Dan had used more than one kind of tree in the construction. The inlaid pieces gave the whole a unique quality she found quite beautiful.

"Like it?" When she nodded, he pressed it back into her hands. "Take it. A gift."

"I couldn't—"

"Why not? Think of it as my version of flowers and candy." When his brows lifted questioningly, Liss knew her expression had betrayed her. "What?"

"I have to ask you something."

He caught her by the elbows, holding her so that they were facing each other with the clock between them. "Ask."

But she couldn't quite pose it as a question. "There's a page missing from the looseleaf."

Very slowly, he released her. "And you think I took it. Even though someone might have gotten into my un-locked house after searching your place."

"I don't know, Dan. Everybody has secrets. Maybe you found yours in those pages."

"I didn't." Stepping back, he ran his hands over his face, as if trying to clear his thoughts.

"I'm sorry. I know I should automatically trust you, but—"

"No, you shouldn't. You shouldn't trust anybody when there's a murderer running around loose. I did rip out a page."

Liss blinked at him, at a loss. "Why?"

"It wasn't *my* secret." He picked up an awl and put it down again, finally turning to face her from a distance of some six feet. "Hell, I don't know if it was anybody's se-cret. But it was too damn close for comfort to something my sister was involved in years ago. I didn't want to take the chance of it getting out. Not now, when everything's going so well for her. I know the cops have Mrs. Norris's computer and that stack of printouts I saw. They might figure it out anyway, but—"

"But they won't. I mean, they aren't even trying. You know they aren't looking into the blackmail angle any-more. The only reason LaVerdiere is still fixated on me is because of Mrs. Norris's will."

"The entries in the looseleaf could still refer to local people."

"Some of them. Maybe. But not all. Not even most of them, which doesn't make much sense." Liss hated being this confused about anything.

"None of this makes any sense. And we have no way of knowing if there are more missing pages. I did leave the house unlocked. It was coming home and realizing someone could have gotten in that gave me the idea to remove that one page in the first place."

Chapter Eighteen

On Monday morning, Liss awoke to the realization that she was running out of time. More than a week had passed since the murder and in a little less than two weeks her aunt would be home. Liss wanted this mess resolved before Aunt Margaret returned.

Unfortunately, she still didn't have any clear idea how to proceed.

With the shop closed for the day, she took her time with her morning exercises and breakfast. This time the scones were *almost* edible. After she tossed them in the trash and made do with whole-wheat toast and cornflakes, she ventured out into the town square. Although it was a pleasant summer day, dry and not too hot, the playground was deserted. Liss put one foot on the merry-go-round and used the other to set it spinning.

Fond memories rushed back. When she was in grade school, all the kids in town had come here to play. The merry-go-round had served as the magic castle when they reenacted fairy tales. She glanced at Dan's house, suddenly reminded that the favorite game among the boys had also involved the merry-go-round. They'd used it for puke competitions.

She made a face. They'd piled onto the merry-go-round,

all except the designated spinner. He'd set it in motion, around and around, faster and faster, until everyone aboard was dizzy . . . and more. The "winner" was the one who *didn't* puke. *Charming* game, and yet she could view even that with nostalgia now.

Children, she thought, didn't appreciate childhood. She'd give anything to be young and carefree again. Aside from the family interest in things Scottish, she'd had a pretty normal rural childhood. Although she'd grown up with computers and video games, there had been plenty of times when she and the others had amused themselves with nothing more than imagination.

She let the merry-go-round slow to a stop and only then realized she was no longer alone on the playground. The girl had dark hair that hung in thick waves around a thin face. Her big brown eyes were solemn. "You're Liss Mac-Crimmon," she said in a voice so soft Liss had to strain to catch the words. "My mother says I can ask you."

"Ask me what? And who is your mother?"

She found the answer to the second question for herself. Angie Hogencamp was watching from the doorway of her bookstore. Glancing from the woman to the child, Liss saw the unmistakable resemblance between them.

The girl scuffed one foot in the dirt, overwhelmed by shyness.

"I won't bite." Liss sat on the side of the merry-go-round, which put her at eye-level with the child. "What's your name?"

"Beth."

"Well, Beth, what can I do for you?"

The whispered reply took a moment to interpret. When Liss finally understood, she had no idea how to react. She cut her eyes to Angie and sent Beth's mother a pleading look.

Beth grew bolder, an expression of longing on her small, pinched face. "Please? I really want to learn." She held out a hand. "My mother said I could invite you to come for coffee so she can talk to you about it."

The kid was getting downright chatty, but her smile faded when she realized Liss wasn't exactly jumping for joy. "You want me to teach you to dance." Liss's voice was leaden.

"Yes, please."

Liss sighed. "I'm not making any promises, but I will talk to your mother."

A short time later, after Angie had sent Beth off to play in her room, the two women once more sat at the kitchen table in the apartment above the bookstore, just as they had almost exactly a week earlier. Liss hadn't felt half as uncomfortable then.

"I'm sorry if she put you on the spot," Angie apologized. "I should have approached you first myself, but Beth was so excited. We went to the Highland Games on Sunday and she watched the dance competition. She's talked of nothing else since, and then someone at the memorial service told me that you used to compete. I pointed you out to Beth this morning. I said maybe you could give her a few pointers. Get her started. She jumped from that straight to lessons."

"I'm not a teacher. I'm not even a dancer anymore." To Liss's surprise, it was less painful than she'd expected to explain why to Angie. And somehow she found herself talking about the first competition she'd entered and how much she'd loved learning new steps. Her mother had been her first teacher.

"If you could just get her started. Show her a simple dance—"

"I don't have any experience with children." She took a

sip of the coffee in front of her and found it had grown cold while she'd talked. "I can't even guess how old your Beth is."

"Eight."

"I won my first competition at eight."

"Anything would mean a lot to her, even just talking about your experiences. I tried to find someone for her to take real lessons from on the Web, but there doesn't seem to be a teacher closer than Boston."

"I'll probably be leaving as soon as my aunt comes back," Liss warned her. She could feel herself weakening. So much for her determination never to teach!

"Well, who knows how much longer the Emporium will be around anyway? But any amount of time you'd be able to spare would be much appreciated. I can pay—"

"Wait a minute. What did you just say about the Emporium?"

"Oh, well, it's just that I expect, now that Mrs. Norris is gone, her heirs will sell her place. Graye Realty made her an offer a couple of months ago, so I'm sure Jason Graye will be in touch with whoever inherits."

Liss barely had time to take in the remarkable fact that Angie hadn't heard that Liss herself was the heir before her hostess was speaking again.

"Stu at the ski shop has been talking about selling out to him, too, if he'll just go a bit higher. And since the Emporium sits between those two properties, I'm sure Graye wants your aunt's land, too."

A tight lump formed in Liss's chest. "The Emporium is also my aunt's home."

"Can't stop progress," Angie said cheerfully. "Especially when Jason Graye has the town planning board in his pocket. He's a Moosetookalook selectman, you know. Besides, from what I hear, all the houses on that side of the town square are in terrible shape. They may look nice on the outside, but inside they've got mold and carpenter ants and who knows what all."

By the time Liss left Angie's kitchen a short time later, she'd agreed to give Beth dance lessons at the Emporium during the hours the shop was open.

She'd also learned considerably more about Jason Graye.

Sherri hesitated in the doorway of Willett's Store. She hadn't set foot in the place in almost three years, ever since her father, shocked by the news that she'd come home with a child but no husband, had informed her she was a disgrace and told her she should go back to whatever sewer she'd been living in.

So much for welcoming the prodigal home.

She hadn't left. She'd run into Margaret Boyd at Patsy's and ended up with the offer of a job and a temporary place to stay. Within a month, she'd landed full-time work as a dispatcher and corrections officer at the jail and, with her mother's help, bought a second-hand mobile home. They weren't living in the lap of luxury, but they were getting by . . . without any help from her father.

So why was she here now? Because she owed Margaret Boyd a debt of gratitude and Margaret's niece needed help. Swallowing a lump in her throat that was the size of Cleveland, she went the rest of the way into the store.

"What do you want?"

Sherri ignored the surly tone and ferocious scowl and studied his eyes. The haunted look she saw there floored her . . . and made her remember the affectionate father of her early childhood, before constant quarreling between her parents had turned their home into a battleground.

"I need your help," she said.

"How much?"

"Not money. Answers." She glanced around the store. No customers wandered the aisles. For the moment, at least, they had privacy.

"Liss MacCrimmon came and talked to you. You said there had been 'shady characters' hanging around the Emporium. Who did you mean?"

Someone pulled up to the gas pumps, but for once Ernie Willett ignored a customer. "That real estate fella. Graye. And the bimbo he hangs out with."

Sherri let out a breath she hadn't realized she'd been holding. She'd been afraid her father would refuse to talk to her.

"Never did like that fella. Didn't vote for him when he ran for selectman. He wants to buy the whole block of Pine between Ash and Birch and tear down the old houses."

The impatient blare of a horn interrupted them. "Go," Sherri said.

He hesitated. "You'll still be here when I come back?"

"If you want."

A curt nod conveyed his satisfaction with her answer. Sherri wiped her hands on the sides of her jeans, wishing she could relax. She didn't know where she stood with her father, but she hoped she was about to find out.

Once again seated in Jason Graye's office, Liss studied the realtor with a new intensity. He was up to no good. Of that she was certain. What she couldn't tell was just how big a villain he really was.

If he'd killed Mrs. Norris, she was foolish to have come here. On the other hand, the plate glass window looked out onto the main street in Fallstown. Surely someone would notice if he tried to strangle her or inflict other bodily harm.

"I have some time this afternoon," Graye said.

"I just don't know." Liss didn't have to fake her distress. "It's so soon after Mrs. Norris's murder."

"A walk through the place. That's all I need. I can't set a price until I've seen what shape it's in."

Did he expect mold and carpenter ants? He'd already mentioned the possibility of dry rot at their last meeting. Did any of those things actually need to be present for him to claim he'd spotted them?

"This is all so upsetting. And just think—if I'd loaned you the key to the shop when you asked for it, you might have been there to prevent what happened to Mrs. Norris."

"My dear Ms. MacCrimmon, surely that's unlikely." Graye looked genuinely taken aback by her observation.

"When I was here before, you said you'd never met Mrs. Norris. But you made her an offer for her house. A very low offer, as I understand it."

Graye hit the intercom button. "Barbara, get in here."

When she entered the office, he waved her into the second client's chair. His own, behind the desk, was higher and arranged so that he was slightly in shadow while full sunlight fell on whomever he faced. He didn't miss a trick when it came to getting the upper hand.

"Ms. MacCrimmon was asking me about her poor neighbor. Did I ever meet her?"

"I don't believe so."

Graye tented his fingers on his chest and looked properly solemn. "And the day she was killed—back me up, please, Barbara—we thought it worth a try to stop by Mrs. Boyd's little shop to see if anyone else might be around to let us in. You were most anxious to get a look at that cloth, weren't you, my dear?"

Liss slanted a look at Barbara. The woman nodded warily but seemed a bit anxious about what Graye might say next.

"Naturally, we found the shop locked, so we went ahead with our plans for the evening. We spent it together, at my place."

Only a slight start gave away Barbara's surprise at this statement.

"I don't think that's quite true," Liss said.

They both stared at her, but neither gave any more away.

"You stopped in at the clothing store. The owner was quite pleased to have made a sale."

Barbara flushed a deep red. "I don't ordinarily buy second-hand clothes. I was just trying to help her out. Small businesses have such a hard time of it these days."

"And you asked her if she had a key to the Emporium," Liss continued, shifting her gaze to Graye.

His expression bland, he nodded. "I had forgotten that. Yes, you're right, of course."

"You seemed so anxious to get in. I wondered if you might have gone back again later. Perhaps you saw something on your second visit that—"

"I told you. Barbara and I spent the rest of the day together. The night, too. At my place. We didn't go out."

Again Barbara gave a slight start, but she didn't contradict him.

Was she just embarrassed to have her private life discussed with a stranger, or was she trying to hide something? Liss couldn't decide.

"Thank you, Barbara. That will be all." But she'd no sooner left the room than he was on his feet and going after her. "Excuse me a moment, Ms. MacCrimmon. I've just remembered an errand I have for Barbara. Not something that can wait, I'm afraid."

He closed the door between his office and the reception area, making it impossible for Liss to hear more than the murmur of voices, but he was quick to return. She had no chance to snoop in his file cabinet or among the papers on the desk.

"Now, then, Ms. MacCrimmon, if you've satisfied your curiosity, shall we set a date for me to go through the house? It is essential, I assure you, that this be done as soon as possible." If he'd been insulted by her implication that he'd had something to do with Mrs. Norris's death, he wasn't about to let that keep him from earning a commission.

"It will have to be in the evening. I'm tied up with my aunt's store during the day." And in the evening, she could make sure she was not alone with Graye. Dan . . . or Sherri could watch her back.

"Wednesday?" Graye was nothing if not persistent.

"Yes. Fine. Wednesday at eight?" Suddenly she wanted nothing more than to get out of there. She felt claustrophobic in the office and the cloying scent of Barbara's perfume lingered, making her slightly sick to her stomach.

Graye delayed her for another ten minutes, hunting for and finding various bits of paperwork he wanted her to have. Barbara was just coming back into the building as Liss fled. Graye's lady friend couldn't meet Liss's eyes and her cheeks turned a bright, betraying pink as she rushed past.

This entire visit had been a wasted effort, Liss decided, except for that tell-tale blush. Barbara was nervous. *But what did that mean?*

Liss went directly back to her car, parked in the quiet, tree-shaded parking lot behind the real estate office, momentarily distracted by the realization that she'd forgotten to lock it . . . again. She didn't suppose it mattered. She'd also left the sunroof open to take advantage of the cooler temperature. If anyone had wanted to steal the CD player badly enough, they could have gotten to it that way. She hadn't left anything else of value in the car.

Sliding in behind the wheel, Liss started the engine and headed for home. Her thoughts circled back to Barbara Zathros. She was certain Graye had lied, and the best way to prove it was to talk to his lady friend when he wasn't around. That would have to wait until evening. She knew where the other woman lived. Hermione Biggs's house was exactly one block away from the Emporium, on the corner of Ash Street and Maple Avenue.

Liss had driven less than a mile before she decided against confronting Barbara on her own. Much better to have back-up. She pulled onto the shoulder of the road and punched Sherri's number into her cell phone.

"I want to question Barbara Zathros," she said when her friend answered, "but on the off chance she's the one who killed Mrs. Norris, it would be pretty stupid of me to confront her by myself."

"That's easily fixed. We'll do it together. This evening, after she gets home from work?"

"Come by the apartment. I'll feed you first."

"No scones."

"No scones."

"Liss? I talked to my father today. I was wrong. One of the 'shady characters' he mentioned to you was Jason Graye. The other was Barbara."

"Well, well."

"Yeah." Suddenly her voice went up an octave. "Adam! Take your hand out of the toaster! Got to go." And the line went dead.

Satisfied that she'd done everything she could for the moment, Liss eased back onto the road. A short time later she turned onto the hilly, twisting byway that was the time-honored shortcut to Moosetookalook and increased her speed. There wasn't much traffic and she made good time, cresting the first of two long, curving hills five miles south of the town line fifteen minutes after leaving Fallstown. She applied the brakes as she started down the other side, nervous about taking the descent too fast, but when she let up, the PT Cruiser accelerated on its own. She tapped the brakes again, relieved when the car slowed. It had been running perfectly. She couldn't think what the matter might be. She'd have to get it checked out.

For another mile, nothing happened. Then, without warning, the throttle stuck again. The first tendrils of alarm made Liss's hands tighten on the wheel and had her heart doing a step dance. This time when she touched her foot to the brake and let up, the car seemed to leap forward. Reacting out of panic, she slammed both feet down on the brake pedal. It was a mistake. The engine was still accelerating. She'd crested the second hill. Her action sent the car spinning out of control just as it started to descend a treacherously curving slope.

Disbelief slowed Liss's response time. This couldn't be happening. By the time she jerked at the emergency brake, she was flying down the hill. A horrendous sound, a grinding and squealing, told her the brake was trying to do its job, but the car didn't slow. And then, to her horror, she saw that an SUV was coming the other way. She jerked the wheel, desperate to stay on her own side of the road, but she overcompensated. The next thing she knew, she was heading straight for the guard rail.

Impact came a moment later as her car struck with bone-jarring force. Metal screamed as the barrier gave way. Her airbag deployed, smacking her in the face with enough force to make her wonder if her nose had been broken. It brought with it a smell and a cloud of fine powder that had her choking. And while she sputtered and coughed, her car continued on, bumping over a few feet of gravel before it reached the edge. Dimly, Liss realized she was airborne . . . and headed straight for a hard landing in the middle of the Kenebscot River.

Chapter Nineteen

"*If you feel yourself start to fall, go limp.*"
The long-ago voice of a ski instructor came back to Liss as her car plummeted. The air bag was already deflating. Big help that was going to be! The skiing hadn't gone well either. She'd taken a total of five lessons before deciding she didn't like being out in icy cold weather on the top of a mountain.

Relax! Her mind screamed the message in her own voice this time, and she willed herself not to tense up in the split-second before water geysered up on all sides. Liss's seat belt jerked tight, knocking the breath out of her. For a moment she felt as if she were still suspended in space. Then her stomach settled, her heart dropped back out of her throat, and she realized that the car had landed right-side up. It was moving sluggishly downriver.

Fumbling to shove the useless air bag out of the way, still coughing from the dust it had released, Liss needed two tries to unlatch her seat belt. She clawed at the door, trying to open it, but the car was sinking. There was already too much pressure against the outside. It wouldn't budge.

Spurred on by the sound of water lapping against the sides of the car, Liss pushed at the button to lower the driver's side window. Nothing happened. She made a sound of ex-asperation. The engine had stalled. No power, no power windows.

Through the cracked windshield she could see the water rising. It was over the hood of the car, inching toward her. All right. She wouldn't panic. If the car sank, it would fill slowly with water until the pressure equalized enough for her to open the door.

All she had to do was find a pocket of air and wait it out.

A drop of water landed on her nose, jerking her attention upward to the open sunroof. Damn! Without power, she couldn't close it. Another couple of minutes and water was going to come gushing in. So much for waiting it out.

Liss blinked. *Idiot.* She was looking at an *open* sunroof.

Pushing aside her seat belt and the remains of the air bag, her heart thudding like a jackhammer, she eased herself out from behind the steering wheel and up onto the seat. As she got her legs beneath her, her bad knee gave a warning twinge. She ignored it, distracted by the way the car tilted with the shift of weight.

Don't rock the boat!

She was trembling and couldn't seem to stop as she clambered awkwardly upright, standing on the seat to thrust the upper half of her body through the opening. With every movement, the sinking vehicle swayed. If it tipped over and sank, she'd probably be trapped beneath it. Bracing her hands against the sides of the sunroof, Liss levered herself upward until she was sitting on the roof of the car.

The water had reached the top of the windows. With no time to lose, Liss pulled the rest of the way out of the opening and launched herself into the water. It wasn't the most graceful of dives, but it took her far enough away from the sinking vehicle to keep her from being caught in the whirlpool as it disappeared beneath the surface.

She didn't look back. The river was deep but not wide. Ignoring a growing number of aches and pains, she struck out for shore. Cars had stopped along the road, including the SUV she'd swerved to avoid. Someone was scrambling down the bank toward her.

Strangers helped her out of the river and bundled her into blankets. One of them used his cell phone to call the police and it wasn't long before a deputy sheriff showed up.

"I can't show you my driver's license," Liss told him when he asked for her name. "I left my purse in the car."

Paramedics arrived next, wanting to take her to the hospital to be checked over. "You're in shock," one of them said.

"I'll get over it. I want to go home."

"You wouldn't if you could get a good look at yourself."

She had no real concept of time passing while she sat in the back of the deputy's cruiser, but more and more people kept showing up. The sheriff herself. Then Sherri. Then LaVerdiere.

"The throttle stuck?" LaVerdiere sounded skeptical.

"I don't understand it," Liss murmured. "The car isn't that old. I suppose it's a total loss." Her mind was starting to function again, now that she'd stopped shaking, but slowly. The car, her purse with her identification and credit cards, and her cell phone—everything was at the bottom of the river.

Sherri touched her arm, waited until Liss met her worried gaze. "Liss, where did you park in Fallstown? Could someone have tampered with the car?"

Liss took a deep breath and closed her eyes. "You think someone tried to kill me? Like they cut the brakes or something?" Unable to absorb the enormity of that possibility, she tried to make a joke of it. "Oh, goody. That must mean I've been promoted from prime suspect to second victim."

"Let's not jump to any conclusions here," LaVerdiere warned. "We'll pull your car out of the river and take a look at it, but at the moment this is just another traffic accident. Unless the guilt's getting to you. Maybe what we have here is a case of attempted suicide."

"He *is* joking, right?" Liss asked of no one in particular.

"Why would anyone try to kill you, Ms. MacCrimmon?" Sheriff Lassiter asked. "Do you know something about Amanda Norris's murder that you haven't shared with the police?"

"She's been asking questions, okay?" Sherri ignored La-Verdiere and spoke to her boss. "So have I. Maybe someone's getting nervous."

"Who do you suspect?" Unwilling to let another officer interfere in his case, LaVerdiere reluctantly pulled out his notebook and prepared to write down names.

Liss, with interjections from Sherri, told him everything. Unfortunately, it didn't amount to much. He showed minimal interest in the blue looseleaf and dismissed her suspicions of Jason Graye and Barbara Zathros as the result of too much imagination.

It was getting dark by the time Sherri drove Liss home. "I still want to talk to Barbara," Liss told her as they turned onto Pine Street. "It's a cinch LaVerdiere won't."

"No way. Not tonight. You're going straight to bed. If you don't hurt all over now, you will by morning. I hate to tell you this, but you have a fat lip and burns on your hands and I'm betting you've got some spectacular bruises all across your torso from the seat belt. Besides—Well, damn."

Ned was parked in front of the Emporium. He jumped out of his car as soon as he saw Sherri's truck. His face blanched when Liss eased herself out of the passenger side.

"What—? You look like . . . what happened to you?"

"Little accident. I'm fine."

Ned took a moment to process that, then reverted to form. "Where have you been all day? I've been sitting in the car for hours. You never did give me a key after you changed the locks."

"Sorry, Ned. What did you want?" She was limping as she started up the walk to the porch.

"I've been thinking about what you said the other day. About snooping around on your own. If you're still determined to do that, there's someone you should take a hard look at. Guy named Jason Graye. He has a real estate office in Fallstown."

Liss exchanged a look with Sherri. "I know who he is."

"Yeah? Well watch out for him. He's shifty."

"And how is it that you know that, Ned?"

"He tried to con me. Wanted me to give him information about the Emporium, or better yet, let him inside to look around."

"Why?"

"That's the way he operates. So I hear. Snoops around properties he wants to buy, looking for structural problems and the like. Figures if he can point out that the place needs expensive repairs, the owner will be quicker to sell and for less."

Struck by a thought, Liss turned slowly to face her cousin. "Ned, did you tell Jason Graye about the key over the back door?"

"No! Of course not." His innocent look faded into a frown. "I don't think so."

"You're the one who just suggested he might be the killer," she reminded him. "That could explain how he got in."

"Yeah, but that would mean it was partly my fault."

She could see he didn't like *that* idea. Typical Ned—self-centered and inconsiderate, but probably sincere in his concern for his mother's future, at least insofar as he expected to one day inherit whatever she had left. Now that Liss knew how precarious Aunt Margaret's finances were, she had some sympathy for her cousin . . . but more for her aunt.

Sherri stayed after Ned had gone, accepting Liss's offer of a cup of tea. "If your car was somehow tampered with, you should let the police handle things from now on."

"I might, if I thought LaVerdiere knew what he was doing. Ned's claims make me even more certain someone needs to follow up with Barbara. You said your father thinks Graye is a suspicious character, too?"

Sherri gave Liss a brief account of her visit to Ernie Willett. "When he came back in from pumping gas," she added, "he told me he wanted a chance to get to know Adam, be a real grandfather to him. I was floored. All this time, he's never shown any interest. I thought he didn't care. I guess that just proves you can never predict what other people will do."

"I can't even predict what *I'll* do half the time."

"You're not going to stop asking questions, are you?"

"Not unless LaVerdiere gets off his duff and does his job."

If anything, her close brush with death had made her more determined to clear her name. It would have been unbearable to die and have people believe, as LaVerdiere did, that she'd killed herself out of guilt.

"Meet me here tomorrow afternoon? We can talk to Barbara then. I'm pretty sure Graye lied about the two of them being together to give himself an alibi."

"That gave her one, too," Sherri pointed out.

"Yes, but what if that was the final straw? He seems to constantly take advantage of her. He's rude about it, too. She must be getting fed up with that treatment by now."

"The worm is about to turn?"

"Exactly."

Sherri thought it over while she finished her tea. "Okay. I'm on the day-shift tomorrow. I'll stop at home to check on Adam, then come straight here."

Dan was furious. By the time he got home there were no fewer than six messages on his machine about Liss's accident. None of them were from her.

"You could have called me!" he shouted when she opened her door.

"How? My cell phone is at the bottom of the river."

"Jesus!" He wanted to grab her and hold on and held back only because he knew she had to be bruised and hurting. Her face was puffy, in spite of the application of ice—she held the bag in one hand and looked as if she were contemplating smacking him upside the head with it.

Sitting her down on the sofa in Margaret's apartment, he listened in growing horror as she briefed him on what had happened. An accident? Coming on top of the break-in, he had to wonder. But whatever had caused her car to plunge into the river, he'd almost lost her. The thought chilled him to the bone.

"Sherri left just a couple of minutes before you got

here." Liss's voice was absurdly calm, as if she'd been talking about someone other than herself. "I haven't had a chance to feed Lumpkin yet."

"Let him live on his fat for one night."

"Dan!"

"Okay. Okay. I'll come with you."

He took care of the cat-minding chores himself. By the time he finished, she'd left the kitchen for the library. He expected to find her scouring the shelves for something to read, but instead she was flipping through the business-card holder on the desk. She looked up when he came in. "I'm curious to see if Graye's card is here. He claims he never met Mrs. Norris. All I've seen so far are cards for the doctor, the dentist, the vet, the florist, and the Chinese restaurant."

As he watched, she turned over cards for a hairdresser; a copy center; the animal emergency clinic in Three Cities; Fallstown Hearing Services; an eye doctor; a bank; an orthopedist; and one that showed an old fashioned inkwell and read "Will Shakespeare, freelance writer."

Liss put the cardholder back where she'd found it and opened the desk drawer. "If the police didn't take anything besides the computer and printouts, then logically that means they left everything else." She shifted a checkbook register and an address book and there, stuffed beneath the latter, found what she'd been looking for.

The card bore the logo of Graye Real Estate, but the name embossed beneath was not Jason Graye. It was Barbara Zathros. "So, maybe he wasn't lying. Maybe it was Barbara who dealt with Mrs. Norris. Guess I'll have to ask her."

"You're not going anywhere near her."

"I beg your pardon?"

"Are you crazy, Liss? Stay away from these people. Let the cops—"

"We've been through all that. The cops think I did it. I don't have any choice but to keep poking around on my own. I'll be careful."

"Damn it, Liss. You have no idea what careful is."

One look at her expression had him mentally kicking himself. The only thing he'd accomplished by yelling at her was to make her dig in her heels.

"Look, I know I can't stop you from doing what you think you need to do. But can you at least wait until I can go with you?" There'd been more trouble at the work site. It had begun to look as if that employee his father had fired for theft had been up to more than petty pilfering.

"You have obligations of your own," Liss said in a practical tone of voice. "Besides, Sherri can back me up."

The blind leading the blind! "I'm tied up till late again tomorrow, but—"

"Dan, it will be all right. I'm not some Gothic heroine racing out in my nightgown to confront—" She broke off, a wry twist of the lips acknowledging that she'd already done just that. "Well, I won't do it again! Really."

He wished he could believe her, but Liss MacCrimmon had never been known for her patience.

Stiff and sore as she was, Liss opened the Emporium on time the next day. Better to stay active, she told herself, but she spent most of her time on the phone trying to cancel and/or replace what had been in her purse and dealing with her insurance company. Her car was still at the bottom of the river. There weren't that many divers in the area and the one who usually handled retrieval of drowned vehicles was out of commission with a broken wrist.

One by one, she ticked off driver's license, health insurance card, and various credit cards. She'd have to get a new cell phone, too, but she could leave that for the moment. Dan had loaned her one of the extras Ruskin Construction kept on hand for workers to use.

She spent a little time on-line as well, exploring what might have gone wrong with her car. She found an explanation—or at least a clue where to look for one. Apparently the throttle could stick if something went wrong with one of the engine hoses. The website did not tell her just what that something might be, but since it had obviously happened to other people, that meant it was a fluke, not sabotage.

Good, she thought. She hadn't liked Sherri's suggestion that her car might have been tampered with.

Her friend had just been upset. She'd let her imagination run away with her.

A wry smile tugged at the corners of Liss's mouth. It wasn't as if she'd lost her brakes. Wouldn't *that* have been a cliché? Out of curiosity, she spent a bit more time researching potential car problems on-line. It reassured her to discover that cutting a brake line was nowhere near as simple a process as murder mysteries made it seem.

In early evening, after the shop was closed, Liss and Sherri headed for Mrs. Biggs's house. The previous day's cool, pleasant temperature was a thing of the past. They were both dripping with sweat by the time they'd walked the short distance from the Emporium. They spotted Barbara while they were still half a block away. She had changed into shorts and a halter top after getting home from work and was sitting on the glider in the side yard, sipping a tall glass of lemonade—the picture of the exhausted working girl after a hard day.

"Do you think LaVerdiere questioned her about my accident?" Liss asked.

"Doubt it. I heard he was in Augusta all day today."

Two Adirondack chairs flanked Barbara's glider. Liss and Sherri slid into them before their quarry was even aware of their presence.

"What the hell—?"

"Hello, Barbara. It appears we're neighbors," Liss said.

"So?" She gave Liss's all-too-obvious bruises a sharp look but did not comment on them.

"Call this a neighborly visit. I've been talking to quite a few folks who live near the Emporium, trying to jog memories about the day Mrs. Norris was killed."

"A: I live a little far away to have seen anything. B: you already asked me about this. I told you all I know, which is nothing."

Liss glanced sideways, across Maple Avenue. Beyond the pretty little cape cod with dormers she could clearly see the back of Mrs. Norris's house.

"Besides, I wasn't here when she was killed."

"Forgot for a minute, didn't you? Let's drop the pretense, Barbara. I know you weren't with your boss. What did he do? Drop you here as soon as he realized he couldn't get into the Emporium? Oh, no—I forgot. You got a scarf out of the deal first, didn't you?"

"What are you implying?"

"I'm *asking* if you want to change your story. Maybe you saw something Graye didn't or maybe you know that Jason Graye went back to the Emporium later, on his own."

"You were seen, you know," Sherri said.

Both Liss and Barbara turned to her in surprise.

Sherri nodded earnestly but Liss was pretty sure she was lying through her teeth. "Your neighbor over there—" she gestured toward the cape cod—"saw him drop you off."

"Okay. Fine. Jase brought me straight home after the stop at the vintage clothing place. I have no idea what he did during the rest of that afternoon and evening. Or that night. But he wasn't with me. And I was right here, minding my own business the whole time."

Well, that hit a nerve, Liss thought. Barbara looked like she might bolt if she had to answer any more questions.

"Are you afraid of him?" Sherri asked.

Barbara's look of surprise was answer enough. "What? You think he beats me or something? He's inconsiderate and rude, that's all."

"Why do you put up with that kind of behavior?" If he'd been her boss, Liss would have walked out the first time he shouted at her. He'd never have gotten as far as boyfriend status.

Barbara shrugged. "The money's good. You don't see many starving realtors around, do you?"

"I understand Graye put a bid in on the hotel," Liss began.

Barbara abruptly stood. "That's none of your business. I'll thank you to leave now."

"Hey, we're just two gals out for a stroll." Neither Sherri nor Liss made any move to rise.

When a glare didn't unseat them either, Barbara stalked off toward the outside stairs that led to her apartment. Liss stayed put a moment longer, wondering what to do next. Graye had lied, but that didn't mean he'd killed Mrs. Norris.

"Psssst! Over here!"

Startled, Liss turned toward the voice. She hadn't realized how close the chairs and glider were to the side of Mrs. Biggs's house, or that the kitchen window had been open. Mrs. Biggs herself stood just on the other side of the screen, beckoning to them.

A few minutes later they were inside, seated at yet another kitchen table, tall glasses of lemonade of their own in front of them.

"I couldn't help overhearing," Mrs. Biggs said, after she'd tut-tutted over the visible reminders of Liss's accident—she'd heard all about it at Angie's Books.

"We didn't mean to disturb you, Mrs. Biggs," Liss apologized.

"Call me Hermione, dear. And you didn't disturb me one bit. But my tenant's lies, well that's another thing."

Liss and Sherri exchanged a look.

"She went back out that day, after Jason Graye dropped her off. And she was heading toward the Emporium when she left here."

"Perhaps she had to pick up groceries," Liss suggested, playing devil's advocate.

"Store's in the other direction. Besides, I thought at the time that her movements were, well, furtive. She kept looking over her shoulder, like she was afraid of being seen."

"Do you know much about her?" Sherri asked.

"She keeps to herself." Disappointment tinged the admission. "She was from New York originally. Came up here to college and stayed. She's only been upstairs for the last six months." She gave a disdainful sniff. "I think she moved here to be closer to her boss. They car-pool, you know. If you ask me, since he didn't ask her to move in with him, it would have made more sense to live in Fallstown, near the office."

Hermione Biggs had been friends with Mrs. Norris, Liss remembered. Apparently she'd taken a similar interest in her neighbors' doings, but she had only speculation to offer about Barbara Zathros. The woman had done a good job of avoiding her landlady's nosy questions.

They had polished off the lemonade, thanked Hermione

for her help, and started to leave when Liss remembered something Hermione had said at the memorial service. "You were close to Mrs. Norris, weren't you?"

"I was. I miss her something awful." She smiled. "She did the right thing leaving everything to you, dear. You're a good girl."

"I . . . it was a surprise."

"Well, of course it was. She'd never have told you. Someone more deserving might have come along before she passed."

"Yes, well . . . I was wondering . . . I found a looseleaf binder in the house. Blue. It seems to be filled with odd notations about fictional characters."

"Oh, that would be the ideas file for her fanfic group." At Liss's blank look, she explained. "It's one of those online e-groups. FarFetchedFanFic. As a hobby, the members come up with their own stories about favorite mystery characters. They especially like to cross-pollinate. You know—take one character from one series and put him or her together with the sleuth from a different set of mystery novels. Oh, I know it isn't strictly legal. The rights to use those characters belong to the authors. Amanda felt a little guilty about that. But she said it was just so much fun to speculate!"

Liss was still shaking her head when she and Sherri arrived back at the Emporium. "Well, that's one mystery solved. We had it backwards. It wasn't gossip about the locals disguised with character names. The scandal was about characters, using bits and pieces of real life."

"Well, why not?" Sherri asked. "I mean, why not take a few ideas from all the gossip she heard? It would have been obvious all along if we'd seen the record of posts she sent to the fanfic group and the printouts the state police took away."

"No wonder the forensics guys knew blackmail wasn't the motive for her murder. And why LaVerdiere looked foolish for thinking it was. So what now? Barbara still didn't tell us the truth, even if she did ruin Graye's alibi."

"Much as I hate to say it, you have to call the cops. Tell LaVerdiere what you just found out and let him take it from there."

"You're kidding, right?"

"I'm dead serious. In fact, if you don't tell him what you discovered, you could be accused of withholding information."

Grumbling all the while, Liss reluctantly had to agree that Sherri was right. "Way back when all this started, LaVerdiere gave me a number to use in case I wanted to change my story." She dug it out and reached for the phone.

Five minutes later, after filling the detective in on what she'd learned and what she suspected, Liss slammed the receiver down in disgust.

"What happened?" Sherri asked.

"He said he'd wasted enough time listening to amateur theories and hung up on me."

Chapter Twenty

After Sherri headed home for an early night, since she was now on the 7 AM to 3 PM shift, Liss fed the cat, fixed herself some supper, and fumed. She'd have gone over to Dan's and shared her troubles with him, but he wasn't home yet.

LaVerdiere's attitude infuriated her. It wasn't as if there weren't grounds to investigate Jason Graye further. Barbara, too.

Impatience had always been her worst failing. As the evening wore on, she gave up trying to convince herself to wait for the police to get a clue. If she wanted to clear her own name, and to have this mess resolved before Aunt Margaret got back from Scotland, then it was up to her to take action. The approach Sherri had used with Barbara earlier—pretending she knew more than she did—had worked once. Why not again?

Liss made the trip back to Mrs. Biggs's house at the fastest trot she could manage with muscles still stiff and sore from the air bag and seatbelt bruises. The lights were on downstairs, reassuring her that a good scream would bring help if Barbara took exception to her questions. Liss rapped firmly on the door to the second-floor apartment and pushed her way in the instant it opened.

"What do you want?" Barbara demanded.

"The truth. For a change." Barbara started to protest, but Liss cut her off. "Here's the thing—I'm sure it was an accident. If you'll just turn yourself in, you won't be charged with murder."

"Are you crazy?"

"Not at all. I understand exactly how it happened. You wanted to get in to look around the building for structural flaws. Not exactly an honorable reason, but we'll let that pass. You knew a key was kept above the back door. Mrs. Biggs probably mentioned it. She saw you leave here again after Graye dropped you off, by the way. So you let yourself in and started snooping around and Mrs. Norris caught you at it. You'd been after her to sell her house, so I don't imagine she was willing to listen to any feeble excuses. Did she threaten to call the cops?"

"You're wrong. I never—"

"She was a teacher for years, you know. She had that disciplinarian thing down pat. Didn't need to use it often, but when she gave you that look and pointed her finger at you, you knew you were in trouble."

"This is ridiculous. I never went inside."

"But you planned to."

Barbara didn't have enough chutzpah to brazen it out. "Alright. I admit I did return to the shop, and I did know about the key, but I went away again when I realized there was someone inside already."

"Who?"

"I . . . I don't know. I just saw a shadow moving in front of a window."

"Guess."

"It could have been anybody."

Liss held her breath.

"It could have been Jase. At the time I thought it was. I

didn't try the door because I didn't want to talk to him. We'd quarreled earlier. He said I wasn't doing much lately to earn my keep. Jerk. I put on one of my best performances over that damned kilt." She gave a humorless laugh when she saw Liss's expression. "You didn't guess. Damn I'm good. It was all an act. Jase wanted to get a look at the building, just as you said. He thought he could con you into lending him the key. He didn't know about the one over the door."

"And you didn't tell him?"

"I would have if he hadn't been so snarky. Then I thought, why don't I take a look around for myself. If I found something we could use to convince your aunt to sell cheap, he'd give me credit for it. I've got to say that much for him—he's fair with commissions."

"Did he kill Mrs. Norris?"

"How would I know?"

Barbara's perfume, Liss thought, wasn't the only thing about her that stank to high heaven. "You must have suspicions. He claimed he was with you, as if he needed an alibi."

She shrugged. "Could have been something else he didn't want people to know about. Maybe out at the ho—" She bit off the word, then shrugged. "Oh, hell, I've said this much. If he killed that old woman it won't make much difference anyway. He'd been talking about doing a little sabotage out at The Spruces. Helping Joe Ruskin along toward failure so he could step in and scoop up the pieces. I don't know if he did anything or not, but he did talk to some guy Joe'd fired."

Some alibi for the time of the murder if he did, Liss thought.

"You need to go to the police," she said aloud.

"I'll think about it."

"Think about this. If you don't tell them your suspicions about him, what's to stop him from pointing a finger at you?"

"I don't *know* it was Jase in there. Could have been anybody." And with that, Barbara refused to say more.

In the middle of the night, Liss woke from an uneasy sleep. No matter how she tried, she could not drop off again. She kept going over what Barbara had said and what didn't fit.

Barbara wasn't the murderer. Her perfume would have lingered in the stockroom if she'd killed Mrs. Norris. And if she'd broken into Aunt Margaret's apartment, Liss would have smelled it throughout the living room and kitchen.

Jason Graye was a more likely killer. She could imagine him pushing Mrs. Norris. What she couldn't fathom was why he'd return to the scene of the crime. It had not been to steal the blue binder. Graye didn't even know it existed.

So who had searched the apartment and what had he or she been looking for?

Whoever it was had to be the same someone who'd taken Aunt Margaret's key, and that was the murderer. Wasn't it?

For some reason, Liss found herself thinking about the safe and what was in it. And what wasn't. She'd found the papers Aunt Margaret had said would be there, but not her diamond ring. She'd meant to check her aunt's jewelry box for it, but so much else had been going on that it had slipped her mind.

Throwing back the covers, Liss padded barefoot into the other bedroom. A quick search revealed that the ring was not there, either.

Wrapped in an afghan, legs curled beneath her on the living room sofa, Liss sat in the dark and considered what that meant. There was no escaping the unpalatable conclusion.

She thought about calling the police to tell them what she suspected, but there didn't seem much point in it. Twice burned, third time shy. She had a pretty good idea what LaVerdiere's reaction would be to any suggestion she made.

By the time the sun came up, Liss had already downed three cups of coffee. She watched Dan head off for work. She'd have called him after her return from Barbara's if he'd been home. He hadn't yet returned by the time she went to bed. This morning . . . well, he'd only try to talk her out of what she wanted . . . needed to do.

At a little past seven, she left Aunt Margaret's apartment, too impatient to wait any longer. She was halfway to her destination, walking swiftly, before second thoughts overtook her. She did not believe she would be in any danger, but it wouldn't hurt to take one simple precaution. As she continued on, she pulled out the cell phone Dan had insisted she borrow and called the sheriff's office in Fallstown. Sherri had just started her shift.

Liss was standing in front of Ned's building by the time she'd filled Sherri in on what she'd decided to do and why. "Promise you won't say anything yet," she added. "If I'm wrong, I don't want to embarrass myself or my cousin. If I'm right, Ned deserves the chance to do the right thing."

"Liss, you're making a mistake. A big one."

"I'll be fine. I'll call you back in a couple of hours and let you know what happened."

"Liss—"

"Relax. This is Ned."

As she returned the phone to her purse, clicking "end" as she did so, she thought she heard Sherri say, "That's what worries me."

*   *   *

This time Ned didn't see her coming. Everything else was the same. His disheveled appearance, the piles of discarded clothing, the miasma of neglect about the entire apartment.

Suddenly feeling awkward, Liss said the first thing that came into her head: "You need a cleaning lady."

"Can't afford one." He sounded testy. "Look, Liss, can't this wait? You got me out of bed. I haven't even had coffee yet."

She hung a left into his tiny kitchen. "I'll make you some." Wrinkling her nose in distaste at the sight and smell of dirty dishes in the sink, she foraged for the makings. It surprised her a little to find a fancy French press instead of a coffee pot. The coffee blend she found in the refrigerator had been fresh-ground at Patsy's within the last few days.

Ned disappeared while she was filling a glass measuring cup with water. He returned just as it came out of the microwave. He'd washed his face and combed his hair, but hadn't bothered to change from the baggy sweats and t-shirt he'd slept in. Well, why should he? She was family, and uninvited, besides.

"Ned, we need to talk." Keeping one eye on him and one on what she was doing, Liss poured the boiling water over the coffee in the French press and gave it a stir with a long-handled spoon.

"Sheesh. Why do women always say that?"

His attempt at humor fell flat. Liss set the microwave timer for five minutes and turned to face him. "You were the one in Aunt Margaret's apartment the other night."

Ned was not awake enough to hide the flash of guilt that accompanied his automatic denial. Liss felt as if she'd just taken a body blow. She'd had her suspicions, but she'd kept hoping she was wrong. This was going to kill Aunt Margaret.

"You can't lie your way out of this one, Ned. I know what you did. I even know why. The only thing left is to decide where we go from here."

The timer dinged. Automatically, she finished making the coffee and poured two cups, adding sugar and cream to Ned's. She knew how he liked his coffee, but until now she'd had no clue what he was capable of. Abruptly, Liss sat, wrapping both hands around her mug, but she didn't want more coffee. She wanted something much stronger.

Ned took the chair opposite her. "What do you think you've figured out?"

"You knew Lumpkin bit ankles. But you also claimed you hadn't been in Mrs. Norris's house in years. So how did you know that? Lumpkin is an indoor cat. The only place you could have encountered him, and his teeth, was in your mother's apartment in the middle of the night."

His smile was more of a sneer. "*That's* your logic?"

"There's more. I know what you were after. When I talked to Aunt Margaret, she told me what was in the safe. She wasn't sure about one item—her engagement ring—so when it wasn't there, I wasn't too concerned. But then I got to thinking." She gestured at their surroundings. "You were short of cash, out of a job. Maybe you decided to help yourself to something you expected to inherit one day anyhow. You didn't find it in the safe, so you tried again later and took it from her jewelry box."

"Think you're smart, don't you?"

"I think there was a terrible accident on the the day you broke into the safe. Obviously you didn't intend to hurt Mrs. Norris." If he'd only admit the truth to her, turn himself in to the authorities, she'd help him all she could. He was family. She couldn't abandon him just because of one terrible mistake.

He drank more coffee, watching her intently over the rim. "You're right about a couple of things," he said at last, "but not all of it. I spent an hour or more going through the shop and the apartment looking for cash. Mom used to stash twenties all over the place—for emergencies."

"I remember finding one in the cookie jar once." Liss almost smiled.

"Yeah. Well, I came up empty there and everywhere else I looked. I didn't dare take any of your stuff. All that was left was Mom's jewelry box. She only has a couple of good pieces and I figured she'd notice if they went missing, but I needed rent money. I was all set to take them and hock them down to Fallstown, even if she would figure out I took them, when I found a slip of paper in the bottom of the jewelry box with the combination to the safe on it. That's when I remembered her diamond ring."

"Wait a minute. The ring *was* in the safe? I thought that's what you were looking for when you came back."

"I had the ring."

"Then why were you in the apartment the other night?"

He shrugged. "You're a list-maker. Always have been. Just like my mother. After you said you were going to snoop around, I figured you'd be keeping track of what you found. I wanted to see if my name was on one of your little lists. I couldn't find any," he added in an accusatory tone.

"I had them in the bedroom with me."

"Figures." The look he sent her over the rim of his coffee mug was full of resentment and something else she could not quite identify.

Increasingly uneasy, Liss kept her eyes on her cousin. As long as he was willing to talk, she'd listen. She wasn't prepared to give up on him quite yet, although it was getting harder not to be judgmental. He didn't seem to be sorry for anything he'd done, just angry that she'd found out too much to be put off by his lies.

"I'd just taken the ring out of the safe when Amanda Norris walked in the back door, bold as you please. She had the nerve to ask me what I was doing there."

"She saw the ring box?"

"Of course she did." Ned sounded disgusted. "That eagle-eyed old bat never missed anything." He took another swig of coffee.

"But why did she come in just then? If you'd been in the house for hours—"

"Said she saw someone snooping around outside and wanted to check on things."

Barbara, Liss thought.

"Probably just made that up as an excuse to snoop. I'd left the back door unlocked and she just waltzed right in. Caught me red-handed. I was ticked at myself for being so careless. I'd put the key in my pocket and never given it another thought. Well, I never expected anyone to question my being there. It's my mother's place, after all."

He was *still* irritated that Mrs. Norris had challenged him, Liss realized. Surely that wasn't a normal reaction.

"Anyway, there she was in the stockroom, acting like I was still in third grade. Said I'd better put that ring back or she'd tell on me. I said, 'Get out of my way, old woman,' and I started to leave. I wasn't about to put up with a lecture from an old busybody like her. She stepped right into my path, like she thought she could stop me. I swear, Liss, I just meant to shove her out of my way, but I was pretty mad." He raked his fingers through his hair, the first outward sign of agitation Liss had seen from him. "I guess I pushed her too hard, because the next thing I knew, she'd bounced off the shelving and was lying on the floor and bleeding."

On the last word, his bravado evaporated. His face suddenly ashen, he shuddered convulsively. "She hit real hard, Liss. Her head made an awful sound when it struck the shelving."

Liss covered his trembling hand with one of hers. "It was an accident, Ned. You didn't mean to kill her."

"She was dead. She was dead and if I'd stayed there everyone would have known I was the one responsible."

"It was an accident," Liss repeated. "If you'd turned yourself in, the authorities would have seen that right away. Manslaughter at worst. Not murder. That will still be the verdict if you contact them now."

"You can't be sure of that. *I* can't be sure of that. I did the smart thing, the sensible thing. I got the hell out of there before anyone else came along."

He was sweating and his eyes had a glazed look. He was remembering. Liss had no respect for the choice he'd made, but she felt sorry for him.

"Ned? Ned, you have to do the *right* thing. You know that."

"The right thing?"

"You have to call the police. I'll hire a lawyer for you. A good one." Given the circumstances, he might not even have to serve time in jail.

Ned's eyes blinked back into focus. "Do you know what I thought about doing when I was in Mom's apartment that night and you were sleeping blissfully in the guestroom?"

"No, Ned, I don't."

"I thought, what if Liss were to commit suicide? Then everyone would be sure she killed Mrs. Norris. They'd say she couldn't live with the guilt."

Liss stared at him, horrified to realize that he was perfectly serious. And that was exactly what LaVerdiere *had* thought, after her car—

"Ohmigod! You did something to my car! I could have drowned," she added in a horrified whisper.

"That wasn't supposed to happen. You were just supposed to go into a tree or something."

"Oh, thank you very much!"

He shrugged.

"What . . . what did you do?"

"Poked a hole in an intake hose." He sounded proud of himself. "Created a vacuum leak. Figured it would take you up to maximum speed and when you tried to brake, you'd lose control."

"But you didn't intend for me to end up dead." She couldn't quite keep the sarcasm out of her voice.

"Well, no. I just wanted to put you out of commission for awhile. And if the cops thought it was a suicide attempt, so much the better. You were sniffing around, getting too close. Besides, it's your own fault I was able to pop the hood. You're the one who left your car unlocked. I just happened to be in Fallstown that day. I saw you go into the real estate office, realized the car was out of sight in that little parking lot. . . ." He shrugged.

Temper provoked her into speech. "You're lying, Ned. You didn't just happen to know how to rig an accident with my car. You aren't an expert on engines. You had to have gone on-line and done some research."

His eyes narrowed. "That's my story and I'm sticking to it. Besides, I'd never have had to do anything to the car if Ruskin hadn't shown up at the wrong time at Mrs. Norris's house."

She thought back to the day she and Ned had gone in together to feed the cat and blanched. "What did you plan to do? Push me down the stairs?"

"I was thinking about it. You just had to meddle, didn't you? I didn't really want to hurt you. Liss. I'd probably have changed my mind that day. But now—now I've got no choice. You know too much."

Liss stood so rapidly that her chair toppled over. Ned mirrored her action in slow motion, making her excruciatingly aware that he was taller, wider, and stronger than she.

"This won't work," she whispered. "I told Sherri I was coming here."

"Not a problem. I'll be properly distraught when your body is found."

"How on earth are you going to make it look like suicide, Ned? You can't strangle or shoot me. That would pretty obviously be murder." Her heart hammered in her ears. She hoped she wasn't going to faint.

"Scared, Liss? You should be. You always were annoying. Tagging along where you weren't wanted. Snooping. And then that old bat left you all her money! Was that fair?"

She'd always thought of Ned as lazy and laid-back. She'd have described his eyes, if she'd considered them at all, as dull or sleepy. Now they blazed with hatred. Fear of exposure had driven him over some invisible edge. He was beyond listening to reason.

"A fall is always good." He sounded as calm as if they were discussing the weather or what to have for supper. "We'll go up on the roof. It's not all that high, but it'll do the job. And I can tell everyone how you came here to confess to me, then ran up there and threw yourself off."

She might survive a fall. Maybe. But she had no desire to find out. "How are you going to get me up there?"

"You can walk. Or I can clip you on the jaw and carry you."

"I'll walk." And hope she'd be able to get away.

Pushing her ahead of him, one hand firmly clasped around her upper arm, he guided her into the hallway, deserted at this time of the morning, and up the roof stairs. They came out onto a nearly flat surface. Low parapets surrounded it, just at a convenient level to trip over. Someone had left an aluminum lawn chair set up. Liss supposed the roof was occasionally used for sunbathing, but no one was there today, nor were the odds good that anyone would notice them up here. Even if they did, a struggle at the edge of the roof would be interpreted in hindsight as Ned trying to keep her from jumping. *Winners wrote the history books.* Hadn't Mrs. Norris said that, way back in third grade?

Liss bided her time. If she was going to escape, she had to lull Ned into a false sense of security. He hadn't seen that much of her in the last ten years. She was still the much-younger cousin to him. The tag-along.

"Can't we talk about this?" She tried to make herself sound desperate and weak.

"Sorry, Liss. This is the best solution all around." He gave her a shove toward the edge of the roof.

She wasn't going to get a better chance. The moment his hand left her shoulder, she whirled and kicked. Even after three months of retirement, in spite of the bumps and bruises she'd sustained in the last few days, years of dancing had left Liss with strong legs and an agility her cousin lacked. Her flying foot caught him in the shoulder.

"You bitch!" he bellowed, staggering backward. He stared at her, enraged and disbelieving.

The jarring force of the blow had Liss's newly-healed knee protesting the sudden resumption of high-impact exercise, but she ignored the pain and took advantage of Ned's surprise to grab the lawn chair. She swung it hard, connecting first with the middle of his chest, then with the side of his head. Ned's eyes rolled back as he went down.

They both landed hard, Ned in an ungainly, unmoving sprawl and Liss, backpeddling to get out of the way, with a yelp as she lost her balance. The wind knocked out of her, it took her a moment to pull herself upright on the sun-warmed gravel that covered the roof. She looked around for her cousin, but he was still down for the count.

Don't kid yourself, she thought. He could revive at any moment and she was a long way from a phone. The one she'd used to call Sherri was in her purse and her purse was in Ned's apartment.

Liss did a quick assessment of her injuries. She had scrapes, bruises, maybe even a twisted ankle on her good leg. She was alive and relatively undamaged, but she wasn't sure she could walk, let alone do stairs, and this time she had no dance team to support her until she reached the wings.

"Crawling it is," she muttered after her first attempt to stand verified that she'd done damage to both her ankle and her knee.

The sound of footsteps pounding up the stairs was music to her ears. When she recognized Dan's voice calling her name she could have wept.

"Sherri will pick you up at the airport," Liss told her aunt.

She didn't want to go into detail on the phone about the twisted ankle that made it impossible for her to drive to Portland Jetport. Nor did she explain that Sherri had realized before Liss did that Ned wasn't going to quietly confess to killing Mrs. Norris. Stuck in Fallstown, Sherri had not been about to sit tight and do nothing when she was certain Liss was walking straight into danger. She'd been unable to send in the local constabulary—they were tied up with a tractor-trailer accident out on the Ridge Road—so she'd called Dan at the construction site. He'd arrived at Ned's apartment building just in time to hear Ned shout, "You bitch!"

"How's she holding up?" Dan asked when Liss hung up.

"Hard to tell. I think she's still in shock." Twenty-four hours after Ned's arrest, Liss was far from sanguine about the situation herself. Her own cousin had tried to kill her. How was she supposed to react to that?

"Did you tell her you were staying here?"

"No. I'll probably be able to hobble up to the apartment by the time she gets home."

Forbidden by the emergency room doctor she'd seen to climb stairs until the swelling in her ankle went down, Liss had temporarily moved into the downstairs of Mrs. Norris's house. *Her* house, she corrected herself. The local grapevine had brought out the neighbors in force to help her settle in. They'd made sure she was comfortable and had plenty to eat, as well as plenty of company. Patsy had paid a visit this morning, bringing a fresh batch of "wicked good" sticky buns.

Dan had stayed the night.

She smiled up at him from the Canadian rocker. Both feet were propped up on a hassock. She had a clear view of the neighborhood but she had realized something—the neighbors were keeping an eye on her, too. In a good way. Horrible as the experience with Ned had been, since then she had truly begun to feel as if she belonged here, as if she was a part of Moosetookalook.

"I'm thinking about staying on here awhile."

"Till you're on your feet again?"

"Maybe longer than that. I have to decide what to do

about this house and Lumpkin. And Aunt Margaret. . . ." She let her voice trail off. On the phone from Scotland, her aunt had been talking about selling the Emporium to raise money for her son's legal defense. Liss wasn't sure how she felt about helping that effort but, in spite of everything Ned had done, she knew she couldn't abandon his mother. "I'll stay as long as Aunt Margaret needs me."

Leaning against the wall, he grinned down at her. "Stick around long enough and you may even be able to get that scone recipe to come out right."

In spite of her worries about her aunt, Liss couldn't help but respond to his teasing. "That last batch wasn't so bad."

"Wasn't too good, either."

She made a face at him. "The next batch will be good," she promised. "And the batch after that—" She paused for effect. "—will be *wicked* good."